CLEARWATER BLUES

BOOK TWO OF THE MARSHA O'SHEA SERIES

JOHN A. HODA

CHAPTER 1

"FOR CHRIST'S SAKE, What is Egypt? I knew that answer," Marsha barked.

The bartender and other happy-hour patrons belly-up to the hotel bar gave her more than a few raised eyebrows and scowls.

Her vocal participation in *Jeopardy* was wearing on them. The breaking news story out of Arizona had just interrupted her boozy streak of right answers.

The hi-def screen showed the all-too-familiar scene of high-schoolers fleeing single file from campus in yet another school shooting. The story then cut to the on-scene reporter doing her best to describe the carnage. At the same time, RoboCop SWAT team members milled behind her inside the fluttering yellow crime scene tape with their military rifles and visor helmets clearly on display.

This local current events reporter of cancer 5K runs and bakery openings, along with her cameraman, were nearby when they were suddenly thrust into the national spotlight. She was doing her best to report the facts without the horror or her excitement bleeding through.

The shooter was dead, this much she had been told. Around his body lay his AR-15 and high-capacity magazines. His name and motive were not clear at this time, she said. The number of dead and wounded were unknown, but area hospitals were swamped with ambulances from all over the county, she reported.

"Hey, barkeep, I'm a little dry here." Marsha held up her mug and waggled it upside down for him to see. She took this break from the game show to get her refill.

"Are you a guest here, ma'am?" he asked quietly upon his arrival to her stool. The empty shot glasses and peanut shells made for proper accounting of her afternoon's decision to get shit-faced.

"Yes, I am, and don't call me ma'am." Marsha snorted.

"I had to ask because if you were driving, I would have to cut you off and recommend you get a cab."

Marsha was primed and ready to smart ass him when she looked at the others at the bar. They stared at her. *I'm the train wreck they are looking at.*

The talking head caught her attention on the screen sadly informing the viewers about the uptick in mass shootings in just this year alone. Marsha looked down at the mess in front of her.

Where did all these shot glasses come from? She closed her eyes and the room began to spin.

"Lady, are you alright?" the bartender asked.

Slowly tears came to her eyes. Marsha tried tightening them to stanch the flow. He slowly removed the mug from her grip. She wobbled forward, eyes clenched closed, and whispered, "No, I am not."

She opened her eyes briefly to acquire a bar napkin to dab her eyes, and then she let the room know she was blowing her nose.

She looked around. Alex just then announced the *Daily Double*.

The other patrons returned to their own business.

"I'll cash out now if you don't mind." Marsha exhaled.

* * *

Sobering up was not the goal this evening. Water gently lapping against the boats moored in the Gulf of Mexico by the Clearwater Beach Hotel provided sights and sounds she needed to focus on. The two six-packs she grabbed at the gas station next to the hotel supplied fuel for her despair. A pool deck chair wrangled over the fence and down to the soft white sand cooling from the unseasonably warm March sun completed her plan.

She toasted herself for not making a further scene at the hotel bar. Bartenders wanting to call cabs for her or bouncers flexing their biceps while pointing to the door had been non-existent in her life until the last month or so.

Getting out of Philly was the right thing to do. The change of scenery with palm trees and spring training baseball was much better than the ice-rutted streets and mountains of snow piled up in shopping center parking lots back home. Not to mention all the dead bodies.

She had always wanted to spend some time watching the Phillies play in the Grapefruit League. With no direct ties back in the City of Brotherly Love, she jettisoned out of town after her last interview with the stern-faced FBI agents trying to make sense of the carnage left in her wake.

Earlier that day, she had started drinking her lunch at Bright House Field and watched the game from the lawn in left field. She was giving the business to some Mets fans when she noticed a young family fold up their picnic blanket and move away from her as the Mets fans gave it right back to her. From there, her drinking picked up again in the cool, dark hotel bar where many fans and snowbirds had retreated from a sunny day at the game or the beach.

The gentle Gulf waters reflected the half-moon when it peeked out between the steady parade of puffy clouds. Commercial shipping traversed north and south parallel to the beach further out to sea. There was no hurry to their movements. The coal stripped from Tennessee and Kentucky mountain tops would eventually arrive in China, and the Hyundai parts would float into Mobile before sunrise.

Here she sat, cooling her sunburn and steadily sipping her sixteen-ouncers. She needed to drink to forget. She needed to drink to remember why she became an FBI agent in the first place. She needed to drink to get numb. She needed to curse her own mistakes and stubbornness that she had replayed over again in daydreams and nightmares. Mostly, she needed to grieve. She had no safe outlet.

Everything was twisted inside. Shunned by her family and kryptonite to her co-workers, she found solace with Mr. Heineken and Mr. Daniels. All alone in Clearwater, Florida, she was doing a horrible job of chasing away the blues.

CHAPTER 2

THE CONSTANT SCREAMING of the dying rabbit was giving Willis a headache. The electronic caller bleated the call to the area predators on a regular preset. His feet were freezing. Here he was at over 5,000-feet elevation near Glendo, Wyoming in the late March winter sagebrush landscape, lying on his stomach in full camouflage as dusk approached. He had moved every hour on the hour further into the brush, and once settled, he would only move to chase away the vultures, circling for the rabbit, with his pellet gun.

When he was growing up, the cartoons always depicted the coyote as wily, but not as smart or lucky as the roadrunner. Sportsmen knew better. There were several reasons why this animal was hunted when other seasons closed. They were skittish, crafty, and stealthy. The private ranch owner had no problem granting access to the Teesdale boys. Local coyotes were wreaking havoc on his wintering sheep.

The setting sun was to Willis's back and the brisk wind to his face. Perfect setup. If the little varmint didn't show up soon, his last day would be a bust. Both his brothers had gotten theirs and were mocking their little brother once again. Even though he bagged as much big game as they had, his bull elk was the smallest, or his deer antler spread was the shortest. There was always something belittling said about the fish he angled or birds he blasted out of the sky.

These hunting trips were getting more costly too. Licenses, hunting packages, airfare, and lodging were a pretty penny, and of course, he had to keep up with them when outfitting and equipping for the trips. Whether it was Marlin fishing off the east coast of Florida or getting an out of state one-day bowhunting lottery berth in Upper Michigan, the Teesdale boys would not hesitate to pony up the money and go.

It was times like this at the end of a fruitless day when he thought about the first time he shot an animal. The whitetail deer wasn't dead yet when he ran up to it. Its back legs were paralyzed, and its breathing was labored as it struggled to drag itself upright. His father must have heard the shot and came upon the scene.

"Well, boy, you have to finish it off," he said and handed him a revolver.

Willis took the gun and shakily pointed it at the deer's head as it stared at him and snorted.

"Not there, Willis," his father yelled. "You don't want to spoil the mount. Shoot him in the heart."

He walked around to the other side away from the flailing front legs, and his father followed him.

"Get closer. Dammit!"

His older brothers approached with their rifles slung over their shoulders. The eldest, Bryce said, "This is what happens when you don't make a kill shot. What a mess."

Jazz was next to add more insult to the buck's injury. "What's all that adrenaline gonna do to the meat, Dad?"

Their father just shook his head. "Finish it off, Willis. You still have work to do."

He inched closer, and the buck craned its neck to stare at Willis. Its breathing more labored. Willis fired a round into its back just below the shoulders and neck and stepped back. The buck writhed and tried to rub out the new bullet hole in its back with the ground.

"Again," his father commanded.

Willis shot two more times in rapid succession, and the buck collapsed with a final exhalation. There was stillness now among the Teesdale men. A crow called in the distance. The wind rustled the trees and fallen leaves. The buck gave Willis a dead-eye stare.

He sobbed as he gutted it, while the boys stood around and made fun of him. It was not easy for this twelve year old to reach into a still-warm animal and cut out its organs. This rite of passage in front of their scowling father didn't get any more comfortable when they made him drag the spike buck back to the roadside where their father parked their pickup.

Breathe. Willis could feel his hearting pounding at his temples. The snug shooter glasses provided the extra pressure on both sides of his head. That memory never escaped him. Over the years, it had gotten easier to ignore the little boy's voice in the back of his head, warning him not to pull the trigger.

Proving himself to his family was not required only when they hunted or fished, either. It extended to sports, games, jobs, girls, earnings, trucks, and anything where a snide comparison could be made.

He saw movement at about 200 yards. He brought up the scope on his .204 Ruger and tried to find it. He slowly scanned the line of brush leading to a draw between rock outcroppings. Nothing. He pulled his eye off the scope and caught a glimpse of a bushy tail glinting off the sun. Back on the scope again, he now acquired the coyote's fur, which was golden brown and matched perfectly with the winter grass.

Only when it moved by the gray rocks in the background did its shape and contours appear. It was sniffing for field mice and nudged sticks and leaves out of the way. Either it was going to retreat from whence it came, or it would cross the draw. How quickly it would run across the opening, he was not sure. Just then, the caller bleated out the call, and the coyote's ears perked up.

It took a few tentative steps in his direction. Again the digital dying rabbit screamed. The coyote took a few more steps toward the sound, but stopped and retreated into the bush.

Damn. Willis took his eye from the scope and sucked in a full breath. *This little guy is a smart one.* His back was talking to him now, but he decided to give it a couple more minutes and was rewarded for his patience. *He's hungry too.*

The coyote edged along the brush line and didn't present a clear target. Zig-zagging towards him made it difficult to get more than a small target profile, even though the creature was getting closer. The wind swirled around, Willis glanced at the windsock on top of the caller and saw that in a couple of seconds his scent would be on the coyote's nose. He put his eye on the scope, zeroed in and exhaled softly. *When he turns, I'll nail him.*

The predator stopped still and smelled the human. Just as Willis predicted, the coyote turned broadside, and Willis squeezed off a round. The impacting high-velocity bullet spun the animal around with its paws and tail kicking up dust and debris. Willis stood slowly and took out his binoculars. It was down and not moving. He walked over to the caller and turned it off. It took him a few minutes to get his legs under him. The release of tension and lying so long on the cold ground made it hard for him to ambulate. He lurched closer, looking for any sign of movement. He kept his rifle pointed downrange.

In the moments before sunset, he came upon the still animal and nudged it with his rifle barrel. Nothing. The entry wound was behind the left front shoulder, and there was no exit wound. There was no deformity to the head or teeth. This was a healthy male. It would make a beautiful trophy for the living room wall.

* * *

"Hi, honey, it's me," Willis said.

"Hi, Willis. Is everything alright," Jessalyn replied.

"Couldn't be better." He angled away from the jukebox music at the country-western bar where he and his brothers were celebrating their last night in God's country. "I got my coyote just before dark. I couldn't let Bryce and Jazz bust my chops about coming home empty-handed."

"That's nice," she said.

"You don't sound excited for me." He thought about how freaking cold it was all day and that he stayed steady on a 175-yard kill shot.

"W-well," she stammered. "Some bills came in while you were away, and I don't know how we are going to pay them. This last trip really put a dent in our checking account."

"Don't worry, honey. I grab as much overtime as I can take to cover us. I always do."

"How much do you think you charged on the credit card for this trip?"

Willis was getting a little steamed here. He wanted to share his excitement with his wife, and she was throwing a damper on it. "I am standing by the bathrooms at a bar. I can't count credit card receipts. You figure it out. Okay?"

"Sorry, I sounded down. You had a good day doing what you love to do. I guess I got all wound up about the bills. It just doesn't look like we are ever getting ahead. I'll just go look online."

Willis asked. "Ahead of who? Ahead of the Joneses? Ahead of Charlie next door? Who?"

"I mean ahead of our bills. We are paying on a refi on our mortgage. After our tithe, we barely have enough to make ends meet."

"Hey, Jessalyn, we are doing okay. I provide. I bring home every penny. Don't I?"

"Willis, what about Briana's college fund? She's bright, and she's going to college in three years. What are we going to do?"

Willis was shaking his head when he spotted his big brother waving an empty mug at him. "Listen, Jess. I gotta go. We will talk about that when I get home."

"Hold on a second, Willis. I hear a strange noise in the laundry room."

He was left standing there, fuming and listening to dead air. He had great news, and all she wanted to do was complain about the bills. That thing about Briana came from left field. What was that about? Finally, he heard her muttering as she entered the laundry room.

"It's the washing machine, Willis. It's making an awful noise."

He could hear it squealing, and something was grinding. "Okay, unplug it. I will look at it when I get home."

"I have school clothes for Briana in there, what am I gonna do?"

"I dunno, take them to a laundromat. What do you want me to do? I'm in Wyoming."

The noise stopped. It was quiet. She picked up the phone. "When it rains, it pours. Tell your brothers I said hello. Have a swell time."

The emphasis on *swell* wasn't lost on Willis.

He hung up the phone and returned to the bar.

"What was that about, lil' bro," Jazz said.

"Nothing much. The washing machine decided to give up the ghost as we were talking. She was happy about the coyote."

Bryce asked, "Did you tell her how much it's gonna cost to get it stuffed and mounted?"

"Naw, she had her hands full. Let's sit down. I'm starved."

"Your turn to buy, Willis," Bryce said.

"I'm gettin' me the lumberjack special," Jazz said.

* * *

"Why you crying, Mom?" Briana asked as she walked in the front door from a study date.

"Washer broke, honey. I've got to take your stuff to a laundromat." Jessalyn was wringing out the clothes and stuffing them into a garbage bag.

"Mom, was that soup for me?" Brianna called from the kitchen.

"Yeah, I turned it off when I heard the washer going kablooey. You can heat it up and have it."

Jessalyn hauled the laundry outside and put it in the trunk of her car. As she was pulling out, her neighbor Charlie, with whom they shared a driveway, was pulling in.

"Howzitgoin', Jess?"

With a tired shrug, she said, "It's going. Washer broke. Willis is away on one of his hunting trips, and I am off to the laundromat."

"Don't be silly, use mine. I have more Chinese take-out than I can eat. Do you want some?" He held up the plastic bag.

Charlie was old enough to be retired for ten years, but he chose to work most days. He was a widower. Jessalyn had been close friends with Mary, his wife, before she died a few years back from cancer. Jessalyn figured it would be nice to catch up with him, and the smell of the food reminded her how hungry she was.

"And after the rain, comes the rainbow."

"What was that, Jess?"

"Nothing, Charlie. I'll tell Briana I'll be right next door."

CHAPTER 3

DURING HER LUNCH break the following day, Jessalyn looked at the credit card bill. It was what she feared. This trip put them close to the limit. While online, she studied the statements going back for a year. When he went on his journeys, the card got dangerously close to the max.

She couldn't take another part-time job. Working at home as a customer rep handling service issues for a large mortgage company, Jessalyn had no overtime opportunity. Still, it had allowed her to be at home with her daughter when Briana was little. They saved on day-care until Briana went to school all day. Jess also worked a Saturday night dinner shift at an upscale restaurant on Clearwater Beach.

She had worked there since her teen years, and it was an excellent way to get out of the house and make some extra spending money.

Her husband, Willis, had a good job doing alarm installations and maintenance. He had the seniority to accept or reject night and weekend callouts, which paid overtime. When they would get upside down like this, he would work the OT until they paid off the bills.

Their church had taught them about tithing first, managing family expenses, and debt. Everything seemed okay, but they were just getting by. That was the problem, they were always just getting by, and now she figured out why.

She was a coupon clipper, shopped sales, and made dresses for Briana growing up, but now their fifteen-year-old was becoming class-conscious at school and didn't like getting teased about all the Walmart markdowns.

Jessalyn didn't belong to a gym, cooked every night except for Friday night pizza, and didn't overspend on hair or nails. She drove a used Corolla built in the previous decade and knew that it would become Briana's car next year. All the paychecks went into the bank, and her tip money was her household spending money. They didn't take vacations and led a tranquil life around church and Briana's activities. Neither she nor Willis were big spenders, or so she thought.

After her shift, she decided to look at their spending. She pulled together all of their records. Willis had handled the checkbook for all their years together. Since Willis was coming home late at night from the hunting trip, she was alone after dinner and decided to track their discretionary spending. Jess had to get all the financial paperwork out anyway for him to do the taxes online, and it was not difficult for her to sift through the checking account register and credit card statements. She built a spreadsheet and started laying out the transactions. Jess was astounded by what she saw.

To be sure, she went back to the previous year's registers and statements that they kept in case of an IRS audit. A disturbing spending trend was becoming apparent. One column far outpaced all the others and the dollar amounts being entered weren't for using the debit card to buy a cup of coffee. She went back another year and then another.

She looked around while nibbling on some oyster crackers she kept in her apron from work. They had already refinanced their double-wide once before and had no equity in the house now. Willis was handy, but their furniture, carpets, and window treatments were tired. When reality hit her hard, she immediately slumped into her kitchen chair.

The money that Willis was spending on his hobbies was astronomical. When she added it all up, they could have quickly paid off the mortgage, have no credit card debt, and could have put more than the minimum in their 401Ks.

Her temper began to boil when she thought about how his new pick-up truck every three years kept getting bigger and bigger. He was supplied a company truck for his job. Every workday, his shiny truck sat in the parking lot at work. He was turning in a leased low-mileage truck every 36 months.

She went back to the checkbook registers and tabulated the nine years of monthly payments for trucks that basically sat around on weekdays.

It's over $25,000! That could have been used for Briana's college.

That's when it all hit her. How many years had they been treading water?

Later that night, when she heard his truck rumble into the driveway, she quickly undressed and got in bed, pretending to be asleep.

The mighty hunter has arrived.

CHAPTER 4

MARSHA'S sparring partner at the Krav Maga morning class was a younger guy, about her 5'9" height, but beefy. He had 75 pounds on her for sure. Using her federal government law enforcement discount, she had bought a ten pack of classes at the studio in a crowded shopping plaza on the outskirts of Tampa.

During the week, it had been a steady diet of punching, kicking, and ab work. Saturday was promised to be a light contact day, but she wasn't sure if this sweaty guy with a brush cut was a poor striker or if he was trying to cop a cheap feel.

"Let's try to be a little bit more careful there, pardner," she warned him.

The instructor, a black-haired woman barely over five feett tall with zero body fat and barbed-wired tattoos across her biceps, noted Marsha's warning and moved closer to them.

"Wha-?" He offered an open palm shrug.

Their next exchange was cleaner, and both their jabs and kicks were more forceful. Marsha could give it as good as taking it, and beefy brush-cut appeared none too happy with her speed or accuracy.

Marsha had been punishing herself all week with these workouts. It was an excellent release for her anger and self-loathing. After the classes, she felt physically spent, but before long, her sadness would return, and so did the need to drown it in alcohol. Never allowing herself to feel sadness or even the remotest form of self-compassion, she had always translated sadness into anger and action.

Female FBI agents working in the field had trouble expressing sadness to their male counterparts, who would take it as weakness, and this athlete with a full-ride scholarship for volleyball to Penn State would never show the boys any weakness. When she was a younger agent working fugitives and bank robbery details in Miami, she worked harder, talked tougher, and walked taller than most of her male counterparts. She protected her image even when she returned to Philly to finish her career with the bureau.

After their second exchange, where she was able to block and counter, Beefy threw a right overhead that Marsha moved in on and blocked, only to close the distance to his left straight jab into her stomach. Light contact just became full contact, and the instructor moved in, issuing a warning to him.

Her crisp middle-eastern accent made the command more forceful. "Break."

Marsha staggered back and fought the involuntary contraction of her abdomen. *Shit. Breathe. Shit. Don't show the pain.* She closed her eyes until the room stopped spinning.

The instructor had her nose about six inches from his chest. Over her head, Marsha heard him say, "She walked into it. I couldn't pull it in time." His hands were on his hips as he shifted from side to side, unsure if the teacher was going to teach him a lesson.

The instructor looked at Marsha. Marsha nodded that she was ready to go.

The women nodded with mutual recognition of what was coming next. Beefy and Marsha moved closer. They circled clockwise and feigned jabs and kicks. Marsha feigned another left jab, then leaned in and landed the left to his throat. As he bent forward, her snap kick with her right foot caught him flush between the legs. Beefy crumbled to the ground, and the teacher moved in to stop Marsha from causing further damage.

* * *

"Maybe you should find another studio for the rest of your vacation," the former Israeli soldier said to Marsha, who was changing into her street clothes after her shower. The red welt on her stomach was starting to rise. Tomorrow, it would be an ugly bruise.

"He pissed me off," Marsha managed as she slipped her Chase Utley Phillies jersey over her head.

"You come in every day with an attitude, Ms. O'Shea. Shit attracts flies. I am not surprised by what happened. It doesn't make his actions justifiable, but I was hoping that you could work out your anger by exhausting yourself here."

Marsha shimmied into her jeans as she stood up. "Me too. I guess I screwed that up." She grabbed her bag and started walking past the instructor.

The instructor stepped in front of Marsha. "For what it's worth, I knew what was coming and didn't stop you. He'll play nice the next time he has to spar with a woman. Here's my card. I give private lessons."

Marsha looked at it, before slipping it into her credit card holder on the back of her cell phone and nodded. "Thank you, Shira. I might just do that."

Walking out to her car in the bright sunshine, Marsha slipped on her sunglasses. She was sore and tired from her workout and was in no mood to heal her mental pain, nor forgive herself. Was her problem with Beefy, or was it with all her pent-up self-hatred?

She got into her Phillies-red Mustang convertible and fired up the V-8.

As she was waiting for the red light, she turned on her radio. Her preset country music station was a 24-hour talk radio down here. The syndicated talk show host agreed with the caller that guns don't kill people, but that people kill people in response to the outrage over the mass killings at the Arizona high school.

The next caller tried explaining that people killing people with AR-15s and high-capacity magazines were much more deadly than any other instrument of death. Walking onto a school campus with a musket would not produce the same carnage, the caller opined. Immediately, the host defended his constitutional right to bear arms.

Before turning it off, Marsha silently agreed with him. *Fuckin'A. If he wants to bare arms, he could wear a strapless black cocktail dress for all I care.*

She slammed a CD into the slot and tried relaxing to the latest country crooner as she went hunting for a breakfast place.

* * *

It was the middle of the fourth inning at Spectrum Stadium, and the Phillies squad were hosting the Red Sox. It was the final tune-up for both staff's aces before heading up North next week. It was still exhibition baseball, but for some players, a good run could mean the difference between making it to the Bigs or being relegated to the minor leagues. Earlier in the game, a camera operator had settled on her, and Marsha pointed to her face splashed on the high-def screen in the outfield.

Marsha had just come back to her seat about ten rows up on the third-base line from the left-field food court with her cheesesteak, peanuts, and the two beer limit.

"Hi, Marsha. Remember me?" The wiry fisherman-tanned older gent with perfect white teeth and a steel-gray military cut head of hair peered down at her.

She squinted her eyes and tried to place the face and voice. He was backlit at first, but as he moved further down the aisle to give her a better look, they both grinned at the same time. "Charlie Akers, what are you doing here?"

"I saw you on the big screen and figured out where you were sitting."

"No, I mean here." Marsha waved her cheesesteak in a large circle.

"I'm a Sox fan and figured I wouldn't see them again until I visited my cousins back in Brockton this summer when it's too frigging hot down here."

"I'm confused. Did you drive all the way from Miami to watch an exhibition game?"

"No, after I retired, we moved here to Clearwater to get away from all the craziness."

"Sit down, Charlie. Nobody has claimed the seat."

"I can't. I bet my buddies that I was going to try to pick-up that beautiful blonde we saw on the jumbotron."

"Where are they? I'll blow them a kiss."

"Would you?"

Charlie and Marsha looked back behind home plate and waved to his buddies. The joke worked, and for the first time in a month, Marsha had a good laugh. The inning was about to start.

"How long you in town for, Marsha?"

"Dunno, Charlie. It's a long story."

"Well, here is my card. Call me, and we can reminisce about the good ole days."

Marsha put down her food, stood up, and hugged him. "I'll do that, Charlie."

She settled back in her seat and took a long pull on her cup of beer. She looked out at the sky across the field. *Chamber of Commerce weather,* she mused.

The cool breeze off the Gulf and gorgeous white pillow-like clouds drifting by made it a perfect day for the national pastime. Passing the time is what Marsha knew she was doing. Nowhere to be, nothing to do but try and relax and let the knots in her heart unravel.

A glance at the scoreboard revealed Boston's left-handed clean-up hitter was coming up to bat. She dove into her foot-long, savoring the taste, and then the memories of going to ballgames with her father and brother came back. She put down her sandwich and recalled getting their cheesesteaks from the stand-up joint at Tenth and Oregon.

Her dad, a now-retired Philly PD captain, would wave his magic credentials at the gate, and before you knew it, they would be whisked like royalty to seats behind the visitor's dugout on the third-base side.

Not much different from where she was sitting now. Was it by design or accident that she picked this seat? Knowing that she could never do that again with her two favorite men made her melancholy on this drop-dead gorgeous day. She reached down to pick up her beer just as the batter failed to catch up with a fastball and fouled a screaming live drive into the stands. A fan tried barehanding the heat-seeking missile. It barely deflected off his hands two seats away and into her head, knocking Marsha and her beer into the empty seat next to her.

* * *

Morton Plant Hospital was over 100 years old. Better than some coastal medical facilities that catered to the snowbirds and retirees, it had grown in size and had a decent neuro-unit. Fortunately for Marsha, it was also the nearest ER to the stadium. The EMTs took no chances at the stadium and put her on a backboard and in a neck brace and hurried her out of there. She was out like a light.

Now, the throbbing started before she could open her eyes. When she did, the fluorescent lighting above her bed made her want to close them tighter.

"Mrs. O'Shea? Mrs. O'Shea? Hello? Hello? Can you hear me?" the nurse asked while adjusting an IV.

Marsha nodded. "What happened?"

"What's the last thing you remember?"

"I was sitting at the ballgame, just finished talking to an old friend."

"Mr. Akers?"

Painful as it was, she looked at the nurse. "And how did you know that?"

"He's in the waiting room. He was concerned for you. And one of the Phillies is out there too."

"Huh?"

"He said he was a friend too."

"Joe DiNatale?"

The nurse got excited. "You're friends with Joe DiNatale? Do you think I can get an autograph?"

Marsha sunk back on the pillow and nodded again.

"The doctor has to check for a subdural hematoma. She will probably order a full scan of your brain. Do you know what day it is, Mrs. O'Shea?"

"Call me Marsha. Mr. O'Shea is long out of the picture. It's Saturday."

"Who is Stew and Nicky, Marsha? You were repeating their names?"

Marsha closed her eyes and leaned back into the pillow.

"Are they really dead?"

"'Fraid so." Marsha's eyes moistened.

Awkwardly, the nurse made her way past the end of the bed, and with a hand on the curtain said, "Sorry to hear that. Well, the doctor will be in shortly to check on you."

So my nightmares even happen when I'm unconscious. That's great to know. Maybe if I had my head in the game instead of on my problems, I could have a souvenir baseball instead of a knot growing on the side of my scalp. Marsha rubbed her head.

Charlie and Joe entered. Charlie was the first to speak. "You're slowing down, O'Shea, Twenty years on the mean streets of Miami and not a scratch. Now, look at you. It's a good thing you don't work for me now. I'd have to fill out all that paperwork."

"Charlie, you could always make me smile." Looking at Joe. "Did they make you wear your uniform to see me?"

"I ran down from the bullpen when I saw it was you. Charlie gave me a ride."

Marsha realized that since they first met in college, Joe had always been straightforward and honest with her. On their brief encounters in Philly, he always talked to her with a complete absence of guile. "No dice, D, I'm holding out for the Philly Phanatic. It's him or nothing."

"The Red Sox hitter was so distraught that he struck out. He asked me to text him as soon as I found out what was happening," Joe said.

"See, Charlie, I am still a team player, taking one for the team." Then to Joe, "Tell him a lobster dinner at the stadium club in Fenway will help my aching head feel better, I think."

Both men were grinning as the doctor came in. She was as tall as both of them, olive-skinned with long black hair. "Ms. O'Shea, I am going to ask your visitors to step out while I examine you."

The star ballplayer and former FBI Area Supervisor in Charge of the Miami field office took their leave.

"You were unresponsive at the scene, knocked out. Would you like to see the instant replay?" The ER doctor held up her phone. "The Phillies were so concerned that they sent the footage to the hospital."

Marsha watched the video. *It seems I've been on video in too many dangerous situations lately.*

The camera operator barely had time to move the camera to catch the action. The video was in slo-mo first. The ball deflected off the fan's hands and into the side of her head. Then at regular speed. Then again in slo-mo.

"We are not taking this lightly. You are fortunate not to be in a coma or ....worse. We are going to run all the tests and follow all the concussion protocols."

Off the gurney and into a wheelchair, the aide pushed her to X-ray and then MRI. Luckily, it was a slow afternoon on a winter's day at the hospital in this sleepy seaside community. No fractures, no masses were forming under the scalp. Her dizziness was abating, but the headache was still there.

The doctor reappeared. "Ms. O'Shea, are you staying with family or friends here?"

"No, I'm alone."

"Is there anyone you can stay with for a few days to keep an eye on you, especially at night?"

"I don't have anyone."

"We will have to keep you under observation then for a few days to make sure."

"It is what it is. Can you let my visitors know I can't sing Karaoke tonight?" Marsha replied.

"I'll make the preparations to get you a room upstairs." And with that, the doctor smiled and waved good-bye.

"Whaddyamean, you have no friends here?" Charlie wasn't smiling.

Joe piped up. "I can arrange for you to have twenty-four hour care at the timeshares where the rookies are staying. After today's game, there will be a couple of vacancies."

"You'd rather stay in a hospital and eat hospital food?" Charlie asked.

"It's the least we can do, seeing how you got hurt in our ballpark," Joe said.

Scanning their faces, Marsha said, "Look, guys, I couldn't impose—"

"Nonsense, O'Shea. When will you stop insulting your friends?"

"Okay, okay, you guys can fight over me, and the winner gets to put up with me for a couple of days, but as soon as I'm okay, I'll decide what I'm gonna do next. Capisce?"

The men corralled her nurse and explained the plan. Charlie and Joe would take her to her hotel and check her out. Then they would move her into one the vacant condo units reserved for the departing spring training players. Joe talked the Phillies training staff into arranging for round the clock aides.

When the endless paperwork was finished, Joe and Charlie wheeled her to the ER exit. As the doors opened, an ambulance pulled up, cut its siren, and the trauma team rushed out to it while the vehicle's rear door opened wide and a gurney came barreling towards them. They couldn't see the person being rushed inside. The team accepted the hand-off with an EMT holding a plasma bottle up high. They were followed by a couple of grim-faced uniformed officers. Marsha, Charlie, and Joe couldn't see the person being rushed inside.

Charlie reached for his credentials and quietly steered an officer to the side.

"What happened?"

"Kid got into his father's unlocked gun cabinet," the officer said, turning down the squelch on her portable radio.

"How old?"

"Eleven."

CHAPTER 5

"THEY'RE MAKING fun of me, Mom. I can't keep wearing baggy sweaters every day," Briana said.

Warm spring-like weather had descended on the Gulf Coast over the last couple of weeks. Her little girl wasn't so little anymore. Taller and leaner, Briana was taking on the shape of a pretty young woman, Jessalyn realized. The older boys in her high school were starting to take notice, but the popular girls called her trailer trash behind her back. It broke Jessalyn's heart.

Worse, some of the bad boys thought her daughter was easy and were sniffing around. Fortunately, Briana had strong relationships with both boys and girls from their church, and she wasn't easily swayed by the excitement of weekend partying and fast hook-ups.

Jessalyn reached above the sink to the wooden shelf and pulled down the brown ceramic cookie jar with a Disney drawing of Mickey and Minnie. This is where she kept her tip money. The fives, tens, and a couple of twenties almost hit a hundred. She quietly took the money and slipped it into her bathrobe pocket.

"Yes, I think we need some girl time together, maybe even get our nails done tonight after dinner. How's that sound, baby?"

Briana brightened up, pecked her mother on the cheek and rinsed her cereal bowl before putting it in the dishwasher. "Thanks, Mom."

When Jessalyn heard the shower turn on and knew that Briana was probably under a head full of suds, she called her mother. "Hi, Mom, it's me."

"Hey, Jessie, what's up."

"Mom, I gotta ask you for a favor." She paused. It hurt to ask her mother for money. Favors from Leona always came with strings attached.

"What's it this time, dear?"

"Look, Mom, it's not for me. Briana is growing like a weed and none of her spring clothes fit her anymore. The kids at school are teasing her."

"I wouldn't know, honey. Last time I saw her was for Christmas at Nicole's house. She barely said hello to me."

"She's a teenager, Mom, she'll come around, you know that."

"How come you can't put it on the credit card?"

"The washing machine finally kicked the bucket. I have to put that on the card and I'm real close to the limit."

Silence.

"Since your father ran out on me and I got sick, it's hard for me. I can't work and Social Security only goes so far. Can you ask Nickie?"

Jessalyn was constantly reminded that her younger sister Nicole married a successful man, that she had gotten her college degree and worked as an OB-GYN nurse making good money. Her sister was living the American Dream.

"I could, but that's not what I had in mind. I wanted to treat us and get our nails done and then I was thinking you could help her pick out clothes. You do such a good job at that. You always made sure I looked good, Mom. It would be a girl's night out. How's that sound?"

The silence on the other end of the line stretched on. Jessalyn knew that her mother liked the idea, but didn't want to say yes.

She added the kicker. "We can go for ice cream when we're done. My treat."

"Well, we can't be too late. I tire easy these days."

"Thanks, Mom. I'll pick you up at six." Jess hung up and shook her head. *Social Security only goes so far, my ass. She buys a carton of Indian cigarettes every Saturday when she gambles at the casinos. She's on disability and gets tired because she has smoking-induced emphysema. I hate asking her for money.* Jess closed her eyes and tried breathing away her anger and sadness. *Be nice, she's your mother. She won't be around forever.*

***

"Hey, Willis, long time no see. How ya doin'?" An obviously surprised Lane stuck out his hand.

"Doin' great, Lane. How's retirement?" Willis juggled a couple of control panels to his left hand and chest to shake his friend's hand.

Lane was walking from the management offices of the security alarm company where he had worked since its inception until his retirement. He had trained Willis, and now Willis was the senior installation and repair tech. "Going stir crazy. Belinda's tired of having me hanging around. I started driving Uber, but I'm sick of cleaning up from college kids puking in the back seat all the time."

Willis winced and laughed simultaneously. "Yeah, it's hard to get that smell out of fabric."

Nervously looking at his watch, Lane said, "Well, I gotta get going. This is about the time that the flights start pouring in at the airport carrying all the snowbirds and tourists to the Sunshine State."

"Okay. See ya, Lane. Take care."

Willis finished loading his work truck with all the repair parts and installs he needed for his run and walked back to the offices and knocked on the new operations manager's door. A recent college graduate with connections to the owner, she was still learning the ropes.

"Hi, Lisa. Have a minute?"

"Hi, Willis, how was your vacation?" Lisa Andre looked up from her monitor and slid a manila folder closed and put it into the personnel filing cabinet.

"It was fantastic. We all bagged one. Wyoming was beautiful." He pulled out his cell phone and showed her a photo of him kneeling behind the coyote holding the head up by the scruff of the neck. Its glazed eyes and tongue lolling showed it to be dead.

"What's that? Is it a dog?" She recoiled back to her chair.

Stung. Willis retorted, "No, it's a coyote. They attack rancher's sheep and other livestock. The ranchers gladly let us on their property to help save their animals."

"Oh, that's good, I guess," she said.

Willis made a mental note not to share his kill photos with the young woman. "I just saw Lane Peters coming from back here. It was good seeing him again. You never knew Lane, did you, Lisa? He retired a couple years ago. Taught me everything I know."

Lisa smiled coolly. "How can I help you, Willis?"

"Just wanted to let you know, I can jump on the overtime wagon again. These hunting trips aren't getting any cheaper and we gotta start thinking about Briana's college education."

"How is your daughter doing, Willis?"

"She's doing good. She's a sophomore, getting straight A's and staying out of trouble. She's gonna be taking the PSATs next week."

Something was off with Lisa. She was struggling to come up with the words. "What's up?" he asked.

Lisa took a deep breath and stared as his chest, avoiding eye contact. "Sometimes, overtime is a sign that a company is growing faster than they can add employees, but for the last two quarters, sales have been stagnant." Looking at the dashboard on her monitor, she added. "This quarter isn't any better. Our residential sales have dropped off tremendously. The doorbell cameras that anybody can buy online are killing us. We are holding our own on commercial installs, but many of our customers are holding off on replacing their older systems in this economy."

Willis just shrugged. "Well, that means more failures on older equipment, more call-outs on nights and weekends, more overtime, right?"

"We've budgeted only so much for salaries. When sales go flat and revenue slows down, OT is harder to justify. We—"

He interrupted. "I've got seniority. I am first to pick and choose overtime assignments. You can't be assigning overtime to any of the other techs before me, Lisa."

"That is true, Willis. We wouldn't do that to you."

"Then what are you saying?" he asked.

"Lane knows the older systems better than anybody. You just admitted that. He is offering to come back part-time to work the call outs. That service still has to be done. He can do up to forty hours a week of it as straight-time, after that you would be first in line for overtime." Lisa added, "I can't discuss salaries, but we created a 'repair tech' rate just for him."

Stunned, Willis didn't know what to say. Torn between his feeling of loss and feelings for his mentor, he couldn't come up with a ready answer. Finally, he sighed. "Well, I'm still first for call outs if Lane can't handle it all, right?"

Lisa nodded.

* * *

"I'm sorry, ma'am, but the system is rejecting your credit card."

Jessalyn said, "That can't be. Can you run it again?"

She was there to buy the washing machine and Willis would pick it up and install it while she was out with her mother and daughter.

He tried it again and waited. "I'm sorry." Glancing at the line forming behind her at the big box appliance store, he offered. "Is there another card you can use?"

"No. We only have gas cards, that's it." Red-faced and shocked, Jess left the sales ticket on the belt. Dazed, she walked out to her car.

Sitting there, she brought up the credit card app and began entering her user ID and password. So upset, she entered it incorrectly. The car had been baking in the sun and the humidity made it a cauldron inside. Trying to work quickly, as she was on her lunch hour, she fumbled it again. Now the sweat was pouring down her face. She started her car and lowered the windows while blasting the AC as much as the old used car could muster. Third strike. She was locked out, and the screen said to try back later.

Undeterred, she called the 800 number and went through the phone tree twice before being put on hold. The hold music droned on as she cooled off and calmed down. Only once before, when somebody had gotten hold of their account information and made a series of unauthorized online transactions, had her card ever been denied previously.

Finally, a cheery but robotic sounding service rep from a country on the other side of the world picked up. Luckily, Jess remembered her account password this time and the rep said, "Mrs. Teesdale, the transaction was blocked as it would have put the balance over the limit."

"Nonsense. How can that be? I just looked at it two days ago and it was fine."

"I'm sorry, Mrs. Teesdale, the purchases since then brought you up to $24,440. Your limit is $25,000. That is why the card was rejected."

Perplexed, she said, "Can you read them off to me?"

"3-27, $100.00 Wild West Saloon, Glendo Wyoming."

"Okay. That is where my husband ate dinner."

"3-30, $216.24 Motel Six."

"That is where he stayed on his trip."

"3-30, $1,025.79 Matt Mardell's Taxidermy, LLC."

"What? Repeat that, please."

"3-30, $1,025.79 Matt Mardell's Taxidermy, LLC."

"My washing machine is busted, my daughter is getting laughed at in school, I have to beg my mother for money to buy her clothes and he gets a dead animal stuffed."

"I am sorry, I do not understand what you are saying. Do you wish to dispute the charge?"

"You bet. Wait until I talk to my husband when he gets home from work. Thank you for your time. I am sorry I had to waste it."

Jessalyn Teesdale roared out of the parking lot already late for her afternoon shift.

CHAPTER 6

THEY ONLY HAD three conversations in twenty-plus years, but the connection remained solid. Both had married. Marsha was divorced and childless. Joe DiNatale was finalizing his divorce from his high school sweetheart and had an adult son, Joey, who was at Penn State where Marsha and Joe had met. Joe had attended briefly for less than half of a trimester. Marsha had gone on to graduate and get her CPA before joining the FBI.

Tonight, they sat at an upscale restaurant on Clearwater beach making small talk. The motif combined a beachcomber flair with strategically mounted marlins, sharks and stingrays.

"So, are you going to tell me why you're not pitching this year?" She prodded.

"Not much to say, really. I went to bare-hand a line drive and it affected some of the nerves in my throwing hand. The injury affected my grip and I couldn't throw it effectively anymore."

"It" was a no-seam knuckleball that Joe had perfected

over all the years he threw batting practice to little leaguers.

"That was the no-hitter against the Mets in late September," she said.

Joe nodded. "It's funny how it was just last February that the Phillies saw me pitch down here during Phantasy Baseball Camp. It all started just a little over a year ago."

"And the rest, as they say, was a single season for the record books." Marsha was letting her fan-girl flag fly.

"Don't remind me. I can't go anywhere without getting hounded for autographs. My privacy is non-existent."

"Even in The Big Apple?" she asked.

Joe had waited until after the season to divorce his wife. He had then moved to Queens shortly after that to pursue a relationship with a woman who was just finishing her nursing degree. "You're right, I was just an average Joe up there, but when the Phillies invited me down for Spring Training, I got thrown back into it all over again."

"So, what are your plans?"

"We started talking about a new role for me this winter when my throwing sessions were not showing any progress with the knuckler. I was pretty good at coaching teenagers and a slot opened up for a bench coach for their minor league affiliate that plays here during the season. I still love the game and I can be a contributing member to the Phillies organization. These Single-A kids are barely out of high school themselves and have tons of talent, but still have a lot of growing up to do."

Joe was talking about the promising talent drafted in the Phillies farm system who were on the first rung on their climb to the big leagues.

The dinner and dessert plates were cleared an hour

earlier and both were drinking coffee. Joe was not a drinker and Marsha was trying not to be.

"What does your girlfriend think of the offer?" Marsha broached the subject with only the slightest of ulterior motive. She knew they still felt the chemistry that brought them together for a magical night in Nittany Valley.

"We met while I was a ballplayer during the season. She was going to school in the daytime and was a server at the hotel restaurant where the team was staying. She is a widow of fallen NYFD fireman with a young teenage daughter and no time or energy to get back in the game. She didn't know I was a ballplayer at first and we talked about raising kids under challenging circumstances. We just clicked.

"We treated the Fall and Winter, like an off-season with the expectation that I would heal and be back playing in the Spring.

She is finishing up her nursing degree and is tethered to the school and hospital for this year. Her daughter is a junior in high school and she would not think of moving her until she graduates."

"Sounds serious," she said.

"We are, but we are not in a hurry. Both of us need the time to see if this is what we really want," he replied.

Marsha understood completely. She and Joe had met briefly in college and she always thought they would have made a cute college couple. Joe abruptly withdrew from school without telling her, and eight months later, he was a teenage father of a baby boy and the husband to his high school sweetheart. It was not until his overnight rock-star celebrity, did they reconnect in late summer of last year. Back when her life was mostly healthy. They also shared more personal time at the funeral of Stew Menke. Stew didn't have many friends, but Joe was one of them.

Stew was an acerbic sports columnist who wrote about the Phillies for decades. He covered Joe's meteoric rise last year and then decided to return to his first love, the crime beat after the season ended. Marsha's connection to Stew was part of the reason why she felt badly for his friends and family.

Tonight, she was celebrating her release from the concussion protocols. The ER doctor had given her a clean bill of health, she had then retrieved her car and checked back into her hotel. The night was still young, and she was longing for a drink. She had been cold-turkey since getting hit by the foul ball and was surprised by the strength of her urges that passed over her in waves, making it harder to concentrate on the good-looking, rich, famous, single, but spoken-for man across the table.

"What about you, Marsha? What do the cards hold in store for you?"

"I'm on administrative leave from the bureau while they decide if I'm a hero or the scapegoat. I'm *persona non-grata* in Philly until this all blows over. I haven't heard from my parents, not even to see how I'm doing. I am kryptonite to my friends. I am only catching bits and pieces about the investigation from the internet."

* * *

The snoring woke her. Was it her own? *No.* There was someone else occupying the other side of the bed.

Whose bed am I in? Marsha noticed her unpacked suitcase where she had left it the day before. *My room. Oh God, I hope it's not D. That would be terrible. Mainly because I can't remember shit.*

She gently turned over to see it was a younger man. The

smile on his face spoke volumes. In the dim light, she could see that he was in good shape and was reasonably good-looking. It started to come back to her.

After she and Joe went their separate ways from the restaurant with a hug and a peck on the cheek, she came back to the hotel. Her feet walked her into the bar and onto a barstool and a beer automatically found its way into her hand. After that, it was a blur. She slowly disengaged from covers and pillows and made her way to the bathroom.

Still drunk. She sat naked on the pot and did a quick exam for any bodily fluid exchange. There was none that she could ascertain.

In the trashcan were two spent condoms. *Oh boy, we must have had a helluva time.* Back to the bedroom, she spotted an unopened condom on her side bed stand. *Guess I was saving that for dawn's early light.*

She staggered back into her clothes, wrote a note for lover boy telling him to leave before check-out, and she grabbed her roller suitcase and toiletry bag and quietly let herself out of the room. She swayed down the hallway to the elevator. Waiting there, she glanced in the mirror. *What a wreck!* She didn't like the person staring back at her.

That's it. I'm done with this shit.

Thankfully the doors opened to an empty carriage. She tramped through the almost-deserted lobby to the front desk. While waiting to check out, she stared at the TV screen with its sound muted.

The footage was being replayed of SWAT team members entering a gigantic warehouse. The streaming banner below the photo of the suspected shooter described him as a disgruntled employee. He had gunned down five co-workers before ending up on the wrong side of a firefight with the cops.

Marsha dragged her roller bag into the parking lot, tweaked her car fob and saw where she had parked her car from its blinking lights in the early pre-dawn mist. She threw her stuff in the cramped backseat behind the driver's side, cracked the windows and walked to the other side. Marsha got in and reclined the passenger seat. She fell fast asleep.

CHAPTER 7

"HI, my wife Jessalyn Teesdale picked out a washing machine today, I'm here to pick it up."

The woman behind the counter checked the pick-up log looking puzzled. "How do you spell her name?"

"J-E-S-S-A-L-Y-N last name T-E-E-S-D-A-L-E."

"Sorry, sir, I tried various spelling and we have no record of her buying a washing machine."

"There must be a mistake. Let me call her." His call went to voicemail. He texted her.

Come home and I will explain it to you. Jessalyn texted back.

They hadn't talked all day. Willis didn't know how to explain to her that the overtime spigot was being turned off. On his drive home, he thought about how his brothers were talking about entering a Missouri catfishing tournament. They would have to pony up the registration fees and airfares pretty soon. *The next Teesdale boys' adventure.* He couldn't wait.

His phone buzzed. It was Marty at the GMC dealership where he leased his trucks.

"Hey, Marty, what's up?"

"Hey, Willis. Black and gray are your colors, right?"

"Yeah. Why?"

"Gotta great deal here. Last year's Ram 1500 and I can blow it out on a three-year lease for $2,500 down and $575 a month. It's sweet. It's got all the toys. You're due soon, right?"

"May, Marty. May, two more months."

"Not a problem. We can let you out early. You really take care of your ride. We always get a pretty penny for your trade-ins at auction. Can you come in on Saturday to look her over and take a test-ride?"

Just then, a picture of the truck was texted to Willis. Stopped at the red light, he opened the text and studied it. The truck was more beautiful than what he was driving now and the monthly would be just a little more than he was paying now. "Yeah, Marty, she's a beauty. Ok, I will see you then."

He was thinking about how he could put the down payment on one of those fifteen-month interest-free credit cards as he walked in the house. He would pay it off and cut the card up and never use it again. They had a rule of having only one card with a low limit, but this was the kind of exception when they needed to handle an emergency or make a one-time purchase.

On the kitchen table, where dinner would usually be sitting, was a laundry basket full of his clothes next to a red jug of detergent.

Jessalyn was sitting at the table in her usual spot with what looked like business paperwork spread out in front of her under her folded hands.

"What's all this?" he asked.

"Until we can afford a washing machine, you can do

your own laundry at the laundromat. I separated them into darks and whites, you need to wash them separately, but can dry them together."

"Whaddyamean?" Willis was confused and getting a little perturbed.

"You nearly maxed out our credit card with the taxidermist bill to stuff that animal you killed in Wyoming. I had to stand there in front of all those people at the store when they declined the card. We have less than sixty bucks on the card, Willis."

"I didn't know that. You didn't tell me we were close to max. Is that why you left me looking stupid at the pick-up counter?" His embarrassment was turning to anger.

"Not as stupid as I felt when I found out you paid to have the damn thing stuffed," she retorted and then added, "When you called me up to tell me about your trip, I told you we were having money problems and that the washer broke. What did you think?"

Willis was in full-blown defensive mode now. "I thought that I could fix the washer. Where's dinner? I'm hungry."

Jess pointed to the box of Kraft macaroni and cheese on the counter. "It's that, or we go to Walmart and buy enough food to get us to payday, but before you decide, I want to show you something."

She walked him through the numbers. Four years of spending broken down by each expense item.

After about five minutes of seeing how much each of his trips cost, including the attendant outfitting and equipment, he really started to simmer. He got up from the table and walked over and looked into the barren shelves in the fridge. The cupboards held only spices, flour, and lard.

"I don't like walking into an ambush, especially after a long workday when I am tired and hungry."

"Willis, I am not beating you up. The numbers don't lie." Jessalyn pointed at the spreadsheet. "We can't keep living like this."

The pie chart of what each one was paid compared to what each one spent on themselves was most damning. His spending far outstripped his contribution to the family finances. That hit him the hardest. His view as the breadwinner evaporated like steam off the pavement after an afternoon shower.

"We have to dig out of this hole, and we can't do a re-fi on the house. We are upside down on the loan." She showed him the latest bank statement and what comparable houses were selling in their area.

He hadn't yet told her about Lane coming back to work and how he would suck up all of the overtime that usually bailed them out in the past.

"Can't you work overtime?" he asked.

"My job doesn't allow for OT. You know that. We work shifts and have overflow associates when the call volume spikes. They don't ask me about taking a promotion to Dallas anymore. They know we are here for your job and until Briana graduates high school. Besides working full-time during the week, I work at the restaurant Saturdays. I need Sunday off or I'd go bananas. What about you?"

Willis physically backed himself into the corner and looked away. "No overtime, business is slow."

"What about the call-outs?"

"What did I say, Jess," raising his voice, "No OT. Okay?"

Jess stood up and walked around the table to face him.

"That means you're free to work somewhere else at nights or on the weekend."

Willis was not used to her confronting him this way. "What? You expect me to wash dishes?"

"It's straightforward, Willis, if we can't make more money, then we have to spend less. Where do you suggest we start tightening the belt?"

Avoiding the question, he said, "I'm not eating mac n' cheese. Let's go shopping."

He waited for her in the truck. *First, I find out that the OT has dried up and then she didn't buy the washing machine, and now she is scolding me like a school-boy.*

She climbed in the truck and shuffled through a handful of coupons from the circulars. There was a stony silence between them. "How many miles on your truck, Willis?"

"30,185. Why?"

"My Corolla has over 175,000. We will need to replace that when we give it Bri. The next car we get will have to be for me."

"Mine is going off lease soon and I can get a good deal on a leftover," he chimed in hopefully.

"Can you find out how much and for how long it would cost to buy this off lease?"

Jessalyn tapped on the dashboard. "This is nice, you could keep it for a long time."

"And why would I do that? I have a clean truck with all repairs being done under warranty." *That's the way the Teesdale boys did it.*

"Like you said, hon, you take good care of your vehicle, with proper maintenance it should last a long time. Wouldn't it be nice not to have a car payment for a change? And the insurance will go down as it gets older."

The idea of driving a rust bucket like some of the old

geezers living on the outskirts of the town where he grew up was a non-starter. His stomach was turning in knots. *When is she gonna stop?*

"Bottom line, we need to write up a budget and plan on me getting another used car next year. It gonna be hard enough to swing two car payments while we are upside down on the re-fi and maxed out on the credit card," Jessalyn said.

He knew enough not to argue about the truck. "Look, I've had a lot for one day. I'm sorry about the washer, OK? Can we just let it go for now and get something to cook? I am starved."

They parked and walked silently into the store. It was busy for a weeknight. Willis headed for the hunting and fishing section while Jess grabbed a shopping cart for the food aisles.

Twenty minutes later, Jess was placing the coupons and the five days of hamburger, chicken, pasta, and pre-packaged deli meats on the conveyor belt next to the large Diet Pepsi bottles and paper towels.

"Excuse me. Sorry, I'm with her." Willis weaved between shoppers and their carts in the line behind Jess to bring his armful of stuff to the cashier to ring up. He handed the cashier the first item. Freshwater fishing line with a picture of hooked big-mouth bass on the label. Jess grabbed it from the surprised cashier and looked at it. She then looked at the other items on the belt. Some ammo, thermal socks, and a blaze orange rain poncho.

Jessalyn pointed at the register and said, "This is the last bit of money on the card, we only have enough money for food."

"Do you have any cash?" he asked.

"Yes, but I need to hold onto it until we get paid."

Willis looked in his wallet and came to the same conclusion. He was embarrassed. "I'm sorry, I'll take them back."

He started to gather them up and turn to go back to wade past the irate shoppers in line behind them when the cashier said, "That's okay. Just set it there and I'll call someone from restocking."

The Teesdales stood in silence, both simmering, while their meager food order was completed and bagged.

She strode ahead of him, cutting an angry swath past incoming shoppers. The kindly greeter took one look at the charging mama bear and stepped quickly aside. Into the parking lot with no apparent regard to the cars pulling into and out of parking stalls, Jess slammed the rattling carriage over the weed-covered ruts.

She waited for him to unlock the truck, threw the packages in the back of the extended cab and walked back to confront him as he approached the driver's side.

She raised her voice. "We were going food shopping, Willis, not toy shopping."

He upped the ante. "You embarrassed me in there. You wouldn't talk to Briana that way." He upped the ante.

"That's right. She never put toys in the shopping cart, even as a child, Willis."

Passersby took notice.

"You've been on my case since I came home, Jess."

A few stopped.

Jess moved in close and cut the distance between them. "We can't buy the things we need and you are buying toys. Don't you get it?"

A woman pulled out her cell phone and began filming.

"Listen, I don't drink, I bring my paycheck straight home on payday. I work hard for everything I get. I don't need to hear your crap." They were red face to red face.

"Less than an hour ago, we talked about having to tighten our belts. I bought the cheapest food we could afford to get by and you want to buy your toys. How is that tightening the belt?" she screeched at him.

"Back off, Jess, I am warning you."

"I have to beg my mother for clothes for our child and you spend over a thousand dollars to get a dead animal stuffed." She snorted at him.

"That's enough," he barked, giving the growing crowd a nervous scan.

Others coming out of the store with their carts stopped and stared. A young woman with a toddler in tow put the child in the carriage and began dialing her cell phone.

"No, you listen to me, Willis. I don't have to live like poor white trash while you drive around in a shiny truck and go flying around the country on your adventures." With that, she wheeled around and kicked his truck.

Without thinking, he shoved her to the ground. "Stop acting stupid!" he yelled.

Jess sat on the asphalt and looked at her skinned knees and palms. "Don't you ever put your hands on me again, Willis Teesdale."

"Y'all better knock it off. I called the police, they will be here any minute." The young mom said while trying to placate her crying two-year-old.

Willis looked over at the young woman shaking her cell phone at him. Standing next to her was a teenager with his cell phone camera pointed at them. The crowd had grown.

He reached down to Jessalyn with his hand outstretched.

"I don't need your help. Thank you very much." She got to her feet, brushing the gravel from her skinned knees and walked to the passenger side of the pick-up.

"Show's over, folks," Willis said as he scooted into the driver's seat and revved the engine.

They drove through the empty stall in front of them and out of the parking lot from the opposite direction they had come and away from the two oncoming squad cars.

Neither spoke on the ride home.

Jess quickly fried two burgers while heating frozen mixed veggies in the microwave. Willis was angered by her confrontational posturing from the minute he had gotten home, topping it off with the public humiliation in the parking lot.

Apologizing was not on the agenda for her it seemed. He was not going to say he was sorry for stopping her from making a bigger fool of herself in public. How would he explain the dent in the quarter panel when he went to trade the truck on Saturday?

She plated the food, threw the frying pan in the sink, and stormed off to the bedroom.

There was a knock on the door. Willis got up from the table with his mouth full of dinner. Chewing and trying to swallow, he could see two Clearwater police cruisers parked in front of his double-wide trailer. His food had trouble going down as his heart raced up through his chest. He nearly choked as they knocked again.

He opened the door to two officers standing sideways on either side of the front step.

"Willis Teesdale?"

"Yes?"

"We understand that you and a woman were arguing in the parking lot at Walmart and it got physical."

"No, sir. You must be mistaken."

The female officer spoke next. "We watched the video

of what happened. How do you think we got your license plate and address so quickly?"

Willis had dealings with the police on call-outs to fix broken audible alarms at businesses and he didn't recognize either officer. He had a friendly, helpful attitude with them, knowing that they could not leave the scene until the alarm was fixed or silenced. Tonight, he didn't know what to say or do next.

"What were you two fighting about? It looked pretty heated," the male officer continued.

"We had a difference of opinion, that's all. It's all fixed. Everything is fine."

"May we come in or do you want your neighbors to hear what's going on?" The male officer tried looking past Willis into the interior of the dwelling.

"What do you need to come in for?" Willis was gulping for air.

The female officer spoke first and moved towards him. "We want to hear the lady's side of the story."

"Nothing to tell, like I said. We came home, patched it up, she made dinner and went back to take a shower."

Both officers looked at each other and the female officer spoke first. "I want to see her, and if that's what she tells me, then we'll believe you."

"There's no problem, officer." Jess pushed past Willis in her bathrobe, which covered her knees. Her hands were stuffed in each pocket. "We're starting to have money problems and neither one of us knows how to deal with it. I'm sorry."

"What's your name, ma'am?" the female officer asked.

"Jessalyn Teesdale. I'm his wife."

Quickly the male officer asked, "Mr. Teesdale, do you want to press charges for the damage to your pick-up?"

"God, no."

"Mrs. Teesdale, do you want to press charges for the assault on your person?" the female cop asked.

"I was furious and my husband tried stopping me from hitting his truck again and I fell down. I'm fine." Jess shrugged. "You see me, I'm fine. We are not mad anymore. It won't happen again. I promise."

"Mrs. Teesdale, here is my card. I hope you are right, but just in case you ever want to talk."

Jess snatched it quickly, palm down, without smiling and returned her hand to her bathrobe pocket.

The male cop added, "Mr. Teesdale, we have enough to arrest you both for creating a public disturbance just from the video and the witnesses at the scene. You two put on quite a show."

"We don't have the surveillance cameras from the store yet, but can pull their feed if we need to," the female cop added.

Jess pleaded, "Please, no. We are members in good standing at Clearwater Church of the Rock. Neither of us has ever been in trouble. We both work good jobs, but we got over our heads on our bills. We can get help. I will call you, officer, and tell you where we are going and you can verify it. I promise." Jess shook her hand with the card in her pocket.

The male cop looked at the female cop and, as if it were against her better judgment, she said to Jess, "Call me with your plans and we'll decide what to do next."

The Teesdales watched from their doorway as the police officers departed. No sooner were they off the street, away from the eyes of prying neighbors, a candy apple red Mustang convertible with Pennsylvania plates pulled in behind Charlie's sedan next door.

CHAPTER 8

"THANKS, CHARLIE. I APPRECIATE IT."

"Not a problem."

His living room was cool, the couch comfortable, and with the shades drawn down, Marsha felt like she could tell him everything. So she did.

"I left Miami when the Bank and Fugitive squads were down-sized after 9/11 and I returned home to finish my career on the Organized Crime squad. A Russian mob boss died and we didn't realize who he was until all of Philly's mob bosses showed up at his wake."

Charlie sighed. "I'm glad I retired when I did. The bureau is nothing like what it was when we were the federal alpha-dog crime-fighters."

Sipping from her 7-Eleven Big Gulp, Marsha continued. "His death left a power vacuum and bodies started dropping everywhere. It was like the Wild West. A reporter was tortured to death and I knew that it was related. Philly PD wanted to treat it like a regular homicide, and I was told in no uncertain terms to back off."

Charlie said, "Your friend, the baseball player, filled me

in on the rest of the story while we were waiting at the hospital on your tests. It got a lot worse, I take it, and that's why you are hiding out down here."

Marsha nodded and then looked away. "No family, no friends, cut off from work and being treated like I had leprosy, what was I gonna do?" Another sip and another deep breath. "Needed to get out of Dodge and I figured that this girl could use a little sunshine and warmth in her life." She shrugged, looking down at the floor.

"But?"

"You know, Charlie, I could always keep up with the boys when it came to drinking; learned it as a sorority sister in college."

"Drank me under the table a few times as I recall," Charlie said.

"I would occasionally tie one on, but after the reporter died, my world turned to shit." She pulled on the sugary drink and sat looking at him.

She blurted, "It happened so fast, Charlie. I woke up this morning with a guy in my bed and I didn't know how he got there." She hid her eyes from her former boss.

"He slip you something?"

"If I thought he did, you'd be bailing me out at the police station for aggravated assault. No, I had a blackout, and this wasn't the first time that I blacked out. That's what scares me. I had a nice dinner with DiNatale and left him to go back to my hotel, and the next thing I remember is some total stranger snoring next to me."

"That's not good," he said.

"I know," she replied.

"If it's any consolation, I dove into the bottle after Mary died. Happy hour usually started around noon and I drank only on the days that ended with the letter Y. It took me getting stopped for DUI in the middle of the afternoon on a weekday to wake up."

"You get pinched?"

"Naw, told the trooper that I just lost my wife and had a couple beers with my depression meds."

"Did he buy it?"

"She. It was a female trooper that pulled me over. Not until I showed her my wife's funeral home card and my retired FBI credentials at the same time. She told her dispatch that my car overheated and I'd come back for it later. She gave me a ride to exit. Uber was a lot cheaper than bail and a lawyer, let me tell you." Charlie sipped his cold instant coffee. "I came home and threw out all the booze and became my gang's designated driver."

"How hard was it to quit?"

"It sucked. In hindsight, I should have gone into a program, but being a former supervisory agent in charge, I had too much pride to walk into the AA rooms. I dealt with Mary's death the hard way; no program, no grief counseling, no nothing except...." He drifted off into thought.

"What?"

"Work. I blew the dust off my PI license that I kept renewing after I retired and just started working again. Ex-agents keep the connection and we do jobs for each other. Since I'm down here in Tampa-St.Pete, me and a few other retirees split up all the stuff that comes our way. It keeps me sharp and keeps me out of trouble."

"Do you miss it—the drinking, I mean?" Marsha asked him in such a way that she knew that she would have to say goodbye to Mr. Beam, Mr. Walker, and Old Grandad.

"Naw, I was a lightweight back in the day. It was missing Mary that I had to deal with. I am doing it without the booze one day at a time like the bumper sticker says."

"Well, you know they cut me off from working until they sort out all the bodies. God knows I have my own grieving to do. It's been all bottled up inside." She began to tear up.

"Well, Marsha, it looks like Old Charlie Akers has to bail your sorry ass out again."

She looked at him, puzzled.

"I've got more work than I can shake a stick at, and for some of it, a young woman is better suited for than an old sheepdog like me."

"I can't work for you, Charlie. I'm still in Limbo."

"Not offering you a paying job. You get free room and board and all the corny jokes that you can handle. You can be my 'operative.'" Charlie made the air quotes. "I write the reports, I handle the invoicing. Besides, I always enjoyed watching you figure things out. Humor me."

"I dunno."

"Listen, I gotta go to the bathroom. Close your eyes and when I come back, open them and say yes."

Marsha did as she was instructed. *Never thought I'd be in a position like this. Down and out in Clearwater and craving alcohol. No, I am craving something else and booze is the substitute. No boyfriend or co-workers to confide in. I can talk to Charlie about anything. He's been there and knows what real grief is. Joe, too. He will be around for the season. I can't figure this out on my own.*

Just then, she heard the toilet flush and the water run, the bathroom door squeaked open and his shadow preceded him into the living room. Charlie stood in the door frame and was hard to read.

It's my call. She cleared her voice. "I can't cook worth a damn."

"That's okay," he replied. "You can clean up afterward."

They both smiled.

Marsha was led to the spare bedroom. The covers were turned down with a small box of chocolates on the pillow. *How did he know I would say yes?*

"This is how we roll at the Aker's Airbnb," he said.

She dropped her roller and toiletry bag on the bed and turned, closed their distance and gave him a polite but firm hug. "It's perfect."

CHAPTER 9

"OH MY GAWD!" Marsha was trying on her best New York accent. "How can you sell them soooo cheap?"

They were beautiful, she had to admit. The Balenciaga bags that Marsha touched and was secretly recording with Charlie's pinhole camera could have been legitimate. Wrapping and tagging showed the same markings as the real bags they had studied for the assignment. The PI out of Los Angeles working counterfeits for the big-name designers had his hands full. The secondary market was flooded with knockoffs.

A rack of Prada dresses on one side of the display table competed with a display of Hermès scarves on the other. Back in her Miami days, a visit to the upscale stores on Los Olas in Fort Lauderdale with her girlfriends was not unusual. She always dressed well and accessorized for success when she wasn't scaling backyard fences in Liberty City running down fugitives. She knew the good stuff.

"Sometimes the factory will produce 10,000 of a product and then make 2,000 more on the run and sell them off cheaply," came the reply from the wary saleswoman.

The location was not a high-end boutique, but one of the last remaining drive-in movie theaters that served as a flea market on the weekends during the daytime. The poles that held the drive-ins speakers marked each stall. Marsha could not place the eastern European accent but was glad it was not Russian.

"How do I know it's not a knockoff?" Marsha turned the bag around in her hands, squinting at it from various angles, her cell phone was recording the audio.

"Look at the lining and all the metal clasps. Feel the stitching. Do you see any discolorations anywhere? Original packaging too."

"It's beautiful." Marsha acted indecisively.

The saleswoman waited.

"It's a lot of money." Marsha put it down on the table and started to walk away.

The woman gently touched her elbow to halt Marsha's exit. "Make me an offer."

Marsha pulled out a marked $50.00 bill from her no-name purse and held it before the hidden camera.

Deftly, the bill was snatched, and the bag went into an everyday white shopping bag with its packaging. "I make an exception for you, beautiful lady, you will love it."

"Now, how about that Magenta scarf?" the saleswoman asked. "Look at how it matches your new bag and your eyes."

She left the flea market with the bag and the scarf. Marsha returned to Charlie's car after making sure she wasn't tailed. She was jazzed. "They never let me work undercover back in Miami, Charlie. That was fun."

"Yeah, you didn't have that strung-out junkie look back in the day."

"I dunno Charlie, look what Charlize Theron did in *Monster*."

"We both know what working undercover does to your soul," Charlie volleyed back.

"Tru dat."

She had to admit, she was having fun, getting back in the saddle again, even though it might be for lesser stakes, or so she thought.

Charlie entered the flea market just before closing and videotaped the woman breaking down her stall and he did a foot follow on her to the exit where a windowless cargo van marked up with gang graffiti was waiting. As she and her companions pulled out, Marsha, now wearing a Tampa Bay Rays cap over a jeans jacket, both she had bought for peanuts at the Flea. She skidded to a stop where Charlie was standing. Marsha's aviator glasses completed the disguise. The goodies that Marsha had bought were in the trunk.

"They only authorized us for a one-car follow," Charlie said. "I didn't think the lit-up Christmas tree of a car you drive would be suitable for a second chase car."

"What? You have no eyes in the sky? What kind of rinky-dink operation are you running Charlie?" Marsha quipped.

"Welcome to the world of private investigations, Marsha," he said. "Let's do a loose tail. It's better not to spook them. I may be able to get a two-car authorization next week if they're still around."

The van meandered on surface roads past the airport's air cargo terminals to a gated storage facility. The bar raised and they went in. The corrugated tin storage sheds all had the roll-up gates held shut by a single padlock. The van disappeared into the interior of the sprawling complex.

Marsha spotted security cameras mounted high on the ends of the rows. "We can come back Monday and pull the tapes." She began to relax.

Charlie interrupted her chill with, "Follow that car and honk when you get behind them."

Marsha pulled in behind the rust-bucket loaded down with clothes in the back seat and a used mattress on the roof that the male passenger was holding down with his arm out the window. Charlie was out of the car and up to the guy, scaring the bejesus out of him. She watched the animated conversation and Charlie's quick flash of his credentials. The Camry lurched through and Marsha just made it before the bar came down, and then she picked up Charlie.

"You forget, grasshopper, that we don't have the badge and gun out here. I go in on Monday and they will tell me that I need a subpoena from their corporate offices. That is if they don't just tell me to go shit in my hat."

Twelve rows in, they spotted the van mid-row with the doors up on the unit. "Let's get the money shot," Charlie said, borrowing a phrase from the porn industry.

Marsha went down the row and pretended to slow down so that they didn't hit the van while her co-pilot shot video of the storage unit's interior. The setting sun illuminated the scene and back-lit Charlie's plain vanilla sedan and its occupants. The storage unit was half-filled with product stacked to the ceiling.

"Score," Charlie said.

* * *

Marsha was watching the news from Charlie's couch with the last of her sushi and a Diet Coke.

The video was being replayed of the aftermath of a mass shooting at a festival in Santa Fe, two weeks previously. The talking head explained how the gunman acquired the weapon he used in the shooting because of a fault in the law known as the Charleston Loophole – a loophole in gun laws that permits licensed gun sellers to sell guns if a background check is not completed within three days. The shooter in Charleston walked into an AME church and shot nine people attending a bible study.

She heard a knock on the front door.

She opened it to the surprised look of a woman carrying a laundry basket and detergent.

"Oh, hi, I'm the next-door neighbor. Charlie said I could use his washer until I get a new one."

"Hi, I'm Marsha, come on in."

Just then, Charlie entered the living room as Marsha muted the TV. "Hi, Jess, howzitgoin?"

"Another day in paradise."

The three of them looked at each other in awkward silence until Charlie said, "Marsha used to work with me in Miami, she is visiting for a while."

"I saw your car in the driveway. It's nice. All the way from Pennsylvania, huh? Must be cold up there."

"Yeah, I needed a break. Charlie's nice enough to put me up and put up with me." Marsha grinned at her former boss.

The women walked down to the utility room. Marsha watched as Jess put in the darks first and started the wash cycle.

Jess asked, "Were you in the FBI too?"

"Still am, I've got a few more years before I can retire."

"That's a neat job, you must have a ton of stories."

Marsha flashed on the recent story that had her all twisted up inside and instead deflected with, "You could say that. How about you, Jess?"

She laughed and said, "Lived here all my life, married after I graduated high school and got pregnant right away with my daughter. I work as a telephone rep for a mortgage company. You look familiar to me, I think I know from where."

Oh god, I hope she hadn't seen the coverage after the Philly shoot-out. Marsha remained silent, waiting for the shoe to drop.

"I work Saturday nights at O'Sullivan's and I filled in for a girl that was sick the other night. Were you with an attractive dark-haired man?"

Relieved, Marsha said, "Yes, he's spoken for. We've been friends for over twenty years."

"I wasn't your server, but I thought you two made an attractive couple."

Marsha blushed. "Maybe someday. How about you?"

"I married the first boy that I fell in love with. We've been together ever since."

They moved to the living room and kept the TV muted. Sensing Jess wanted to talk more, Marsha encouraged her with, "And?"

"Well, like any marriage, there are ups and downs, and lately, it seems like it's been a lot more downs."

"I was married once. Mr. O'Shea wanted me to stop playing cops and robbers to settle down and make babies."

"I take it you didn't."

"Nope, but I did keep his name." Marsha smiled.

"Any regrets?" Jess asked.

"Hell yeah, plenty of them, but not divorcing him. I

would have had to quit doing what I loved long before I was ready." She paused. "I regret not having babies and some of my work decisions, but I can't change either of them." As she said that, she accepted maybe for the first time some of the decisions she made recently. With that came a flood of emotions. Startled and unsettled, she moved to change the subject. "How'd you guys meet?"

"My church sponsored a mission trip for the youth group to repair houses after a hurricane ripped through central Florida. His youth group was there and we worked side by side for almost two weeks. We started dating long distance after that."

"That's certainly a different way to get to know somebody."

"Yeah, between the flies and mosquitoes and the summer humidity with no air conditioning, it certainly was not a vacation. Both of us were away from home for the first time and we were given real adult responsibilities. I liked what I saw in him and I guess he liked what he saw in me."

"But now the bloom is off the rose?"

"That's a nice way of saying it. I thought we were working hard and getting by on what we made. He pretty much handled the bills and worked overtime when we needed to pay for the extras."

"But?"

"I never looked at how much he was spending to go hunting and fishing around the country with his brothers, until just the other day when the washer broke."

"And?"

"My daughter and I live like poor white trash while he drives a new shiny truck and goes on his mighty adventures. I'm busting my bunnies six days a week and we are going backward. He just doesn't get it. Worse, he's in denial." Jess shook her head. "And to top it off, there's no overtime."

They both watched the struggling contestant lose everything on the Daily Double on *Jeopardy*.

"I don't know why I'm telling you all this. I'm sorry." Jess bit her lip.

Marsha said, "Don't be sorry, I'm safe. God knows, I am not gonna judge you. I won't blab your business to anybody else. While I'm here, you can always stop by."

"Thanks, Marsha. We are going to talk to a credit counselor. He needs to hear it from somebody else that the party is over."

Charlie came out from his office and interrupted them, "Hey, Jess, how would you like to do some undercover work with Marsha tomorrow night?"

CHAPTER 10

"HOW LATE ARE you going to be?" Willis asked.

"As long as the case takes. I don't know, Willis," Jessalyn replied as she was getting dressed to go out.

"You look like you're going out on a date," Willis complained.

Briana came into their bedroom. "Whoa. Mom, you're looking good." Briana came into their bedroom.

"Thanks, honey. Do you need anything?"

"No, I was just wondering why you were going out on a Sunday night."

"Charlie asked me to work a case for him, baby. He's gonna pay me $200 cash for the night. He said if he went out by himself to some of the bars, they'd be suspicious of him immediately. We are going to make believe that it's my birthday and I'm having a girl's night out. The lady that owns the Mustang used to work for him in Miami before he retired. She is staying with Charlie for her vacation. She's pretending to be my designated driver. We have to go to a list of bars to see if they are showing a fight on their flat screens. If they are, it's called signal piracy. She's gonna get the proof for Charlie. These bars were supposed to pay a fee to run these pay-per-views and they didn't sign up."

"You don't even like watching boxing. Why would you go?" Willis asked.

"Oh that is so exciting, I wish I could go with you, Mom," her daughter said.

To both of them, Jess said, "He's paying me to go out for a night on the town and for all my food and drinks. All I have to do is act like the birthday girl. Woo hoo!"

The women laughed at Jessalyn's transformation into a party girl as the husband sulked into the living room to watch his favorite hunting show.

"This is so cool, Mom. You are gonna be an undercover spy."

"When I was over doing the wash last night, Charlie asked Marsha and me if we would do it. Cable piracy is a big business and he has turned down more of them than he has accepted. He can make really good money if he catches a couple bars doing this. He has the list of those bars that paid for the pay-per-view and he has an idea who's not paying up."

"How does he know?"

"Sorry, Briana, it's a secret."

Just then, Jess heard Marsha's car start up.

"That's my cue. I gotta go. Wish me luck." Jess gave Briana a peck on the cheek. As she made her way out of the house, she said, "Don't wait up for me, Willis."

He didn't bother to look up.

"Do you mind if I put the top down? It's a nice night," Marsha asked. She was dressed up for a night out with the girls with painted-on jeans and a tight black top. She and Charlie agreed that going to bars might be tricky for her. By asking Jess to go, it would give her an excuse not to drink and concentrate on the steps needed to document the piracy.

"It's warm for you snowbirds, Marsha, I'll wear my jacket.

My daughter asked me how Charlie knew would who would be showing the fights without paying for the rights."

"Beer consumption."

"Huh?"

"The reason they steal the feed is to bring more customers in. More customers drink more beer and they will also pay a small cover too. The beer deliveries are usually made Thursdays and Fridays for the weekend. He followed the delivery trucks out of the distribution center and made friends with the drivers. The drivers know exactly how much the normal delivery is, as they have to lug the kegs and cases of beer into the bars.

"He convinced the guys to alert him about this weekend. Some of the places have even advertised the fights. You have March Madness with college basketball, but other than that, the fights are the big attraction. The delivery guys told him who was getting a larger order for the weekend. He subtracted out the bars paying for the feed. Here is the list we have."

Marsha showed it to Jess. "I already put them into my GPS and we are going to work them from furthest away to closest to home. Charlie's going to a couple of shot-and-beer bars in the not so nice part of town where he would fit in just fine. For every solid hit, he will give the delivery guys a hundred dollars per."

"That's amazing how he figured that out."

"Welcome to the world of paid confidential informants."

"What about the other PI's he usually works with?

They all said they were busy and begged off. What's so important on a Sunday night? I don't get it."

"It's not that they were busy, they would only work on an hourly basis, and for a premium at that. The lawyer that hired Charlie pays on an 'eat what you kill' basis. Charlie could not pay these guys to go out all night and get nothing."

Marsha noticed her new friend was hanging on her every word. Reminded her a little bit about how Ramit was when they let him out of the office. "Are you excited, Jess?"

"Absolutely. I have never done anything like this in my whole life."

Marsha admitted, "I worked some thrilling cases in my career and I've got to tell you, this sounds like fun."

Two girls out on the town, top-down, radio on, and hair blowing in the breeze. Marsha drove across Tampa to a locally owned restaurant with a dance floor and a sizable bar.

"They have balls," she said. On the valet stand was a sign for a $5.00 cover next to a picture of the promotional flyer for the fight. She zoomed her cell phone camera on the flyer and then panned out on people forking over the cash and then the exterior of the restaurant. They approached the bouncer who saw they were of age and female.

"Welcome, ladies, are you here for the fights?"

"Fights? On no, we are celebrating my birthday. Hubby is home watching the kids." Jessalyn said, following her script that they rehearsed in the car.

"Girl's night out," Marsha said, giving the black dress-shirt a wink.

"Step right inside, ladies," he said, waiving the cover.

"What shall I order, Marsha?" Jess whispered to her.

Realizing that her own beer and whiskey habit was not

suitable for an amateur, she said, "Ask for a Ketel with ice and a side of water. Nurse half the drink and drink the water until we are ready to leave and then pour the rest into the water."

Marsha found the bar's license on the wall and pretended to take a video of Jessalyn toasting her birthday. Jess took a generous gulp and her eyes bugged out while she stifled a gag. Marsha kept the camera rolling from the license to the hi-def flat screen showing the preliminaries before the first fight on the card. The only way they could have this on the screen was by pirating the feed.

"Smooth." Jess coughed.

Marsha toasted her with ginger ale. "Happy birthday, Jessie." Marsha then surreptitiously took video of the bartenders and servers doing a brisk business, she then walked back to the restrooms and shot video through the swinging doors to the kitchen. Next to the entranceway was the department of health license identifying the restaurant and owner. In the bathroom, she made sure she had captured the video. She moved it to Dropbox and returned to Jess.

A man had wasted no time in approaching Jess and had engaged her in conversation.

Enjoying the attention, Jessalyn declined his offer to buy her a drink and continued to sip her iced vodka.

Marsha sat on the stool on the other side of the man and took more video of the crowd. Chairs and tables had been set up on the dance floor and the servers were busy bringing out food and pitchers of beer. Marsha peeked at her checklist folded up in her credit card holder on the back of her phone. One more chore.

"Excuse me, sir, but I just got a call from the sitter and we've got to leave now," Marsha said.

Jess finished her drink and they left him standing there.

Out of earshot, she asked Marsha, "And what did the sitter tell you?"

"She asked me where did I keep the condoms," Marsha deadpanned.

Jessalyn Teesdale laughed loudly as she teetered out of the bar.

The last thing was to get license plates off the cars parked farthest away from the building in the parking lot. This would be a possible way to identify employees if the case had to go to court. Before arriving at the next bar, Marsha drove and dictated a fill in the blank boilerplate affidavit. She sent it off to Charlie and he gave her a big thumbs up emoticon.

The next restaurant was bustling for a Sunday night. It's reserved dining room held a wedding reception with an open bar. *A good reason for the more significant order of booze,* Marsha surmised.

As they walked into a sports bar, Jessalyn asked, "Do you think we could split a couple of appetizers?"

They immediately saw the place was packed and

lightweights were dancing around the ring on most of the screens. There was one vacant tabletop in the corner away from the screens and most of the noise.

Marsha negotiated with a server for a serving of nachos and wings to go with their sodas. The server yelled back that a cover for the fight would be added to their bill. Marsha nodded, and then to Jess. "This place is a zoo. I don't know how I can get everything Charlie needs." The birthday girl cover was obviated by the press of people. Nobody cared.

As they waited, Marsha got up and walked to the bathroom mostly to do recon. She couldn't find the liquor license or the food license. Except for the screen showing the fight, it was dark and claustrophobic. When she returned, Jess was smiling.

"Look at your place setting," she said.

Right there in four-color art was the calendar of events for the bar. For that night, the fights were featured with a cover charge. It had the bar's logo, address, and social media icons.

"Stupid is as Stupid does. Hey, we should bring Charlie and Willis here for Wednesday all-you-can-eat Wing nite." Marsha smiled as she slipped it into her purse.

They ate, they talked, both took turns going to the bathroom and Marsha took video of bartenders, servers, barbacks, and the glad-handing owner. When the guy in the black trunks was announced as the winner by decision, they settled their tab with Charlie's money, got the receipt, and headed off to the next destination.

At the next place, Marsha asked, "Jess, do you want to wait in the car?"

Roxanne's Red Light was in the industrial area near the airport. No schools or churches were within 1500 feet. Jess figured it out in a couple of beats. "All nude! Oh, my God!"

Breathing deeply as to summon her courage, she said, "Maybe the birthday girl has never been in a place like this and she wants to walk on the wild side just once. I mean, after all, it's for the case, right?"

Marsha laughed. "Just don't order a lap dance. We can't expense that."

The doormen with tuxedos, earpieces, bulging necks, and biceps waved the ladies in without charging them a cover, all the time feigning minimal interest in two women who would frequent an upscale gentlemen's club on a Sunday night.

The cocktail waitress placed a Ketel on ice with a water chaser in front of Jessalyn, who maintained eye-contact with the server, even though the server's cleavage spilled out of her skimpy top. The girl's red hair hung down to either side of her breasts, framing her most-noticeable assets. Marsha's Diet Coke arrived with a similar presentation. She paid cash for both and left the smiling server with the balance of the twenty.

"I don't think Charlie is going to have a problem with identifying this bar by the video."

Marsha carefully hid her cell phone while she taped the middleweights duking it out on the screen through the upside-down V of the dancer's legs on the main stage. The pounding bass notes and flashing lights added to the difficulty of filming while the dancer twirled on the pole. Off to the right side of the spotless main room, scantily-clad dancers were leading men by the hand to the VIP rooms.

"Where are they going?" Jess yelled into Marsha's ear as she nudged her to look.

"Champagne rooms for private dances or VIP rooms for lap dances. Guys can't touch the girls with their hands, but otherwise, it can get pretty frisky."

Jess was taking it all in, and before she knew it, her empty glass was replaced by a full one. Eye contact was not maintained on this visit. The tattoo above the servers left breast of red rose in bloom had an almost 3-D look.

"Oh my, I always wondered what went on in a place like this. Most of these girls are stunning or, or...."

Marsha answered, "Exotic."

"Yes. Exotic, mysterious, and young, very young." Jessalyn continued to sip and surveil.

Marsha said, "They are selling the promise of something more to come. Do you mind if we leave now? I have everything I'm gonna get without getting caught. A camera of any kind in a strip-club is a no-no."

"Okay." Jessalyn pushed off the tabletop with a stagger.

Marsha grabbed her by the arm and guided her to the door. "You know why they think we came?"

"No, why?"

"They think we were on the prowl for a girl to come home with us."

"Really?"

"Really."

"I've lived a sheltered life, Marsha."

"Be thankful for that, Jess. There's more baggage in a place like this than at a Sear's liquidation sale."

Once outside, the valet brought her Mustang around. Marsha helped Jess to her seat, much to the chagrin of the muscle-heads leering at them.

"Do you think you can put the top up Marsha? It's getting cold out."

"Okay, but it's ginger ale for the both of us from now on. I can't bring you home shit-faced. Oh, by the way, how's your Spanish?"

"Why?"

"The next place is Hispanic."

"I speak a little."

"The feature event has a guy from Mexico challenging the light-heavyweight champ. Maybe we should have gone there first," Marsha second-guessed.

"We'll be fine. You're pretty and I'm tipsy. The guys will make room for us."

Marsha looked over at her friend with the loopy smile swaying in her seat to the dance music emitting from the Mustang's speakers.

"What can be better than this?" Marsha asked. They

pulled into a parking spot that just opened up by outdoor seating under a corrugated awning attached to the establishment. In the corner above a serving station was the screen, angled just for them. The fight was on it and Marsha placed her zoom adapter on her cell phone and filled her screen with the contest. She then removed the adapter and slowly filmed the crowd. "I'll get a to-go menu and be right back."

Every worker in the kitchen was transfixed to the hi-def screens above the horseshoe bar that was three-deep with bodies. She got the Department of Health permit, the liquor permit and good facials of the bartenders and servers who were all glued to the fight. She floated around the building like a ghost, nobody paid the least attention to her. The Champ defended his belt with a second-round knock-out, much to the booing of the crowd.

Their work was done for the night. By the time they would have gotten to the last place, regular programming would be on the screens.

Coming back to the car, she was not surprised to see Jess snoozing. Just then, she received a text from Charlie. It read: *Waffle House?*

"Wake up, sleepyhead." Marsha shook Jessalyn's arm.

She woke with a start. "Okay, okay, I'm okay."

"Charlie wants to meet us at the Waffle House. Whaddya think? Should I take you home first?"

"No, the birthday girl needs coffee and some dessert before going home to her same-old, same-old."

They rode with the windows open while Marsha kept Jess talking about the night and her life until they found the back booth of the restaurant where Charlie was looking at the video on his laptop. He looked up at the returning warriors. His steaming coffee sat next to the closed menu.

"Three out of four, that's fantastic," he said.

"How'd you do, Charlie?" Jess asked.

He gave her the peace sign or the victory sign or the number two sign, but it all meant the same thing. "We got five pirates in under four hours. If each affidavit is accepted that means we get $12,500. I can't wait to tell the guys that begged off. I was offering them 30% on each kill."

Marsha said, "I wouldn't tell them anything at all. Next time, you pay them what they want knowing that you are shooting fish in a barrel. They can't bitch about getting paid what they asked for and you take home all the rest."

Charlie thought for a moment and said, "You're right. I figured out how to streamline this. I just need the bodies to scale it."

"You only have to tell them that you are going to do quality control by going out to a couple of places to make sure that they aren't sandbagging you."

"I like your thinking, O'Shea." Charlie looked over at Jess spooning ice cubes into her coffee. "Jess, how did the birthday girl like her first case?"

"It was great, Charlie, but Marsha did all the work."

"Nonsense, you were her wingman, and when I get paid, you both are getting bonuses."

"I can't take the money, Charlie, you know that," Marsha said.

"What's a little cash between friends? Now you're insulting me again. Put it aside for a rainy day."

She nodded.

The waitress with "Dot" on her name tag arrived. "So have y'all decided?"

"I'm ready for dessert. I'll have the chocolate pecan whole slice, please." Jess said, peering over her menu.

"Same for me," Marsha said.

"Make it three." Charlie nodded.

"Whipped cream?"

They all nodded. Charlie solemnly said, "In life, you can never get enough whipped cream."

Even Dot nodded with them. "That is for sure."

After the carb-fest, Marsha and Jess followed Charlie home. Jess was able to walk on her own, but did give Charlie and Marsha crushing hugs for a night she would never forget.

Charlie ambled in, but Marsha stayed in her car and checked news alerts from Philly on her phone as she did most nights. She wanted to see if the bribery scandal at the police department was getting press. She read with passing interest the story of a kid who had gotten hold of his cop father's service weapon and shot him in retaliation for taking away his video-game privileges.

There was a knock on her window. She thought it would be Jess, but instead, she was looking at the angry face of Jess's husband, Willis.

She rolled the window down and said, "I don't think we met. I'm Marsha."

"I know damn well who you are. You got my wife drunk and took her to a strip bar on the Sabbath for Christ's sake!"

"Hold on a second, pardner." Marsha exited her Mustang and walked around behind it and met Willis between her car and his truck. "If you have a beef, you take it up with Charlie. We were only doing what he told us to do."

"Charlie wasn't with her. You were the one buying her drinks and driving her around. What if somebody recognized my wife at that place? What would they think?"

Marsha sighed. "I gave her the choice of going in. Besides, when you see somebody at a strip club that you recognize, you don't go throwing stones in a glasshouse. What can I say? You need to talk to Charlie."

"So, you know a lot about recognizing people in strip clubs?" He sneered.

Marsha realized the futility of talking to this hothead and didn't appreciate the jab. "Doesn't seem like this conversation is getting us anywhere. It's late and I should go. You need to talk to Charlie." She started to walk away, but Willis grabbed her right arm with his right hand.

"I'm not done talking to you, lady." He pulled her back.

In their private sessions, Shira and Marsha had worked the next move dozens of times. Using her free hand, she twisted the wrist of his grabbing hand, straightened his arm and swung him face-first into his driver's side rear quarter panel, putting a second dent there. He crumpled to the ground with a groan.

She pulled the offending hand and arm up and behind his back. She whispered in his left ear. "You so much as look at me funny, I will kick your ass and then call the cops. They will arrest you this time, I promise."

CHAPTER 11

"THIS IS RIDICULOUS," Willis said, showing no interest in what the credit counselor had to say anymore.

Patiently, the counselor looked at him and then at the simple income and expense sheet on the table between the Teesdales. "What don't you like about this plan?" she asked.

"You are putting me on a $50.00 a week allowance? That's what's wrong with it," he said.

"Where would you like the money to come from? Clothing for your wife and child?" She pushed a hot button.

"What about my truck payments?" he said, stabbing his stubby index finger on the sheet.

"By turning it back in on lease, you will save $575 a month and can pay down your credit card faster and move to a 15-year fixed-rate on your home. The sooner you start having equity in the trailer, the sooner you can start moving that money to discretionary spending."

"What will I drive?" he barked.

"Mr. Teesdale, there is no need to get loud with me." She paused and stared at him until he looked away. "I am told you don't need your truck for work. You are a one-car family until your finances are under control. Your credit card is maxed out and you are upside down on your trailer. You need a new washer and there is other required long-overdue maintenance to your home."

Jess, who was sitting quietly until then, said, "On the days that I need the car, I can drive you to work and pick you up. Otherwise, you can take my car."

"*Your car?*" The only time he drove her car was when they had to take it into the shop.

"You're saying it like it's beneath you to drive the only car I have ever owned." Jess glared at him.

He tried changing the subject. "You've got nothing here for vacation, either."

"Oh, I'm sorry." The counselor pulled the sheet back from between them. "How much did you spend on the last *family* vacation?" She held her pen in the air waiting for his response.

He sat there and fumed.

"Eight years ago, we went to Disneyworld for a three-day weekend. We won it as a prize from a 50-50 drawing at church," Jess said.

"So what family vacation are you talking about, Mr. Teesdale?" she asked, not so innocently. "Mrs. Teesdale is working a part-time job. Have you given any thought to getting something on the weekend? As soon as you pay off the credit card, you could use that money for a little bit more spending money."

"I work hard during the week. I used to grab as much overtime as I could when we needed it. I do my share."

The counselor shook her head. "Here is your take-home pay without overtime every month, and here are the expenses that are solely related to you. You need to earn an additional thousand dollars a month to make them balance."

Willis reached for his right shoulder and began messaging the muscles that had gotten wrenched by that bitch who owned the Mustang. He looked at his angry wife and the smart-aleck counselor and he realized that he had gone into a battle of wits unarmed. He abruptly stood up and announced, "I took time off from work for this?" He shook his head. "Game's over." He slithered out of the room and walked briskly to his truck. He fired it up, making sure to rev the engine louder than necessary and peeled out of the parking lot.

The counselor, with an ear cocked to squealing tires, said to Jess, "Sounds like somebody needs an anger management course."

"It's partly my fault." Jess sighed. "I was content to let him run the finances alone for years and didn't realize what was really going on until now. I can't do this alone."

"You're partially right," the other woman said, looking at the numbers, "You can't cover you and your daughter's expense along with his."

"What are you saying?" Jess asked.

"Have you thought of separating, start your own credit, get an apartment and start over with just you and your daughter? If he wants to drive a new truck and fly around North America on his hunting expeditions, you shouldn't have to subsidize it and live like a pauper."

"What about the double-wide?"

"You're upside down on the loan. Walk away from it. Let the bank do a repo. I know that is contrary to what I would normally advise, but if you don't get his cooperation, I don't see how you could afford it. This may the time to talk about cutting your losses."

"You are supposed to be a credit counselor. Do you hear what you're saying?" Jess cried.

"Mrs. Teesdale, do you want to keep living like you are now?"

"No, of course not."

"Does it look like he will do what he needs to do for you and your daughter?"

Jess was silent.

"The only way you are going to get his attention is by making him realize that his focus has to be on his family if that is what he truly wants."

"This is all a real shock to him. He just needs time, that's all," Jess pled.

"What are you really saying, Mrs. Teesdale?"

"My mother divorced when we were young. It was hard on us kids. I don't want to be divorced. My younger sister is happily married. I don't want to look like a failure to her. When the women in our church get divorced, they disappear from worship. They don't come back. They feel ashamed like they let down God."

"Jess, he has to stop spending money on what he is spending money on and he has to start spending money on your family. That is the first step. If he is not willing to take it, you have to think about yourself and your daughter. After he gets his head wrapped around that reality, you have a better chance of success, but he needs a shock to his system."

"I don't know," Jess said, shifting on her chair uncomfortably.

"If he then buys into this plan, he could probably take one hunting trip next year, but remember you still have to start funding your retirement accounts." She tapped the paperwork on her desk. "He could use that money to buy a used truck. Both of you can try to get better-paying jobs once your daughter is in college. You can't work more hours than you already are. Most people can live on what they make once they realize the difference between what they want and what they really need. Concentrate on that first, then think about getting better-paying jobs. Try to visit this with him again after he has cooled down. I am not a marriage counselor. I just look at the numbers and talk to people about what to do about their financial problems, but they have to want to work on it. He just walked out on that advice and on you just now. If I seemed harsh, it's because you both need to be on the same page."

* * *

"Pastor Rick, thank you for seeing me on short notice, I don't know who else to talk to."

Jesslyn had left the counselor's office in a daze. The advice to start over without her husband was brutally honest. Being alone and raising a teenager was not what she had in mind when she asked for financial advice. Her husband's unwillingness to get a part-time job or give up his truck really put a crimp into their plans of recovery. One of their most significant expenses was their tithe, which represented ten percent of their net income.

"Not a problem, Jessalyn, how is Briana doing? We didn't see her at Youth Group last week."

The photos of his life were lined across his desk, credenza, bookcase, and mantle behind the full-size couch where they sat angled on either end with their Kuerig-made coffees on the coffee table. He was young, muscular, and handsome in his ripped jeans, black T-shirt, and pewter cross hanging from a leather necklace. The photos were mostly of his blonde wife and four children that she homeschooled.

High school jock, bible college scholar and pastoral-team member doing outreach in the more impoverished neighborhoods completed the charismatic montage of the man looking at her with bright blue eyes.

"She had a biology test to study for and stayed home to cram for it." This was the same night that Jess had done her "birthday girl" routine. She didn't mention that part.

"So, how can I help you?"

Before Jess answered, she realized she was in a fishbowl and that word would get out that she was having a heart to heart with Pastor Rick. This executive-style room behind the administrative offices to the left of the worship hall entrance was quiet and spacious. The hum of running a mega-church with satellite campuses swirled outside the glass-paneled walls. Paid workers and volunteers scurried about just outside of earshot.

Clearwater Church of the Rock was the largest of a loosely-affiliated group of evangelical churches in South Florida and had over five thousand worshippers on any given Sunday.

"There were two things. We received some bad news this week, Pastor Rick. Willis will not be able to earn overtime for the foreseeable future. It comes at a time when our finances are in the worse shape they have ever been in. We overspent on some things that we really didn't need." The image of a mounted dead coyote came into her mind.

"Have you prayed on it, Jess?" he asked.

She shook her head, no. Instead, she had been angry and had a temper tantrum in the Walmart parking lot. She had been numbing Willis with number since the washer broke.

"I suggested to Willis that we seek credit counseling and he wasn't interested in what the counselor had to say. He walked out in the middle of the session."

"Have you tried looking at the situation through his eyes?"

She again shook her head no.

"Maybe he is embarrassed and doesn't have an answer for you. Maybe he feels like he let you and Briana down. Do you think that may be part of it?"

"I guess so." Jess sat there and started to feel that their finances were her fault.

"Offer these tribulations to God and you will get your answer," he said.

"Can you talk to Willis? Maybe, he will listen to you," Jess asked.

This time Pastor Rick shook his head. "My advice is for you to make him a nice meal with his favorite dessert. Tell him all the good things that he is and ask him to pray with you to find a solution to these problems. Tell him you need his strength and guidance while you both get back on your feet."

Two unspoken words came through loud and clear. *Submit and Obey*. She nodded and stood up. "Thank you, Pastor Rick. That's good advice."

"What was the other thing you wanted to talk about, Jess?"

"Huh?"

"You said there were two things you needed to see me about," he said.

"Oh, I did, yes I did." Jess didn't want to burn this bridge but was scrambling for an answer.

"We will still make a plate offering during worship, but

we are suspending our tithe until we are sure we can make our mortgage and truck payments."

He withdrew the hand he had held out to shake with and the smile disappeared. "Don't be hasty. Pray on that decision as well."

"No," she said, lowering her unshaken hand. She fixed a cold stare into his eyes. "I think God will understand."

She walked out of the immaculate lobby with the welcoming smiling-face signage and into the bright sunshine and expansive well-marked parking lot. Jess thought of her best friend in high school who had taken her to her church, where the female preacher talked about how their church was a hospital for sinners and not a hotel for saints.

Jess remembered feeling welcome there and didn't worry what the people in the pews around her were thinking. Although her friend and partner moved to Austin, Texas, years ago, the little church was still there and had a very active food pantry and consignment store where the classrooms used to be.

Her phone vibrated as she was putting it on the car charger. It was her sister-in-law Brenda. "Hey, girlfriend, how you doing?"

Jess was a little suspicious. Brenda only called when they needed to coordinate travel to Folkston, Georgia where the Teesdale clan lived. Brenda was Willis's oldest sister whom they usually stayed with when visiting for the birthdays, baptisms, and funerals.

"S'all good. How about you, Brenda, what's up?" Jess replied with a neutral tone.

"Bryce tells me that you lost your temper and kicked a dent in Willis's truck and then had a girl's night out at a strip club. I can't believe that. Is that true?"

"And where did Bryce learn that? I don't remember posting anything on social media lately." Jess kept it cool.

"Don't play coy with me, Jess, you know the Teesdale boys talk almost every day." She added, "I'm worried about you, girlfriend."

"Did Bryce tell you that I couldn't replace my broken washing machine because Willis maxed out our credit card on their last hunting trip?"

"No, I...."

"Did Bryce tell you that Willis isn't getting overtime anymore and that he refuses to get a part-time job to pay for his share of the bills?"

Brenda cleared her throat.

"Did Bryce tell you that we didn't have enough money to buy food for the whole week and that's when Willis handed the cashier more hunting and fishing toys?"

"Look, Jess, I was—"

"Hey, I got an idea, Brenda. Your husband makes good money working for the county. Right?"

"Ugh, yeah. Why?"

"Why don't you buy a new washer and send Bryce down with the old one, that way it doesn't look like charity. He can report back to you how worn out and beat the rest of my house looks. Do you think you can help a *girlfriend* out?"

"Sorry I bothered you, Jess, you take care now."

Often thought but never said out loud, Jess stared at the call ended sign on her phone and muttered, "And screw you very much."

CHAPTER 12

"I DON'T KNOW MUCH about religion, I was raised Catholic," Marsha offered to Jess.

"Pastor Rick's answer was to pray and make Willis his favorite meal."

"Both ideas are better than getting lottery scratch-offs, I guess."

"What really zinged me was that he wanted me to let Willis drive the bus again," Jess said. "That's what got us into trouble in the first place. Then I got thinking of all those years where we were scraping by. It took a broken washing machine to bring it all to a head. I don't want to drive the bus, I just need to be able to see where we are headed."

"Was he spoiled as a child?"

"No, just the opposite. He was the youngest, and by then, his parents were tired and worn out. He was last on the totem pole."

"That might explain why he has to prove to his family that he is worthy," Marsha offered.

"I married into a very toxic family, but who am I to talk.

You oughta sit down for a holiday meal with my mother at my sister's house. When he came home from work, I waited until after Brianna went to sleep to ask him why he stormed out of the counseling session. He said that no matter what he said, that 'bitchy' woman had an answer for him. He had to leave before he lost his temper."

Marsha looked over at her temporary neighbor and fast-becoming friend as they drove to downtown Clearwater. The morning mist leftover from the overnight rain was now giving way to humid sunshine. Her car was shedding water droplets as she sped along. "Maybe he's learning."

"Learning what?"

"How not to act out when confronted by a strong woman."

Jess seemed puzzled but agreeable with that response. "We didn't talk about what needs to be done and he hasn't brought it up since."

"So, you didn't kiss and make-up?" Marsha joked.

"Hardly, I asked him to tell his brother the whole story the next time he complains about his crazy wife."

"What?"

"Yeah, I got a call from his oldest sister, who is a witch, asking me why I was in a strip club?"

"No, shit." Marsha whistled.

"Yeah, I waited until he put his hands on me. Maybe I shouldn't be telling you that," Jess confided.

"I take it things got a little frosty then."

"Most definitely. I was still smarting from some of the names he called you and me when I got home from the case."

"Like what?"

"I don't want to repeat what he said about you. It was neither nice nor accurate."

"I bet he called me butch, a dike, or a lezbo?"

"Dyke."

Marsha just shook her head wanly. "I've heard it all my adult life, except from the men that I have been with." She pulled into the parking spot right in front of their destination. "Some men confuse strength with masculinity or bitchiness."

Jess realized there was a price to pay for taking charge.

"How do you see fixing this mess?"

"Didn't you say to me never to go into a gunfight with a knife?"

Marsha was impressed with Jess's memory. "That's why we are here, isn't it?"

They got out of the Mustang and walked into Clearwater Legal Aid in time for the 10:00 a.m. appointment.

The offices were downtown. The name of the lawyer who had once worked from this storefront operation was fading from the plate glass next to the rolled-up security gate. The brick facade was faded and crumbling along the roofline and in each corner. The rubber matting of the entranceway was scuffed almost bare.

All the people sitting on plastic chairs in the entrance lobby, along with the receptionist, were transfixed, mouths agape to the wall-mounted TV. News from half-way across the world was breaking of a man with a modified military-style assault gun who stormed into two houses of worship, killing fifty-one people. If not for the brave actions of a couple of seriously out-gunned police officers, there may have been more carnage at a third location. Crime scene tape and body bags filled the screen. The scene changed to the shell-shocked leader of that country who was offering condolences to the families and survivors.

"My God, that is awful," Jess said.

"I understand cops and robbers, but this stuff goes way past anything that I ever was involved in. It seems like it happens every day," Marsha replied.

"And it's getting worse," Jess added.

The clinic's executive director motioned them to her office and closed the door.

"Hello, Mrs. Teesdale. My name is Thelma Madsen. As you can see, it's a little crazy around here today."

"Thank you for meeting me. This is my friend Marsha O'Shea. She came with me today for moral support."

"Nice to meet you, Marsha. It is good that Mrs. Teesdale has someone to talk to. So many women feel alone in these situations," she said as the women took their seats.

"Call me, Jess," Jessalyn said.

The office was cluttered with files on every available chair and table surface. Some of the thicker files were stacked in the overflowing wall cabinets and others were set out in bins.

Noticing their stares at all the files, Thelma began first. "We handle a variety of matters here. We help persons get their Medicaid benefits. We work on landlord-tenant disputes that have gotten to the eviction stage." Pointing to a free-standing two-drawer cabinet on wheels. "These are the files of people victimized by predatory lenders and pay-day loan outfits. I am the only paid attorney, and we have two paid part-time paralegals. Our receptionists are volunteers."

"This is way too much work for one person," Marsha surmised.

"You're right. Besides my own caseload, I supervise third-year law students and a steady stream of first-strike attorneys."

"First-strike attorneys?" Jess asked.

"The local and state Bar Associations give lawyers who

have committed ethical infractions the opportunity to do the equivalent of 'community service' to keep their licenses. The disciplinary committees order the lawyers to work so many hours in a specified time frame and I have to sign off on the work. I try to figure out who is best at what and where others can do the least damage. I won't sign off for hours of non-effort, so everybody learns very quickly that I hold the Ace card in any games they want to play."

Both women nodded.

"Many of those folks out in the lobby are waiting for their assigned lawyers to come back from court so they can discuss their cases." Addressing Jess now, Thelma said, "So you wanted to talk about your credit counselor's suggestions of separation and filing personal bankruptcy?"

"It's like I have woken up from a bad dream, but the nightmare is continuing. Just this morning, my husband asked me to co-sign on a truck lease. He said that it would be only a little more than the current lease, and we could take out another credit card for the down payment. This is ***after*** he was told we had to downsize."

Marsha looked over at Jess. "Why not dig yourselves into a deeper hole for Christ's sake?"

Thelma asked, "Did he say how he would pay for it?"

"We'll figure it out, he said."

"Did he offer to get a part-time job?" Marsha asked.

Jess shook her head no.

"Doesn't sound like a plan," Marsha offered.

"I pulled out the counselor's expense sheet and told him to show me what to cut and where we could make up the difference to handle another credit card," Jess said.

"I take it you didn't sign the papers," Thelma said.

"He walked out in a huff, cursing under his breath. I didn't tell him that we were cutting off our tithe until we get back on our feet. That would start another war. I don't know enough about the legal process of separation and filing for bankruptcy. I want to know if that is an option."

"You are doing the right thing by getting legal advice while you still have options. The easy answer is that there is no such thing as a 'legal separation,' no forms or filings need to be made in court. This state doesn't recognize separation as a legal status. Before you decide to leave him, you should establish a post office box for a mailing address and set up your own separate checking account and debit card. Then get pre-approved on your earnings alone for an apartment if you're going to a place offering a yearly lease. Those are the options to have in place before doing anything else," Thelma advised.

"If that doesn't wake him up to the fact that we have to work together and find the way to dig ourselves out of this hole, then he isn't giving me a choice. Is he?"

"No, it seems like from what you told me on the phone, his spending behavior has to change drastically."

Jessalyn's words spilled out, "I did the extra math, Thelma. If we suspend the tithe, turn in the truck, and he stops flying around the country on his adventures for just a couple of years we could pay off all our credit debt. After that, we could help our daughter with college and start building our retirement account while we still have time. It's doable. What makes me crazy is that he still doesn't see how selfish he is. Now that my eyes are open, I am very hurt that my daughter and I were never put on equal footing with his hobbies. I hold a lot of resentment and it will take some time for me to get over it."

"If you tell him this, what do you think would happen?" Thelma asked.

Jess shuddered and shook her head. "He'll go ballistic."

"And if you tell him that his response is unacceptable and that you will leave him?" Thelma took Jess to the line in the sand.

"When it sinks in that I won't be there to cover my share of the mortgage, part of his truck payments and his adventures, that's when he'll be forced to face reality. Am I unreasonable?"

Thelma shook her head no.

Marsha said, "Put the shoe on the other foot, Jess. If you drove around in a brand new sports car every couple of years and jetted off to Vegas to gamble all the time while he stayed at home, kept a low profile, and worked six days every week, how long would it be before he'd divorce you?"

"I never looked at it that way."

"That's because you would never do that to your spouse and child," Marsha said.

The realization of the unfairness settled on Jessalyn like a dense fog rolling in from the Gulf.

Thelma nodded. "It's premature to talk about bankruptcy today. If you decide to leave, then you come see me again and we'll talk you through it. I hope for your sake that he can change his lifestyle and you guys can get back on your feet." And with that, she got to her feet, walked from behind her desk to shake her visitors' hands.

The meeting was over.

Marsha and Jess made their way back through the office. In the interim, some first-strike attorneys had made it back from court and were listening to their new clients. The pained expressions on their faces had less to do with their client's woes than with their own.

On the sidewalk, both women stared at that now completely dry Mustang. The passenger side had been keyed from bumper to bumper.

CHAPTER 13

THE GUY at the NRA booth at the South Florida Rod & Gun show had a captive audience on this rainy Saturday. "It's a disgrace. How much warning do the authorities need before they will intervene? Some nut goes on social media for months making threats, but his constitutional rights to privacy are more important than your right to safety and to defend yourselves." He had the semi-circle around his booth nodding their heads. "Mental health care in this country is a joke. Most health plans treat mental health not as a medical necessity. The co-pays alone are enough for people not to seek help. Try to get a board-certified psychiatrist to accept Obamacare reimbursements." He was starting to rev up as families began filling out the spots behind the gun owners. "Yeah, good luck with getting someone good."

His booth assistant, a blonde-haired beach-bunny with the tight top and short shorts was doing a brisk business of handing out bumper stickers and collecting emails. No need to solicit memberships today. They were preaching to the choir.

"None of the high-profile shooters in recent history

purchased their weapons at a gun show. In fact, the vast majority of them purchased their guns legally and passed a background check."

The Korean War vet next to Willis spoke up next. "The VA ain't much better. Denying PTSD existed for years. Guys who saw too much over there are coming home wrapped a little too tight, now they're wondering why they are unraveling. For years the VA would shrug their shoulders." His cap showed that he had been a tin can sailor on the *USS Jarvis DD-799* during the conflict.

Willis could understand about things unraveling. One day everything was fine and the next day the dark clouds arrived. When she was not giving him the stink eye, Jess was giving him the cold shoulder. He had done nothing wrong. Now he couldn't do anything right. He disengaged from the NRA booth and continued walking around.

He loved coming to this show. The African safari booths with the stuffed rhino and lion heads always drew a crowd. Videos of hunters on the Savannah with their local guides captivated him.

Someday, he sighed.

There was a booth for hunting in Maine displaying kill photos of a smiling teenager kneeling between the antler spread of an unlucky moose.

From the next booth came the sound of polka music. The fellows behind the table both were speaking in half English and half Polish with a woman about guided hunting tours in Poland for big game.

The pleasure boats, bass boats, trolling motors, fishing rigs and lures were all on display. He nodded to the captain of the fishing charter *Luna Sea*. He and his brothers had a great day off of Daytona snagging tuna and marlins a few years back with the captain.

There was a cordoned off area for shooting pellet guns that looked like pink and lavender assault rifles. Some of the guns were bigger than the kids trying to heft them to their shoulders. He remembered the first time his brothers took him into the woods and let him fire their shotguns. The first shot he ever took about knocked him on his ass. They laughed at him.

"Hey, Willis," the shooting range instructor called over to him.

"Hey, Billy."

He adjusted the stock of the pellet gun into the shoulder of the woman on the firing line and stood to her gun side. "Haven't seen you since your Wyoming trip. Howzitgoin'?"

"It's goin'. Got my varmint on the last day just before dusk."

The woman settled her eye onto the scope and began squeezing off rounds at the paper target of a menacing villain twenty-five yards away.

"Nothing like putting a little pressure on yourself, huh?"

Willis smiled. "I'm glad I got some work in at the range with the Ruger before I left. I was able to keep her steady on a tough shot. I was only getting one chance."

Billy smiled in appreciation. "Wednesday night is Full Auto Night. Would you like a fifty percent-off pass?"

Without thinking Willis said, "Sure."

After the woman exhausted her magazine and returned the rifle to Billy, he reached into his breast pocket and handed Willis a discount card.

"Thanks."

The woman turned around to her pre-teen daughter and said. "See how easy that was? Give it a try."

"No way," the daughter said, "I hate guns!"

Silent stares fell upon her and the mother.

Sorta like cursing in church, Willis thought.

Willis nodded to Billy and moved on. He entered all the drawings for the rifles and the fresh-water fishing reels with cash. The show discounts on some equipment that he wanted proved to be irresistible.

With all the crap coming down on him at home, it was comforting to be with his own people on his day off. Walking the convention floor, he was pleased with himself that he took out the new credit card in his own name with his employer's address for the billing statement. He would take his goodies to his locker at work and keep them there until he planned to use them.

CHAPTER 14

"HELLO, Mr. Teesdale, this is Principal Jenkins from the high school. You need to come for Briana."

Willis didn't think that Briana was sick that morning when he left for work. "I'm in the middle of an important alarm installation. I can't leave until it's finished. Did you try my wife?"

"Yes, the call went to voicemail."

"Did you try texting her?"

"When I didn't get her, I called you."

"What do you want me to do? I can't walk away from this job right now. Can't she stay at the nurses office until my wife can come for her?"

"Brianna's not sick, Mr. Teesdale, she is being suspended from school and must leave immediately."

Willis's head was spinning. "What? Suspended?"

"I can explain it to you when you get here. How long will it take you."

"Let me text my wife and I will get back to you." He hung up before she could reply.

Brianna's been suspended from school. Call me ASAP,

he texted and waited. He looked at the job and saw that he couldn't leave it unfinished. The new customer had to have the system up and running by close of business. He already removed the existing hardware. Federal credit unions don't take too kindly to having their vaults go unprotected. He pasted the same text in again.

Can't talk now, I'm on a call with my boss. Jess responded.

"You gotta be kidding me," he muttered. *How long?* he texted back.

Dunno. Gotta go. Bye.

He might be able to leave everything as it is, run to the school, pick up Briana and get back and finish before they had to lock the doors. He called the school and asked for the principal.

"Principal Jenkins."

"Yes, ma'am, this is Wills Teesdale. I was able to reach my wife, but she is not able to come and pick up Brianna right now. Can Brianna stay there until my wife is finished what she is doing?"

"I'm sorry, Mr. Teesdale, she needs to leave the building in the care of her parent immediately."

"Why? What did she do?"

"I can explain it to you when you arrive. How long will it take you to get here, Mr. Teesdale?"

"Can you put her in a taxi and my wife will pay the fare?"

"No, Mr. Teesdale, school policy states that the student must be retrieved by a parent or legal guardian."

"Well I can't drop what I am doing to come and fetch her and my wife is tied up on the phone with her boss. I am sorry."

"Your daughter assaulted another student and I

persuaded the student not to press charges. It's in my power to summon the police to have her arrested. What would you like to do, Mr. Teesdale? Either way, she needs to leave the building immediately."

"One of us will be there in less than twenty minutes." He clicked off.

He called his manger next. "Hi, Lisa."

"Hi, Willis. What's up?"

"I've got a family emergency to take care of. I have to leave the Wellspring FCU job for about an hour and a half."

"Is everything okay?"

"I got a call from the school, Briana has to come home and my wife can't do it."

"Do you think you will be able to finish it before they close this afternoon?"

"If everything goes right, I should be able to do it."

"Let's be safe. I will call Lane and ask him to help you."

Willis didn't like the idea of needing help to do his job, but he couldn't argue with the logic. "Like I said, I will be back in less than two hours. I will leave everything here and tell the manager that I have to run cross town for a part."

He texted Jess. *Bri is suspended for fighting. I am picking her up at school.*

K. Jess responded.

Willis drove towards the school. He realized that he had not been involved in his daughter's school activities. Jess usually handled the parent-teacher conferences. Most of Briana's after school activities were with the church's youth group. He had to drive around the building twice. The signage for the main office was partially hidden behind overgrown shrubbery.

He found no spots in the visitor spots that could accommodate his truck and had to walk the length of the parking lot.

Shifting his weight and clearing his throat got the attention of the secretary who was busy on the phone. She held up her index finger and continued her conversation with no sense of urgency.

Tick tock. Tick tock, he thought. *I'm on the clock.*

Finally she placed the phone in the receiver and made a point of taking the paperwork to the filing cabinet before addressing him. "Yes, sir, how may I help you?"

"I am here to pick up my daughter Briana Teesdale."

"Do you have identification?"

He showed her his work badge which displayed his photo and name.

"Do you have a state issued ID?"

"Yes. Why?" He realized he had left his wallet in the work truck.

"I will need to copy it for our discharge records. Anytime a parent retrieves a child, we need proof and to have them sign the child out."

"A half hour ago, I got a call from the principal that I had to come in and pick up my daughter. I don't think that was enough time to make a phony ID." He must have raised his voice as work in the office came to a standstill and every student and adult stared at him.

She crossed her arms and stared at him.

"My wallet is in my truck. I couldn't park near the entrance and had to park out by the highway."

She returned to her seat and began busying herself with her computer.

With a controlled and even voice, Willis said, "May I speak with the principal please?"

Without looking up from her screen she said, "The principal is in a meeting right now."

For a moment, Willis thought about returning with the .45 auto that he kept under his seat instead of his license. *Maybe you would like to talk to my little friend.* Willis harumphed out of the office and into the baking parking lot.

He remembered why he had hated high school so much. The thought of going to college didn't ever enter his mind. All those rules and put-downs. He didn't dare talk to his family about any of it. His mother and sisters would scold him and his brothers and father would belittle him. He did just enough to get by and kept a very low profile. He didn't play sports or get involved in any other after-school activities. He would do his homework at school and then ride his bike until he was old enough to ride around in his truck.

He texted Jess again.

At the school, will be home in a few.

K.

Willis retrieved the all important driver's license and felt under the seat for his Colt 1911. The metal felt cool to his touch in the warming truck. He was tempted to strap in on, but instead hustled back into the building after working up a good sweat. He hadn't moved that fast in years and labored with his breath.

He saw the secretary glance up from her computer as she continued to busy herself with the keyboard. He was the only one on the other side of the counter and made a show of retrieving his license from his wallet and began tapping it on edge.

She kept typing, he kept tapping. The more she typed, the louder he tapped. He was hot, out of breath and late getting back to the job. His wife was not available to talk, nor take care of this. How he wanted to reach across the counter and grab that woman by the throat.

"Hi, Daddy."

He looked over to a door opening from a side room and spotted Briana walking out in front of the principal. Briana looked distraught as she held her purse in front of her chest.

"Hi, honey," he replied.

The secretary retrieved a three-ring binder from her credenza and said, "Do you have your identification sir?"

"Other than my daughter calling me daddy, yeah." Keeping his eyes on Briana, he tossed his driver's license the way he used to flip baseball cards.

She snatched it before it fell from the counter top to the floor and slowly walked to the photocopier and waited for the teacher finishing making copies of worksheets for his classroom. She returned to the counter and said, "Sign here, Mr. Teesdale."

He scribbled his name on the form. She looked at the form and then squinted at his signature on his driver's license and said. "They don't match."

Briana gave him a pleading look.

He shrugged. "I guess I've gotten lazy with all the pin pad finger signings at stores."

Walking out to the parking lot, he said to Briana, "That woman is a Nazi. The principal said that if me or your mom didn't get you, she could have had you arrested. I had to leave in the middle of an important job."

Getting into the truck, he noticed that her blouse was ripped and her bra showing. He glanced away. "What happened?"

"I don't want to talk about it. I just want to go home. I never want to go back there ever again."

They rode in silence back to the house. Pulling into

the driveway, he saw Charlie holding a ladder for his female guest. Ignoring her, he said, "Hey, Charlie, what's up?"

Charlie looked over at Willis and Briana and said, "You're home early."

Briana sniffed back tears and ran into the house.

"She had some trouble at school today. I had to get her."

Marsha stopped screwing the camera mount into the eaves overlooking the driveway and watched as Briana ran into the house.

Willis nodded to Charlie. "Watcha doin'?"

"Somebody vandalized my friend's car while it sat in the driveway the other night. You wouldn't know anything about it. Would you, Willis?"

"What night?"

"Tuesday into Wednesday morning."

Willis cocked his head for a moment as if to think. "Nope, didn't hear or see anything strange." He still didn't make any eye contact with the woman that had given him the smackdown. He walked into his house.

Willis went right to the dining room table where Jess worked her telephone rep job. She held up her index finger to Willis and pointed to her headset.

"Thank you, Mr. Miele. That is very kind of you to say. I appreciate the advice." There was a pause and a longer pause. Finally Jess responded. "You have a nice day too." She took off her headset and closed her eyes while taking a couple of deep breaths.

"Why couldn't you pick up Briana," Willis demanded.

"What happened at school? She got suspended for fighting?" Jess was looking at her texts on her smartphone.

"Ask her, she wouldn't tell me."

Jess typed in her offline status for the caller queue and got up from her chair. "I told you this morning I was getting my performance evaluation today. That was my boss going over everything with me. What was I supposed to do? Hang up with him to talk to you?"

"I forgot," he said without a hint of apology.

"Or maybe you weren't listening, Willis." Jess started to make her way back to her daughter's room.

"I've got to get back to work Jess. SORRY FOR THE IN-CON-VENI- ENCE." He dripped it out to her louder then intended.

She stopped, whirled around and walked half-way to him. "You don't even care. Do you?"

Open handed he said, "What?"

"Why our A-student, who was never in trouble—*ever*—is suspended from school."

"She wouldn't talk to me."

"And why is that, Willis? Either you are plastered in front of the TV watching hunting or fishing or you are out on your Teesdale boys' adventures."

"I just dropped what I was doing to pick her up from school," he retorted.

"And when was the last time you were at her school?" Seeing the blank look on his face, she snorted. "That's right, never. You make it sound like it is such a big sacrifice. Tell me the names of any of her teachers?"

"I don't need this." He started to walk away.

She advanced to close the distance. "And what makes you think that your job is more important than mine that I can drop what I was doing to get her? That's right. I always got her from school when she was sick or for early dismissals. She stayed home with me on the school holidays. You didn't have to do jack shit."

Offended by her language and still smarting from being treated like an errant schoolboy by the secretary, Willis lashed back. "Seemed like I can't do anything right even when I do something right anymore. You look at me the way you look at dog shit on your shoe."

"You don't even care about the phone call I just finished. Do you?"

He was clueless and taken aback. "Wha—?"

"That was my boss giving me my performance evaluation. He said that I have the highest ranking of his entire department on my customer surveys. Getting people to stay on the line after they had a problem for a survey is like pulling teeth and the customers I talk to are glad do it." Jess began to cry. "You didn't even care."

"Of course I care." He started to move toward her.

She put both hands out to warn him off. "You better care, because he told me that I also take the most time on each call and I'm forcing other reps to handle more calls. They are complaining to him why they get so many rollovers from me."

"That's not fair." Willis shook his head.

"Guess what, Willis? Not only am I not getting a raise this year, I have a warning in my file to turn the calls over faster or I will be placed on probation. So don't tell me about your IN-CON-VENI-ENCE," she mimicked while wiping her eyes with the back of her hands before scurrying to Briana's bedroom.

He stumbled out to his truck under the glare of both Charlie and Marsha.

Next time I won't leave the front door open, he thought.

CHAPTER 15

"THE WIFE HAD POSTED on her Facebook feed that the family was going to Busch Gardens in Tampa for Easter vacation. That was the first mistake." Charlie said as they made their way crosstown.

Marsha found herself enjoying "helping" Charlie out with his private investigations. Every day was different. The work was challenging, but not taxing. It kept her mind occupied and off her troubles. She had the occasional sharp pangs to drink herself into a stupor, but they were less frequent and less severe. The work was fun, plain and simple, and being with Charlie made it that much better.

"The surveillance guys in Chicago had followed them from the suburbs to the airport before dawn and, lucky for us, they determined which airline the family was flying. It makes our job a whole lot easier. We can camp out in one terminal."

"You mean to tell me that Charlie Akers couldn't get TSA to give up the subject's itinerary?" Marsha winked.

"Sorry, kiddo, we have to do it the hard way," he said.

"We're gonna have a tough act to follow. They had gotten a video of hubby humping the family's bags into his car and then lugging them out of the car at the long-term parking lot and again back into the shuttle to the terminal and out again at Departures. That was mistake number two, not thinking that anybody would be watching. Given that he is making a worker's comp temporary-total claim for a soft-tissue back injury, this is just the beginning of documenting his lack of alleged disability. We have to show that today was not just a good day for him."

Marsha staked out the baggage claim carousel area for airlines and she alerted Charlie of their arrival. She covertly videotaped hubby bending at an awkward angle, grabbing the wife's seventy-five-pound oversized bag with one hand from the carousel, and swinging it to the ground. He repeated the process for his luggage and the kids' backpacks. They rolled them curbside, where they waited for the rental car van to take them to the nearby lot for their rental.

Charlie got video of him wrestling their bags into the van. Then Charlie stopped his nondescript sedan long enough to pick up Marsha before following the vacationers to the rental lot. There he got more video of him off-loading from the van and into the rental. Would they go directly to the amusement park or to their hotel?

Some snowbirds made the most of their visits. Airport follows were always fraught with difficulties, especially post 9-11. Add perpetual construction and expansion at the airports, you weren't always sure that this one opportunity to see where they were going would work. On top of that, insurance companies were loath to authorize more than two operatives for most cases. That exponentially increased the odds of losing the subject in traffic or getting made. The goal was to eventually follow them to the hotel where they could start their surveillance each morning. Charlie had already purchased the necessary passes for Marsha and him to enter the park. Both agreed that they would not be riding any of the death-defying rollercoasters.

The "follow" from the airport took them to the Embassy Suites, a short distance from Tampa's favorite attraction. Charlie was able to set up in a spot where he videoed the husband schlep the luggage onto a cart at the front entrance doors. The family stood by the Busch Gardens shuttle, imploring him to hurry.

Marsha went in and saw him hand off the luggage to the bellhop. He came out and deposited the rental in the back-parking lot. He ran around the building under Charlie's watchful eye glued to the lens on his video camera.

They trailed the shuttle to where the family would have fun in the sun. The weather was cooperative. No rain, except for occasional pop-up showers until they returned to the land of breweries and bratwurst.

"To make this a trifecta, we need to capture him on some herky-jerky rides that the insurance doctors can watch tape on after they conduct an independent medical exam on him. He will, of course, tell them that from the time of the accident until the examination that he was in terrible pain and all that time, he had the mobility of a turnip. They will declare him fit to return to work, and if he chooses to fight it, the attorneys for the insurance company will introduce all the video at the comp hearing, but only after he testifies to his crippled status."

"He will be clueless until then?" Marsha asked.

"If he gets a smart attorney, they could ask for any surveillance tapes through discovery before he testifies. The client would have to fly me up and pay me for my time to sit around so that I testify and introduce the tapes."

"Will he get prosecuted for insurance fraud?"

Charlie shook his head. "They might ask for civil restitution, investigative costs, and attorney fees, but it's more about sending a message to the rest of the employees where he works that somebody is watching and not to pull this crap."

As they neared the entrance, the shuttle stopped and the family disembarked. Charlie snagged a snippet of video before being waved to move on.

"Here's your ticket. Let me know where we can meet up after I park."

Marsha hopped out of the car, adjusted her sunglasses, and fell in behind the gaggle of excited visitors.

The family made a beeline for the nearest eatery and queued in line with their trays to grab their food. The pouty pre-teen daughter was putting up a fuss, something about being a vegetarian.

At that moment, Marsha's phone buzzed. She was expecting it to be Charlie and answered without looking at the caller ID. "We are in the Snack Shack next to the Cheetah Hunt."

"You didn't come to see me and have forgotten me already?" came a voice from her recent nightmares.

The restaurant was noisy with cranky sleep-deprived kids who desperately needed naps. The general din made it impossible to carry on a cell phone conversation. She stepped outside and lost the eyeball position on the surveillance.

"Mike, is that you? How are you?"

Philly Organized Crime Detective Sgt. Hollins replied,

"I just got out of the hospital, but it's gonna be a long time before I can swing a golf club with both hands."

Marsha's heart sank. She hadn't seen him since they packed him off in the ambulance and raced off to Lankenau Hospital. She had to explain to the arriving cops at the scene the three dead bodies and why she was hugging a wanted murder suspect.

She turned away from the noise in the restaurant to listen as he filled her in.

Completely engrossed in the conversation, she was startled when Charlie tapped her on the shoulder. She whirled with the phone to her ear.

"They're gone. You had the eyeball and they're not in there," Charlie said none too kindly.

"Hold on a second, Mike." Marsha didn't have time to digest what he had said.

"Charlie, I'm on the phone with Philadelphia. They were lining up with their trays to get food. I thought it would be safe to take the call."

"Start looking that way, I'll go that way past the coaster." Charlie motioned.

"Sorry, Mike, I'm laying low in Clearwater till it's safe to come home. I'm helping a friend out on surveillance while I'm down here. I just lost the subjects."

"That's not good."

"I know. Seems like I can't do anything right lately. They can't go far, they are on foot at Busch Gardens."

"Could be worse, you could be sitting in a cold van watching gangsters."

Marsha realized Mike was right; it could be worse, especially as she didn't envision herself returning to Philly and getting back into that game again.

Marsha was talking to Mike and half-looking for the

family. She watched *Cobra's Curse,* a family spin coaster twisting and turning and the answer came to her when where she spotted the vacationers in question screaming their lungs out. "Hold on, Mike."

She texted Charlie that their quarry was having the time of their lives on the coaster. She zoomed her camera on the family as they came back into view, doing G-force turns and barrel-rolls. Camera in one hand and with her cell phone, she pointed them out to Charlie. The ride was about over.

Ignoring that she was on the phone, "I've got this, O'Shea, you can Uber home." He said none too politely.

Marsha's eyes widened with the phone still stuck to her ear. She nodded in the realization that she had prioritized the phone call over Charlie's business. She slinked away.

"I screwed the pooch, Mike. My old boss was kind enough to take me in when I started to go off the rails down here. All I had to do was keep an eye on a family of very pale-skinned Cheese heads while he parked the car, and I lost them."

"Sorry to hear that, Marsha, but hey, it could be worse. You could be dragging around an arm that you can't lift over your head."

"You're right, Mike." The emotions of their big adventure came surging back now. "I am sorry I didn't visit you or call you. I just thought that I was kryptonite."

"I'm sorry, Marsha, that I didn't do better that day for both of us. It does looks like the bureau is hanging you out to dry. I don't know what I'm gonna do. Maybe I will just take the disability pension and walk. Who needs the bullshit?"

Marsha wandered around all the fun and frivolity with no clue where she was going. "Get better, Mike. This isn't how you want to ride off into the sunset."

"You too, Marsha, whatever happens, you are still good PO-lice. I'd work with you any day. Don't be a stranger."

"Take care, Mike."

Marsha got her bearings, and as she approached the exits, she had to put an address in Uber.

* * *

Shira's borrowed T-shirt and shorts gave Marsha the appearance of a sweat-drenched Hooter's girl, but it worked in a pinch. They trained until Marsha couldn't lift her arms to protect herself. Shira asked, "Feel better now?"

Exhausted, Marsha replied, "Just needed to get my ass-kicked by a pint-size ninja. That's all."

As they took turns showering and changing, Marsha replayed to Shira the day's events. The former Israeli soldier and the FBI agent on administrative leave were teacher and student first but were also comrades in arms when it came to fighting their own demons.

Shira talked about how the discipline of Krav Maga had saved her. It served as a constructive replacement for getting piss-drunk for Marsha.

Shira said, "I am driving to a women's shelter to teach some basic moves. Can I drop you somewhere?"

"I guess I'll go home and wait to face the music with Charlie."

They drove in uncomfortable silence after Shira turned off the radio news report about how the latest synagogue shootings would have been more deadly if the shooter's semi-automatic rifle hadn't jammed. Shira shook her head.

"Hate crimes against Jews are increasing in this country. There is talk of arming some of the worshippers in the congregations."

The veil from Marsha's focus on chasing the bad guys for so many years was lifted now and she started to appreciate the carnage happening from gun violence. "I can't begin to wrap my head around it. It's all so senseless."

"I teach women to run first, but if they can't, they have to close the distance to the gun and attack. That is hard to do in a House of God where there is distance and barriers between the shooter and the intended victims."

As they pulled into the driveway, they spotted Jessalyn standing in the front of her car. The hood was up and the engine was throwing off steam.

Shira got out and looked inside the engine compartment. "It's your exhaust manifold. This is an older car with high mileage, I assume."

Marsha said, "You are correct."

"When I was in the army, I had a rotation in the vehicle repair facilities. I am afraid that this repair is more expensive than the car."

Jessalyn began crying. "I just got back from the school. Briana was not in attendance after her suspension was over. She blew off a meeting with the principal. Briana ran away. She told me last night she was not going back to school. I guess she wasn't kidding."

"Where's Willis?" Marsha asked.

"We've been fighting every night and he is not answering his phone."

"Did you call his work?"

"No."

"Call them and tell them to have him call you, it's an emergency. We'll take my car and go look for her. Jess, this is Shira, Shira, Jess."

The woman nodded as they went their separate ways.

Once Marsha and Jess were in the car, Marsha asked, "What happened?"

"One girl at school has decided to bully Briana. It's been going on all year. She talks behind her back and makes snide comments to Briana's face about her clothes. She started a rumor that Briana was having sex with some of the boys on the wrestling team. Briana found out and confronted her in front of her posse.

"The girl knows how to fight with words. Briana fought with her hands. The posse said that Briana started the fight. The principal had to side with the girl, but kept the police out of it. The girl got a split lip and Briana got three days' suspension."

"That won't look good on her transcripts," Marsha said.

"If she even goes to college. Briana wanted to transfer to the prep school, but that costs more than to going to college. Willis suggested that she go to the vo-tech school and learn a trade the way he did. Briana said if she did that, the cool kids would win and she would always be treated like trailer trash."

"I take it your husband didn't appreciate that."

"Not at all, and after Briana went to bed, the argument continued. He wouldn't admit that she was smarter than both of us and needed to go to a better school if they couldn't work things out at her school."

Jess directed Marsha to the *Heavenly Brew*, the coffeehouse outreach supported by the Clearwater Church of the Rock. Jess walked in and came out, shaking her head. "I asked them to get the word out to Briana's friends to let me know if they see her.

One last place to check before school lets out and we start talking to her friends on Instagram and Snapchat."

"Where's that?"

"It's where we go when the girls need a little happiness."

* * *

Marsha was glad to be out of the sun. Her surveillance and sparring with Shira left her dehydrated, dog-tired, and hot. Walking through the mall, they spotted Briana at a table in the galleria, spooning a sundae. She was in an animated conversation with a pretty girl.

They overheard the girl saying, "My roommate cleans timeshares and condos and I work...." She looked up with eyes of recognition at the women and immediately lowered her sunglasses. Briana turned around to see why the girl stopped talking.

Jess said, "Hi, baby, I was worried about you. I am so glad you are safe."

"I can't go back to that school, Mom."

"Maybe you can get a tutor and finish at home or work out some other kind of deal." Marsha offered. "Your mom and I can go in and talk to the principal. You are a straight-A student, they don't want to lose you to the streets."

The girl busied herself with her milkshake and looked away.

Briana looked at the girl who shrugged and then to her mother and Marsha.

Marsha said, "Close your eyes and think about it, and when we come back with our ice cream, we can go home in my Mustang with the top down."

The big girls got their ice cream fix while the younger ones chatted quickly with their phones out.

"I'm sorry, Mom that I scared you." Briana stood up and hugged Jess.

Marsha smiled and looked down at the other girl who was avoiding eye contact. Her revealing top allowed a view from that angle of her cleavage.

As Jess, Marsha, and Briana walked away, the other girl was now busy looking at her phone. Marsha wondered where she had seen that rose tattoo before.

CHAPTER 16

"WILLIS, I received a call from your wife, please call her," Lisa Andre said. "She said it was about your daughter."

"It can wait till I finish this install," Willis said.

"Is everything okay?" his manager asked.

"Yep. Just need to make sure the new cameras are working okay with their system."

"I meant with your family, Willis."

"Oh, I'm not leaving this job until I am finished. I had to leave a job unfinished last week. I don't want this to become an issue."

"She made it sound kind of urgent," Lisa said.

"I'll check my texts. Thanks, Lisa." He hung up without waiting for her reply.

Willis went back to what he was doing. He wasn't planning on communicating with Jessalyn anytime soon. This wasn't the first time he went deep into himself—silent running like a Russian sub.

It had been a straight couple weeks now of getting yelled at and he was tired of it. Jess didn't give him a break even when he did something right, like picking up the new washer and installing it. She muttered about having two weeks of his laundry to do as he hadn't done any laundry the whole time the old one was broken.

His clothes were getting pretty ripe, he had to admit. He was going right from work to the Wednesday night "Full Auto" at the gun range with his discount card. He'd come home after she went to bed. Not that it mattered much. She turned off the sex spigot and he hadn't had any since before he left for the Wyoming trip.

He'd get up in the morning, take a shower, and grab a couple breakfast sandwiches at the gas station where he got his coffee, and eat them in his company's break room. They had both gotten paid Monday and she had taken over the checkbook. She had listed out the bills and given him the weekly cash allowance that bitch credit counselor told them about.

He had already stripped two screws on camera installs to exterior mounts and was roughly handling the control panel in the manager's office of this low-priced chain hotel. Usually, he was patient and professional with his work, taking pride in not making mistakes or leaving a mess. Today, he bounced back and forth between his swelling anger and day-dreaming about getting his hands on a machine gun that night at the shooting range.

The school suspension had been Saturday night's drama. He had been bullied all throughout high school and he endured it. His father told him to take care of his own problems and to kick their asses. His brothers made fun of him and didn't do anything to the bullies.

Neither Jess nor Briana had gone to church with him Sunday. He felt alone there during the worship and coffee hour. He told them why Briana wasn't in the youth group. She was helping Jess with a catering job that the restaurant had offered them. Jess reminded him she was taking on extra work and he hadn't done anything yet to get a part-time job.

Pastor Rick had pulled Willis aside while they were stacking chairs and asked him to reconsider their decision to suspend their tithe. It blindsided him. He didn't know anything about it. Pastor Rick asked him if Jess had asked him to pray about their financial situation. He was thoroughly embarrassed his dirty laundry was being aired out at the church.

He confessed to Pastor Rick that no, Jessalyn hadn't told him about her visit, nor about suspending the tithe. Sunday night's screaming match erupted minutes after Jess and Briana came home exhausted and dirty. He ended up sleeping on the couch.

He had to listen to Jess lecture him about the bill-paying Monday night. He went to bed that night, vowing he wouldn't say a word to either of the women in his house. Tuesday turned into Wednesday and now she was calling his boss?

His anger was building and he was taking it out on the delicate electronics in this install.

Two of the cameras overlooking on the back doorways leading to the stairwells were not reporting to the monitor. He had to go back there on his ladder and see if they were bad or not wired correctly.

He carried his ladder to the first stairwell and pulled back the ceiling tiles. Balancing on the third rung from the top with his shins grinding into the top step, he was checking the wiring with his probe for electrical current. A housekeeper propped open the exit door, backed into his ladder while dragging her housekeeping cart, and tipped him off balance.

He grabbed the ceiling tile brackets and sliced his left palm on the razor-thin sheet metal. His right side took the full brunt on her metal cart before he crumpled to the ground.

The searing pain in his bleeding hand and ribs caused him to erupt.

"Damn it! Damn it to Hell!" He crawled to his knees and glared at the horrified housekeeper.

"Ay, dios mio!" she stammered, shocked that a man fell from the sky onto her cart.

"Why can't you watch where you're going!" he yelled.

She ran away as Willis staggered to his feet. He watched the blood pouring from his hand as it swelled. The stabbing twitch in his ribs caused him to tilt to his right. He reached with his good hand for the wash clothes in her upper bins and folded one in his palm, tying another around his hand. He had trouble breathing. *Was it from the fall or his anger or both?*

The desk clerk came running into the hallway and saw Willis bent over with his back against the wall as he tried mopping his blood from the carpet.

"What happened?" she implored with her walkie-talkie in hand.

"You're dumbass housekeeper wasn't looking where she was going and knocked me off my ladder." Willis glared at her.

"She came crying to me that you scared her and yelled at her. She was afraid that you were going to hurt her."

"Did she tell you that because of her stupidity I am bleeding and will probably need stitches and X-rays?"

The desk clerk shook her head. "She didn't do it on purpose. It was an accident. She thought you were going to hit her."

"I can't believe this." Willis straightened up, pushed his way past her to the exit.

His intercostal muscles were tightening around his bruised ribs as he limped to his work truck. He got in and started heading for the hospital. He thought about calling Jess and decided not to. *She would find a way to blame him for this.*

Just watch, he thought. He considered calling his boss, but he nixed that idea too. He would call her from the hospital when the hospital would need his employer's worker's comp insurance. Willis vowed to get a lawyer and sue the hotel for this.

Oh, the poor housekeeper's feeling got hurt. Boohoo! I'll teach them a lesson.

Every bump was an adventure. It brought a jolt to his injured ribs and his breathing was labored. He held the steering with the fingertips of his bleeding left hand. The blood began seeping out of the homemade bandage onto the floor mats. His phone rang then. He fished it out of his pocket to see that it was Jess calling.

You can go to hell.

He needed two hands to turn off the phone and just ended the call without picking up.

Less than a minute later, it rang again.

I tell her. He stabbed at the screen without looking at it and yelled, "I'm not talking to you. Stop calling me."

He fumbled ending the call and could barely make out that it was Lisa asking, "Willis, what's going on?"

He put her on speaker. "I'm my way to the hospital to get stitches for my hand and X-rays to see if my ribs are broken."

"What? I got a call from the hotel manager saying that

you shoved a desk clerk and cursed out a housekeeper. What's going on?"

"Is that what they told you?" He raised his voice even louder, "Is that what they told you? I can't believe it."

"They said you got angry and walked off the job."

Willis shook with rage. He pummeled the dashboard with the phone until it went dead.

CHAPTER 17

WILLIS NOTICED that Jess had cooked his favorite dinner of steak, baked potatoes, and corn on the cob. The house was spotless and she was wearing a top and capris hinting that they might get busy later that night. It looked like his campaign of silence was working.

It was exactly one week after his accident. Even though he wasn't talking to either one of them, Briana told her mom that while she was suspended, other students came forward to the principal and guidance counselors and spoke about how the other girl instigated the fight and had been bullying Briana mercilessly all year. When Briana and Jess returned to school, they were told that the school would have zero tolerance for any further bullying from her nemesis and Briana was to report it immediately. Briana then left to go to a friend's house to study for a test on a school night.

When he reached to place his plates on the counter, a shot of pain went up the injured side of his torso. His ribs were not broken. The painkillers helped. They helped a lot.

His hand took twenty stitches and they would be coming out in another couple of weeks or so. He reported the claim from the hospital and told Lisa that his phone was damaged in the fall and that's how he got the company to replace it. He told her about the accident and how one thing led to another. The hotel wasn't about to apologize, but they did pay for the work that Lane Peters finished.

Lisa cautioned Willis about his temper but didn't put a warning in his personnel file, given that he had a valid and documented injury that preceded the incident. She convinced him not to sue the hotel for causing his injuries.

Not getting his balls busted for the week while Jessalyn saw him struggling to take his shirt off, which revealed the awful green and purple bruising just now beginning to fade, gave him a reason to think that they could get back to normal. He was wrong.

She started mid-spoonful of his first bite of chocolate cream pie, his favorite dessert.

"I was hoping that we could talk. Briana's not here and we need to clear the air. Would you mind telling tell me why you have shut us out?"

He put his fork back down on the dish. He was not ready to talk and just shook his head.

"I know it hasn't been easy these last couple of weeks."

Yeah, you've been riding me like a drugstore pony, he thought.

"We have gotten over our heads financially and we have to work together."

Except that everything I do, you have a problem with. He put his hands in his lap.

"You haven't asked me why my car hasn't moved for a week with the hood up. I've had to bother our neighbors to borrow her car to go to the grocery store."

I bet you don't mind driving that dyke's ragtop. He smirked.

"I need to get another car. We need to talk about that too."

He just stared at her. *Eventually, she'll get tired of staring at me and busy herself with something else and leave me to eat my dessert in peace.*

"Look, Willis, I am tired of this game you're playing. You can go on not talking with Briana and me, but someday when you come home, we might not be here to ignore." She crossed her arms and stared at him.

He tried stalling and went to put the spoonful of the cream pie in his mouth, but stopped. He set it down, mind racing. *She planned this. She planned to ambush me during dessert.* He picked it up again, but couldn't eat his favorite treat. He set his fork down for good, stood up, walked over to the counter, grabbed his keys and wallet and walked out to his truck. He sat there for a moment and decided that he was not going to give in.

She had to blink first and then he would demand that things went back to the way it was before she started ragging his ass or he decided that Jess and Briana could go to hell.

He'd rather be alone than deal with a harping wife and a dramatic teenager. Then he remembered it was "Full Auto" night at the range and he had a discount card burning in his wallet. His mood brightened.

* * *

Billy was on the range and greeted Willis with a nod. "You are gonna like what we got tonight," he said.

The stalls at the outdoor range on the outskirts of Clearwater started with targets for handgun users and then targets set further back for pistol marksmen and finally targets set against hay bales by the back berm of the range for guys doping their scopes of long barrel hunting rifles.

Willis had brought his Colt sidearm and his 30-06 scoped rifle. It was all outdoor tonight. No training classes indoors. This night was set aside for the serious shooters. He donned his over-the-ear noise-canceling headphones and his amber-tinted shooting glasses. He stepped into a stall with a bullseye target at 25 yards. He loaded his 1911 .45 auto with Winchester Service Grade 45 ACP 230 Grain bullets and waited for the all-clear signal before pointing and shooting downrange. His combat stance and two-handed grip allowed him to draw a bead with his right eye. As the other shooters started squeezing off rounds, he relaxed and focused on the target.

The recoil from the first round sent some shock waves into his stitched left palm and loosened the wrapping hand's grip. He was in no hurry. Breathe, squeeze, recenter. Rinse and repeat. He released the seven-shot magazine when he finished, checked the slide to make sure nothing was in the chamber, and slapped in his second clip.

This time he focused on accuracy and placed the first couple near the bullseye. At this distance, at twilight and before the mercury vapor lamps fully kicked in, his shooting was impressive. The rest of the clip was all on target, with the last one hitting the bullseye.

His final clip was all about aggression. He fired the seven rounds as fast as he could pull the trigger each time. He remembered setting off a string of firecrackers as a kid, watching them pinwheel on the ground as each one exploded. He was happy that his grouping stayed tight on the paper.

Gun empty, he holstered the hot barreled automatic favored by the armed forces until about 1986 and collected his brass. He was not a reloader but knew that a couple guys there would appreciate the shells.

He watched the marksmen shooting and meticulously write down their scores. There were open competitions year-round and this range had several trophy winners amongst the membership. Willis shot his handguns for fun and saved the serious shooting for his rifles where his practice shots would matter most in the field.

His brothers were already getting excited about hunting after Thanksgiving at a camp in Western Pennsylvania, where the whitetail bucks ran large. They had gone there before and needed to apply for their out of state licenses soon. Bryce gave him a hard time but relented and fronted the money for the permit when he heard how much crap Jess was giving his little brother. He could drive up and back this trip, saving on airfare.

See Jess, I'm already looking for ways to save money.

He was about to settle into a prone position with his rifle when Billy said, "Gather 'round gents, we have some real shooting to do."

The last rounds were spent by the other marksman. Their guns now secured, it was silent on the range as the evening mist began settling in like a cooling moist blanket. A farm tractor rumbled out to the middle of the range and the kids riding on the trailer kicked off some additional hay bales. Against several, they placed bad-guy silhouettes. They built up a cinder block row chest-high and put old-fashioned iron frying pan skillets on it so that the pans faced the shooters.

Names of the shooters were written down on slips of paper. Billy announced the gun and pulled a name from the well-worn Desert Storm Veteran cap. Nothing was said as the group inserted their earplugs and waited in anticipation.

Billy announced the first gun. "Thompson submachine gun, built in 1930 with the round magazine."

This was the gun favored by gangsters in the prohibition days and popularized by the movies. Billy readied the Tommy gun for firing and gave it to the lucky shooter.

Fired at shoulder level and tucked into the shoulder with a forward handgrip, it spewed a hundred .45 caliber bullets with a steady rat-tat-tat until the drum magazine was expended. The smoke cleared and the group then looked at the hay bale he was aiming at. The paper target was shredded from crotch to skull.

Next was the Soviet Union's favorite weapon that still found its way into many countries fighting against the US, The AK-47 Kalashnikov. Its rate of fire was faster, and the smaller bullet was a high-velocity round that cleared the gun with smooth, deadly precision.

Billy then brought out an M-16, the US military's standard-issue until recently. The lucky shooter was able to keep its nose on target for the full duration of the extended magazine.

An exotic gun, by any measure, Billy hefted an AA-12 in camo green. Willis had never seen a shotgun machine gun before. Billy's assistant rolled out a white metal 55-gallon drum between the hay bales.

The next shooter was a smaller guy, but the recoil of this monster was less than the Tommy. It produced a slow, deafening barrage of 12-gauge shotgun lead that kicked the steel drum around like a soccer ball. At twenty-five yards, the spread of each blast was as wide as a grapefruit and each one punched the barrel with an unrelenting beatdown.

Billy then brought out the Heckler & Koch line of

submachine guns and machine pistols. None of these well-worn guns jammed and the shooters began working over the iron skillets.

Billy's last gun was an M-60 belt-fed. So taken up in the fun of watching fully automatic weapons obliterating targets, Willis had forgotten that this was a lottery. His name was called and he gladly accepted the gun saved for the finale.

Set down on the ground with a bi-pod, Willis was able to spare his injured hand from the brunt of the recall. Billy laid out the belt of .308 caliber rounds and fed them into *The Pig*, as it was affectionately called by its users in Vietnam.

Billy tapped him on the shoulder. Willis squeezed off a round at a different metal drum barrel. The recoil was like nothing he had ever experienced before. He squared everything up again and squeezed off a few more, then he let it rip.

He kept the M-60 on the pirouetting barrel until the smoking gun burped its last round to the amazement of those around him to the marksmanship he had just displayed with a rapid-fire machine gun.

The applause and the pats on the back were unexpected. Having been treated like shit at home and work had taken its toll. The release he felt was palpable. His troubles swirled away from his mind like the smoke drifting into the Clearwater sky from all the rounds he had just fired.

He packed up his stuff and strolled out into the cool Clearwater evening to his truck. He made sure to put everything out of sight and retrieved his cell phone. There were repeated voicemails from his older brother Bryce and sisters. He saw text messages from them as well.

Hurry home. Mom is really sick.

CHAPTER 18

"YEAH, he was pissed and he had every right to be," Marsha concluded. She told Joe DiNatale about losing the eyeball on the recent surveillance and Charlie's reaction to it.

They were working on their entrees at what was fast becoming their favorite restaurant. The rain squalls that Wednesday evening had canceled his game and prompted a surprise invitation to an early dinner for him and a second dinner for her.

Just then, Jessalyn stopped by after dropping off a check at another table. "Hi, Marsha."

Not really surprised, Marsha knew that Jess waited tables here and did some emergency fill-ins during the week, she made the quick introduction. "Jess, I'd like you to meet my old college friend, Joe DiNatale."

Always a gentleman, he stood and shook her hand. "Hello, Jess, it's nice to meet you."

"Marsha told me you are coaching the Threshers. How is that goin'?"

"I've been coaching kids all my life. These just have a lot more talent and even bigger egos."

Everybody smiled at that. "It's finally nice to meet you, Marsha has said so many nice things about you."

Now it was time for both Marsha and Joe to blush. Joe replied, "She's never seen me after a blow-out loss."

"True D, but then again, that doesn't happen very often," she said about the previous season's National League Cy Young Award winner.

"It was nice meeting you, Mr. DiNatale." Jess smiled to Joe and then behind his back gave Marsha a face that confirmed she was seated across from a dreamboat.

Marsha shook her head and said, once that Jess was out of earshot, "She's working two jobs, has a teenage daughter and an SAA for a husband and is still a sweetheart."

"SAA?"

Stirring her bottomless refill sweet iced tea with her straw, Marsha quipped, "Self-absorbed Asshole. He's giving her the silent treatment."

"Sorry to hear that," Joe said. "Sounds like she could use a second chance."

Joe's divorce was finally official and he hadn't talked much about his girlfriend, who worked crazy shifts as an ER nurse in Queens, New York. Marsha and Joe always had a natural chemistry, but the timing of their get-togethers never allowed them to discuss their feelings for each other.

"You gotta give yourself a break, Marsha." Joe returned to the original conversation. "It was the first time you talked to the Philly detective since the shoot out. It wasn't like that phone call was a reminder from your dentist's office for a teeth cleaning."

"That's why Charlie didn't throw me out on the street.

He knows I got baggage and that the call caught me off guard."

"Any word from your folks?" Joe probed.

Marsha kept working the straw, crunching ice while avoiding eye contact. "Not a peep." They were still reeling from the events that sent Marsha careening to Clearwater.

"They'll come around," Joe said.

He set his fork and knife down and stared at the pelting rain on the floor to ceiling windows facing the Gulf. "Your mom will figure a way to get through to him. Even though my ex-wife was bopping the local Cadillac dealer when I was off playing away games, she harped on me regularly to patch things up with my own son. I was pretty much a hard head too. I could have lost him forever."

She missed her family and they were blaming her for kicking over the hornet's nest.

Joe remained silent and held her space.

"More tea, Hon'?" the older server asked before realizing the situation. "Ugh, I'll come back later with the dessert menus."

Marsha reached for a napkin, swiped her eyes and blew her nose. "On my way to the bathroom, I'll just tell her that you're breaking up with me and refuse to admit that you are the father of my unborn child." Marsha left Joe speechless.

"What's wrong, Marsha?" Jess asked. The server pipeline was working just fine. She hovered while Marsha studied her red, watery eyes and streaking mascara.

"So I picked tonight to wear makeup." She shook her head. "I am a mess."

"Did he say something to hurt you? I'll go out there and tell him he's no longer welcome here." She was on her way to the bathroom door when Marsha grabbed her.

"No. He's a sweet man. He knows what happened to

me in Philly and is helping me work through it. I will tell you all about it, but not tonight. I promise."

The next patron to use the ladies' room found the two women embracing and stifling back sobs. She shimmied around them to get into a stall.

* * *

Marsha pulled into her driveway behind Charlie's car. The Teesdale truck was not in its usual spot on the shared driveway. *Jess could use a break from that asshole,* she thought.

Charlie was in his lounger in front of the hi-def flat screen when Marsha came in from her late evening with Joe. She saw that the Red Sox were in extra-innings with the Oakland A's out on the West Coast. Charlie motioned her to pause.

"Watch this replay," he said.

A soft fly-ball lifted out to centerfield. The runner on third base decided to test the outfielder's arm. The throw rocketed to home plate on the fly and the catcher leaped back and made a diving tag on the runner's hand before it touched the plate. The double play ended the inning.

"Christ, they better win. I'd hate to think I gave up my precious sleep time for another extra-inning loss."

Marsha, a long-time Phillies fan, knew what those sleep-deprived weekday mornings felt like all too well, along with the guilt of eating everything in the house during the extra-inning losses. She sat down while the MLB app played the same boring beer and truck commercials.

He looked at her and asked, "Nice night?"

Marsha turned away from the TV and replied evenly, "He's a good man. He's taken and he's never kissed me if that is what you're asking."

"Seems like you are less uptight, that's all." Charlie held his hands up in surrender.

Marsha sighed. "You're right, Charlie. In a way, I do feel better. Christ, I don't know what I would do without you, Joe and Shira."

"Shira?"

"She's my martial arts instructor. She kicks my ass a couple times a week. Keeps me from diving into the pity bag."

"How's the drinking coming along?" he probed.

I'm staying in his house, eating his food and working for him, which is really like he's babysitting me, Marsha thought before replying, "I've replaced it with her workouts along with high dosages of chocolate and sweet iced tea, but I still get the urges, y'know?"

"When?"

"Oh, morning, noon and night and even while I'm dreaming. I've had dreams I was drinking like a Vegas party-girl and woke up hungover."

Charlie said, "I get the drunk dreams, too, now and then. At first, I am terrified that I drank again before I realize that it was just a dream."

While they were talking, the game came back on and the A's hit back to back first-pitch doubles, and just like that, they hung another loss on the Sox.

"Christ." Charlie shook his head, acquired the remote and silence enveloped his double-wide.

"Hey, we got a hot one from St Paul, Minnesota. You up for doing some shoe leather tomorrow afternoon?"

"You mean, I am off Charlie Akers double-secret probation?" Marsha responded alluding to the fact that Charlie hadn't given her any work since the Busch Gardens screw up.

Charlie sighed. "Between fishing and golf on sunny days, it's hard to get quality help, y'know."

They both grinned, a truce had been forged.

"She's a runaway." Charlie fished the picture out of his file on the coffee table.

"Wow, she looks like she could be my daughter," Marsha said. The tall athletic blonde, standing in a high school gymnasium, a volleyball tucked under her arm, was smiling with a mixture of confidence and innocence.

"Wow, she looks like she could be my daughter," Marsha said.

"I remember when you were a young gunslinger back in Miami and I thought the same thing," Charlie said.

"What happened?"

"Everything is wonderful back in the land of a thousand lakes last November, when she cleans out her bank account on a Saturday morning, empties her closet and drawers into the hand-me-down Hyundai Sonata the next day while the family is at church. She leaves a note for them not to worry." Charlie handed her a single sheet of copier paper with the hand-written note centered on it.

Marsha read it and said, "Sounds like she had no choice, but to leave *and* it was not what she really wanted to do?"

"The obvious question is?" Charlie asked.

"The number one answer on *Family Feud*," Marsha played it up, "Survey says—she's pregnant and abortion wasn't an option with her upbringing."

"The Ertz Family is thinking that way too. She Snapchats with her closest girlfriend, who passes it on to her brother that she's okay, but she never has left a clue where she is or where's she's going. The girlfriend won't let them trace Carli's messages. She's eighteen and told them that this is how Carli wants to play it."

"How'd they find her in Clearwater?"

"The family would always take their cars to the dealership where they bought them anytime the idiot light came on. They told their Hyundai dealership to check the vehicle history every month and two warnings for engine work popped up. The local dealership here replaced the timing chain a week ago."

"Oh, that would have been sweet," Marsha said. "To have the car in the shop for a couple days and to be there when she showed up to pick it up."

"In a perfect world...." Charlie's voice trailed off.

"What?"

"Look at her DOB," Charlie said.

Marsha did the math and nodded. "She turns eighteen on May 1st and can tell everybody to go pound sand."

"Doesn't sound like she's brainwashed with a cult or is in imminent danger, so the family wants to find her before she blows out the candles on her next birthday cake."

If she was my daughter, I'd want to know how she's doing. Marsha's eyes began watering again.

Charlie mindlessly turned on the TV while Marsha was studying the rest of the assignment notes. "Oh, Christ, not again."

Marsha blinked away more moisture to see a reporter standing in front of a municipal building up in Virginia describing how an introverted co-worker killed twelve and injured four with two .45 cal pistols that had extended magazines. One had a silencer. No motive was given.

That's one way to give your resignation. I guess.

CHAPTER 19

WILLIS SAT DOWN NEXT to her bed. His father and sisters moved to give him a seat in the crowded ICU at Charlton Memorial Hospital. He hadn't stopped once on the four-hour drive back to his hometown, right to the building where he was born. The frail wisp of a woman that birthed him and his brothers and sisters had been in and out of consciousness before his arrival.

Never one to make a fuss, she had resisted going to the doctors when she thought she just had a nasty cold, which was later diagnosed as a deadly strain of the flu that was resistant to treatment so far. Her condition was worsening. A life-time worrier, she was not healthy, to begin with. The pastor from their church had already been in. Nobody wanted to admit that things looked bleak.

She opened her eyes and saw him sitting there. She must have seen the look on his face. "Willis, you made it." She smiled weakly.

"I'm here, Mom," was all he could manage.

"Where's my pretty granddaughter?"

"Briana has a big test tomorrow," he lied. He had never

told his wife or daughter. He wasn't going to break his silence.

His mom weakly nodded. "That's okay, tell her I always loved her."

"I will, Mom," he lied again. "But, you can tell her yourself when we come up for your birthday."

Looking at him, she said, "Come close, honey."

He shifted weight and stood up, using the railings on each side of the bed. He held his head to the side of hers.

"You were my baby Willis, and I want you to know that I always loved you. God gave me a baby boy later in life to remind me of what a blessing it was to be a mother. I just wanted you to know that."

Good thing she can't see my face, he thought. It hit him like a gut punch. It took every bit of composure to lift his head up and smile back at her. "I always knew that you loved me, Mom."

She closed her eyes and her head fell back on the pillow.

He looked around. His father was stoic as ever. *I don't think I've ever seen him cry.*

His sisters and sisters-in-law were bawling. His brothers and brothers-in-law were hurting as bad as he was but were doing their best not to show it. The monitors beeped and the IV dripped. His mother was resting, a serene look spread across her face.

"She's made her peace with everybody now," the oldest, Bryce, said.

Willis moved from the chair and stumbled to the doorway and into the hall, where he cried unashamedly. He held the wall with his hand, bent over slightly while his sisters handed him wads of tissue and comforted him.

Finally, he looked at them and said. "She's not gonna make it, is she?"

They shook their heads sideways and all three of them starting crying together. It was so sudden. Their mother was not in good health overall, but this turn of events caught them all emotionally unprepared.

"Where's Jess and Bri'?" Brenda asked.

"Like I said, Briana has a big test tomorrow and she's still too young to leave at home by herself." Willis reinforced his lie. He felt trapped in a corner, a corner that his wife and daughter had placed him in.

Before he could think of a way out, there was a flurry of activity in his mother's room. Bryce was yelling, "Mom! Mom!"

Nurses and doctors ran from the nursing station to the room. The family collided with them as the doorway could not accommodate the entrance of cool professionals and the exit of the frantic family. Wills stood helplessly as a crash cart with a defibrillator was wheeled in.

"Clear!"

A long pause.

"Clear!"

A longer pause.

"Clear!"

An even longer pause. The rustling stopped. A silence filled the room. Everyone was holding their breath.

"Mark time of death as....."

Willis stood motionless. *This is all a bad dream. This is not happening. No! No! No!*

* * *

2:38am. The time on her TV cable box read. His side of the bed was empty. Jesslyn looked at her phone, the ringer had woken her. She had it on ring just in case Willis would call her. A text from her sister-in-law read: *Call me.* That's it. Just *call me*.

Jess rolled over and started to drift off to sleep, but something nagged her to return the call.

"Why didn't you come?" Brenda was crying. Jess could hear other people crying in the background.

"Come where? What are you talking about? What's going on?"

"Willis said that Briana has a test today and you couldn't come to see Mom. You know damn well that they would let her take her test another time."

"What? What test? Willis said, what?" Jess was fully awake now and her heart was pounding and throbbing her temple against the phone.

"Mom's dead," Brenda wailed. "She asked for Briana before she died and Briana wasn't here. It's all your fault."

Jess let the phone drop to the bed. Her thoughts went back to her wedding day and the day she came home from the hospital with her newborn to a house full of out-of-state relatives.

Folkston, Georgia family picnics, baptisms, birthdays, and funerals all blurred together.

She was the only one of them to treat me decent. She understood what it was like being married to a Teesdale man.

She stumbled down the hallway to tell Briana that Grammy Teesdale was dead.

How am I going to get there? My car is broke and I have no money to fix it.

CHAPTER 20

HE HAD BEEN HOME from the funeral for a couple of days. On his first day back to work, Lane and Lisa offered their condolences in person. They had covered for him while he was away. He returned to no backlog. Lane had even gotten Willis's work truck washed and vacuumed. He had everything he needed for his run that day packed neatly. He didn't think he had any tears left, but he was wrong.

These were tears of gratefulness. Grateful that he wasn't being judged by his know-it-all wife. Thankful that he was away from his condescending family. Thankful that his employer and co-workers valued him.

It was Friday night—pizza night when his family would usually enjoy a cheap night out, talk about the past week and what they were planning for the weekend. But that was back when they acted like a family, back when he was the king over his domain.

After the stunt his wife and daughter pulled at the funeral, he was more determined to wait them out. Five minutes before the casket was closed, they came into the church and went right to it, ignoring his family. They made their peace with his mother and then sat on the other side of the hot and crowded church with people from town who had come to pay their respects.

After the service, they had driven Charlie's car to the cemetery, tossed flowers into the grave and drove away. The worst insult was that they didn't even stay for the food that all the neighbors had kept bringing in waves to his sister's house.

His sadness at his mother's sudden passing was giving way to his anger at his impotence at not being able to change that outcome. Of course, he got an earful from his father and brothers about how he couldn't manage his womenfolk. His sisters and sister-in-laws harped about how Jess and Briana were too selfish to come while their mother was still alive. He didn't bother to correct them. It was all he could do to manage his grief.

So there he sat in his favorite chair, wolfing down a sausage and meatball while channel-surfing. *So much for family night.*

He heard a car come into the driveway. Before Jess had stopped talking to him in response to his campaign of silence, she informed him that she got nothing for her trade-in, but the dealer towed it from the driveway and put her in a Honda Fit. He didn't know how she paid for it or if she had a co-signer. He was just glad that he didn't have to hear her yak at him about her car problems.

They came in carrying groceries. Briana helped her mother put them away and they talked as if he wasn't even there.

He raised the volume on his remote and got the stink eye from both of them. Jess carried the laundry detergent to the washer and Briana walked into the living room and stood directly in front of the TV.

The hunters were on safari and were stalking big game. He always dreamed about going on safari and those dreams were interrupted by Briana standing between him and the African bush. She was staring at him, hands on hips, waiting to get a response.

None came. He sipped his soft drink and munched his pizza.

She waited until the commercial came on. "I am pretty sure that you stopped talking to Mom because of money, but I don't know why you stopped talking to me."

He put the slice and remote down and stared at her.

"I don't understand. Can you tell me what I did to deserve it?"

He focused on the stuffed and mounted heads on the walls and recalled how he bagged each one.

Briana shifted position and moved to a kneeling position at eye level right in front of him and touched his knee.

"Please, Daddy, I want to know what I did."

He caught sight of Jess lurking in the hallway and he stiffened.

As calmly as he could, Willis looked at her and said, "Daddy's really upset about Grammy Teesdale passing. I will talk to you when I feel better."

He looked over her shoulder to the Cape Buffalo moving warily in the distance away from the hunters. *They have to take their shot soon.*

Briana blinked twice at that response, looked over at her mother and stood up, blocking his view again. He wanted to see if they got it and leaned to the left. She moved to the right, blocking his sight again.

He scolded loudly."Briana Jane," he scolded loudly,

using her middle name and the given name of his dead mother. "I'll talk to you when I am damn good and ready."

She jumped back, startled by his outburst. He wished he could take it back, but it was too late.

Jess moved in. "What the hell is wrong with you, Willis? Your daughter is reaching out to you, and you scream at her."

"Stay out of it, Jess, I am warning you. Leave me alone," he yelled even louder. They were the first spoken words to his bride of seventeen years in as many days.

Briana turned around and saw on the TV the mighty hunters had slain the big lumbering beast and now stood with their grinning guides next to their trophy. Her eyes raised to the mounted coyote. The animal which had caused all the problems to start with.

In a couple of quick, determined steps, she was underneath it and began jumping and reaching over the TV stand to try to snag it. In doing so, the flat screen wobbled precariously and Willis realized what she was doing. He jumped to his feet, closed the distance and grabbed her by the shoulders and threw her roughly to the couch.

She rebounded and went after her father's prize from along the wall and jumped up between the wall and the TV. He started to move and was blindsided by Jess, who shouldered him right in his still-smarting ribs.

"Don't you touch her again, you bastard," Jess said, knocking him to the ground and standing between them.

He saw the fierce look on her face. One that he had never seen before.

Stunned and hurting, Willis looked up to see Briana jump twice and, on the second attempt, slapped the dead animal with the forever sneer from the wall. He staggered to his feet and bull-rushed both of them, knocking them like bowling pins into the hi-def, which crashed onto the coyote's legs, snapping them like twigs.

"Look what you did? You're crazy, both of you. See what you caused? You couldn't leave me alone. Could you? Could you?" he wailed. Willis tried to connect its legs, but they fell like felt-covered Pick-up Sticks to the rug.

He slumped to his knees, staring at the carnage while Jessalyn and Briana scrambled back to her bedroom. He heard her bedroom door close and lock.

The upended TV, the stuffed animal with broken legs, his marriage, his crazy daughter, his dead mother, the stupid maid, the dyke neighbor—all came rushing to his mind like lighting bursts with the deafening roar of rolling thunder.

His vision narrowed. He became dizzy. His heart pounded through his chest.

Calling him from afar, he heard a sharp female voice.

"Mr. Teesdale.... Mr. Teesdale?"

He felt a nudge and opened his eyes to see that he was holding the coyote's paws in both hands, pressed against his thumbs like the handles and trigger of a tripod-mounted .50 cal machine gun.

"Mr. Teesdale?"

He blinked and looked up into the eyes of the female Clearwater police officer who had come to his house on the night he had a fight with Jess in the Walmart parking lot. She held her long metal flashlight backward in one hand and had her other resting on her TASER.

Behind her, he could see her partner shepherding his limping wife and bawling daughter out of the house. He was sure she was lying to him, saying something wrong about him. He was positive.

He looked at the carnage in his living room. He fixated on the TV. It could be repaired, he just needed to reset it.

Looking at the trophy mount, he figured that a little Super Glue would do the trick. He tried putting the paws in place manually.

If this female cop would just shut up and let me concentrate. He carefully placed each one next to the corresponding kneecap.

How did he become so thirsty? His Mountain Dew Big Gulp was just out of reach next to his chair and overturned pizza box.

Hey, I was still eating that. Who is going to put it in the fridge? He found it difficult to reach for his soda, especially with his hands somehow now secured behind his back. *Why can't I move my hands?*

He moved one and the other one pulled with it. The throbbing in his ribs returned and he felt strong, plastic-gloved hands lift him to his feet. He remembered his mother lifting him as a toddler from underneath his armpits from his toys and into her warm embrace.

"I miss you, Mommy," he muttered.

He was led outside and immediately recognized Charlie and his female friend scowling at him from their side of the driveway.

What's their problem?

The neighbors from the other side of his double-wide and from across the street were huddled in the street under the streetlight with their arms crossed, silent witnesses to the dust-up at the Teesdale house.

Okay, I was at a funeral, gimme a break. I'll mow the lawn this weekend.

It was chilly outside. He felt a shudder. The blinding lights on the ambulance next to the gawking bystanders made it hard for him to squint and deduce who the EMTs were tending to.

The gloved hand firmly grasped his head as he was then seated in the back of their car. It only took a few minutes for them to set their clipboards down, remove their caps and radio to dispatch that they were doing a prisoner transport.

As they left his neighborhood and turned onto the main drag, he could hear his brother Bryce's voice while his tight-lipped taciturn father just shook his head.

You done screwed the pooch this time, Willis.

CHAPTER 21

"CAN I talk to the service writer?" Marsha handed the young receptionist the print-out of the service record for the St. Paul Sonata.

"Wait here," she cheerily said as she disappeared into the bowels of the service department of the dealership.

Service customers were seated along the walls of the waiting area, in beautiful cushioned chairs glued to the TV. The reporter just announced that a sheriff's office fired a sergeant while a deputy was fired and charged with neglect for failing to intervene in a school shooting the year before. The shooter killed seventeen and injured an equal amount with a semi-automatic rifle.

Kids were rolling toy trucks on the floor or playing tag. Free coffee refills placated the adults as the talking heads droned on.

Just another day in paradise, Marsha thought. At least this story had legs and was staying in the news.

"How can I help you, ma'am?" The service manager greeted her wearing a powder blue collared polo displaying a logo for the dealership. The fabric covered his generous belly that hid his belt presumably holding up his tan khakis.

She stuck out her hand for him to shake it and said, "Marsha." Putting a pretty smile on her pretty face, she added, "You can call a woman my mother's age, ma'am."

He blushed back. "How can I help you, Marsha?"

"I'm working for a local private investigator, Charlie Akers. Do you know him?"

"No, I can't say I do."

"Charlie and I worked together with the FBI in Miami."

"FBI." The smile disappeared, replaced by a frown.

"That was then, and this is now." Marsha held a photo of Carli Ertz out and sidled into his comfort zone next to him. "I want to ask the service writer if he remembered her."

His eyes took in the athletic blond high-schooler, and before he could protest, she rolled on with practiced nonchalance but stated her purpose. "She's a runaway teenager from up North and her parents are desperate to contact her. She's a nice-looking girl and I'm pretty sure your writer would remember his contact with her."

"We have a lot of people come through here every day. We are the best Hyundai dealership for several years running in this part of the state. I am not so sure he will."

She looked at his face and then his badge and nodding at the box of donuts on the ledge next to the coffee. "I'll bet you a donut, Derek, he does." She kept the closeness and gaze until he broke it.

"I'll go ask him." He began to tug the photo from her hand.

She firmly tugged it back. "Who is the investigator here? I would never think I could do your job, Derek." Repeating his name again with a smile.

Surrendering the power position, Derek said, "Only for a minute. We're busy today."

"No problema." She tilted her head in agreement. *I'll talk with him as long as I need to,* she thought.

She was learning how to replace her status as an FBI agent and its inherent authority with many different interview approaches. When she first arrived on the Gulf Coast without her badge and her gun, she felt like she was wearing a tight skirt and no undies.

She watched Charlie sweet-talk his way into information from people who didn't have to give him jack-squat. And he was a crusty old man! She would shake her head at him and laugh how easy he made it seem, but she knew it wasn't easy.

Just like figuring out how to do a custodial interrogation or street interview with a recalcitrant witness, she realized that here, as then, she could use a few more arrows in her quiver. Interviewing people was both a science and an art.

Cops or federal agents who relied solely on the badge were like major league pitchers who only relied on their fastballs. After a while, the hitters would time their fastballs and see how far they could hit them.

Always a quick study, she was learning how to get people to cooperate with her. Smiles got more than stern faces and prepping for the interviews was getting more comfortable.

Derek returned with a younger man whose hands told her that he still worked on cars. She observed deeply embedded grease and callouses and felt the handshake of a guy that still turns wrenches. His short sleeve dress shirt covered some of his tattoos on both arms. "This is Eduardo," Derek said.

Standing eyeball to eyeball, she calmly said, "Hi,

Eduardo. Derek probably told you that I am looking for this missing girl from Minnesota." She showed him the photo and let him hold it in his hands. She handed him the service order.

"Thank you, Derek," she said. "I know your busy, I appreciate your help. I think I can take it from here." She smiled the pretty face smile and shook his hand vigorously.

"Uhh, you're welcome, Marsha. If you need anything else, give me a call." He handed her his business card.

"You betcha." She pocketed the card. *Fat chance, doughboy.* Her smile faded and she now looked expectantly at the witness.

"I remember her. We got to her timing belt just before it busted. That would have killed her engine. We had to replace it, though. She wanted to give me a tip and I said no. She paid all cash. It was like she raided her piggy bank. Lots of twenties, tens, and fives. It was like that game. Whatzit called?"

"*Monopoly*," Marsha supplied the correct answer. Anything to keep this kid focused in his memory.

"Yeah, *Monopoly*, yeah, where you got two hundred for passing GO and the Get Out of Jail Free cards."

She nodded. *Good boy.*

He looked at the service report. "Hold on, there is more to this. Let me get the customer notes."

He walked over to the receptionist. "Hi, Missy. Can you help me out?"

"Hey, Eddie. What's up?"

"Can you pull up the customer notes on this service order?"

She looked perplexed. "I don't know how to do that. They didn't show me that yet."

He swung around the counter and leaned over her. "Click here." He pointed. "Now put in this number." The order appeared. "See this tab? Hit the drop-down menu. Yep. Just like that, and there are customer notes."

"Thanks, Eddie," Missy said.

"Can you print them out," Marsha asked.

"They taught me how to do that." Missy giggled.

All three of them stared at the printer. It showed no signs of activity right away, but came to life momentarily and spit out three sheets of paper. To Missy and Eduardo, they were records kept in the normal conduct of business for the dealership. To Marsha, they might solve the case of the missing teen for her frantic parents.

Eduardo handed Marsha back the photo and original service order and studied the customer notes like a general practitioner studying a patient's chart.

"Here is her phone number. I called her a couple of times. You can see by the call log notes. Here is where I told her what we found and how much the repairs would be. She said she used the car for her business. She cleaned Airbnbs, condos, and timeshares. My cousin Maritza cleaned houses and I helped her once in a while.

"This girl kept all her supplies and her back-pack vacuum in the car. She had a friend come and take her home. I helped them unload the car. It was packed with dusters and rags and spray bottles and buckets. It seemed like her friend was her roommate too, 'cause they talked about where they could put the stuff when they got home."

"Do you remember her?" Marsha pried some more.

"Yeah. She was hot too but in a different way."

He moved away from Missy and whispered. Stabbing his finger on the picture. "This girl is All-American-sweet as apple pie. The other girl—kinda slutty. Short shorts and a tight top—you get the picture."

Marsha nodded. "Do you remember her car?"

Eduardo thought for a moment. "A shit-box sedan. Kinda went with her appearance. Sentra, I think, black. I don't think it's seen the inside of a car wash for a long time."

"Well, your customer is a runaway. Maybe you can't always pick your friends when you are on the move. Did she bring her back when the car was ready?"

"Dunno. I didn't see anybody drop her off. I made a point to see her again when she went to the cashier, that's how I knew about the *Monopoly* money."

"Did you think of asking her out on a date?" Marsha asked.

"She's too young and way out of my league. Besides, my girlfriend wouldn't like it too much." He added, "But I did like seeing her again. Like I said, she was All-American Apple Pie. I liked helping her out."

"Can you point out the cameras for me, Eduardo?"

He hesitated.

"I want to see if they picked up her friend's car that picked her up and dropped her off and if we can make out the license plate."

"Let's go," he said. He walked her out into the parking lot and pointed out the cameras on the corners of the building and in the sally port where service reps took the cars from the customers. He introduced Marsha to the general manager.

"Mr. Nelson, this lady is a private detective investigating a runaway girl from up North. The girl brought her parents' car in from repairs on this date and picked it up on this date." He pointed to the repair bill. "She needs to look at the videos to see if she can pick up the marker plate for the car that picked her up and dropped her off."

"Marsha O'Shea." She smiled the pretty girl smile and held out her hand.

"James Nelson," he said and gave her a bone-crushing handshake.

"Whoa, Hoss, I may need that hand later today," she said, shaking her hand to get the bones to align.

"Sorry, I forget that sometimes."

"Right now, I can just record the monitors with my camera until you can download the footage to a thumb drive or a disc." Marsha held her cell phone in her throbbing hand.

He paused to consider her offer.

Eduardo and Marsha looked at him with expectant eyes.

"I'm not sure. I may have to clear it with the own—"

Marsha matter of factly charged ahead, anticipating this objection, "If you are worried about the customer's privacy, I can have them fax down their title and sales agreement with their permission. It's your customer's daughter that they are trying to find and seeing who picked her up and dropped her off may lead us to her."

"We usually deal with the police on external matters," he said weakly.

"I'm sure the police were contacted by the parents the minute the car surfaced here in Clearwater. This is the first logical lead to follow-up on. Have the cops asked for the video yet?" Marsha asked, already knowing the answer.

"Umm, no," he replied.

"Let's go take a look then." She added, "What if this was your daughter Jim?"

"It's James," he said automatically. Everyone was now staring at the photo. "You get the parents to send down the fax to my attention and I will take a look at the video and call you up if we got anything."

"Thanks, Ji—James. I'll write my number on the repair slip." She wrote it down and then offered her still-aching hand but first held it up as if to surrender that he had the stronger grip, and this time, he didn't crush her knuckles when they shook.

She walked Eduardo back to the service bay and asked him to politely nudge James the following day. She then spied the box of donuts and grabbed the double chocolate and offered him half.

"Thank you for helping me, I really appreciate it. Here's my boss's card. If you ever need a PI, it's not as good as a Get Out of Jail Free card but works pretty good."

Two bites later, he cleared his voice while pocketing the card and simply said, "Thanks."

"No. Thank you," Marsha said with a genuine smile this time. She began to walk away then turned back quickly. "Eduardo, one more thing, I almost forgot to ask you."

"What's that?"

"Was the girl from up North pregnant?"

Eduardo shook his head in confusion.

"Did the girl look to be about five months pregnant?"

"No, like I said. All-American apple pie."

She nodded her thanks again. On the way to her car, she checked her watch and saw that she still had time for a quick session with Shira before heading over to her appointment with the missing persons detective at Clearwater PD.

Charlie had the parents' phone in the report and email photos of their daughter, her car and a letter authorizing his agency to work concurrently with the PD. It was not uncommon for private investigators to do legwork when the police were swamped with missing persons and runaways.

CHAPTER 22

WILLIS WISHED that he had requested a higher limit on his credit card. Oh well, he'd have to take out another one. After paying the bail bondsman and his lawyer, there wasn't much left on it. He took the coyote to a local taxidermist and they said they could fix it like it was brand new.

The TV was a different story. He replaced it with one from the pawnshop. He hated to part with a couple of his handguns, but he needed cash until payday, and they had a cheap one to buy.

It was quiet in the house and that's how he liked it. Jess had taken Briana to her sister's house. They had slapped a restraining order on him at the court hearing. The lawyer assured him that he'd get probation. If he got into an anger management program, they might be able to *nolle* the charges after a year or so of good behavior.

That is the word the lawyer used: *nolle*. All he knew was that his life would return to normal and they would throw out the charges like they never happened.

He heard someone come into the driveway.

Probably that bitch staying with Charlie.

He busied himself with cleaning his hunting rifle and heard a knock on the door.

He opened it to an older gentleman with a clipboard and a body cam.

"Willis Teesdale?"

"Yes?" Willis was holding the gun with the cleaning cloth by the barrel, the smell of the solvent wafting out the door and into the morning air.

Seeing the gun, the man dropped the papers on the threshold, "You've been served." He moved quickly without taking his eyes or the GoPro camera off the gun.

Willis bent down to pick up the papers as the breeze began to scatter them. He propped the gun against the door and pinned a few to the ground with his foot as he grabbed with both hands for the remainder before they blew off his front stoop. The man had returned to his coupe and was out of the driveway in a hurry before Willis could find the first page.

Divorce papers? What the hell is this?

He looked up to see a neighbor walking their dog. He was now holding his rifle in one hand and the papers in the other. He quickly retreated to the house as if somehow the nosy neighbor could read his papers.

Slumping back into his comfy chair. He set the gun down and tried to make sense of what all the legal mumbo-jumbo said. He muted the fly-cast special and tried to concentrate.

She got a lawyer at legal aid. Thelma Madsen is her name. What is going on here?

He tried breathing, but it was harder and harder to catch his breath. He forced himself to clear his eyes and focus on the papers.

"The Marriage has broken down over irreconcilable differences...," he read.

That's crazy. All we had is an argument. She started it. Continually harping on me about money. We never had a problem while I controlled the checkbook. She kicked my car and Briana knocked over the TV when she tried to destroy my trophy shot.

Slowly, Willis began to simmer. He flashed back to the funeral, the school secretary. He got hotter. His side was still throbbing from where Jess shouldered him. He was initially hurting there because a stupid housekeeper didn't look where she was going. The smart-ass counselor telling him how to run his life. The faces were jumbling together with the woman next door who got Jess drunk on the Sabbath.

Now a female lawyer is telling her to divorce me.

Willis was furious with what he saw as the unfairness of the entire situation. He couldn't conceive how things had gotten so far out of hand. He didn't want a divorce. He just wanted things to go back to normal. The campaign of silence was over.

Now he wanted her to listen to him. He'd get his sisters to talk to her sister. He'd get Pastor Rick to tell her to pray on it and to reconsider her decision. He was sure that she was getting bad advice. They could take out another loan to buy them time until he could start working overtime again.

He could fix this mess.

CHAPTER 23

"SHE'S ALMOST eighteen years old. She's working cleaning condos and timeshares. She has a car and can pay for her own repairs." The harried Clearwater Police detective looked at his paperwork. "What am I missing here?"

Marsha realized that her "ask" was causing the balding detective to have to work and to have to work on a less pressing case. His caseload had the usual parental abductions, runaways, and occasional demented seniors walking away from their assisted-living home. He had to field tips on cold cases and take constant calls from parents looking for any news, but there was more bothering him.

"Have you seen the news lately?" he asked.

Marsha wasn't aware of anything that would be of interest to both of them. She shrugged. "No, sorry. What do enquiring minds need to know, Detective Feeney?"

He pulled a yellowing missing poster from his wall, next to the framed family photo displaying the same woman and probably her kids and smiling husband. "Sandi Heath. Thirteen years ago, she disappeared, leaving her husband with toddlers. We worked it hard.

Looked at the husband too. He took a polygraph and passed it. We busted our butts working the case, and slowly, the leads dried up. Every serial killer with any connection to Tampa-St. Pete still gets a hard look. The reward is up to $100,000, put up by the guy and her family. Still nothing."

"And?"

He tapped his space bar on his keyboard and his monitor lit up and he pointed to it. "Some laid-off newspaper reporter styles himself as an 'investigative journalist,' now and he's got a podcast with advertisers and all. The chief wants us, excuse me—he wants *me*— to monitor all the social media blowing up over this. Of course, the asshole—the podcaster, not the chief—is painting you know who as the stupidest and laziest flatfoot to ever wear a badge."

Feeney looked at his Police Union Credit Union calendar on the wall and realized he hadn't crossed this day off with his red Sharpie hanging from a piece of twine taped to the wall. He reached up, crossed off the day, and quietly sang his mantra. "'Nother one bites the dust. 'Nother one bites the dust."

Marsha nodded in faux agreement. "Freaking reporters always think they know how to work your case." Going back to her demons in Philly, it wasn't the first time she cursed Stew Menke thinking that he could be a crime-fighting, muckraking, Pulitzer-prize winning reporter. Instead, he got tortured to death and died for his efforts.

"Fuckin' A." Feeney tipped his head slightly while staring at the face of the woman in the photo. "This case has stayed with me since the day I caught it. Gotta admit though, a part of me hopes that the son of bitch breaks it and we get 'a solve.' I'd let him come in wipe it off the board. All these years... What if I missed something or somebody here dropped the ball? It has been nagging me and will probably nag me until the day I die."

"So, you don't think she's snorkeling the Great Barrier Reef with her boyfriend?"

Feeney shook his head. "I'd be on a plane tomorrow if I thought that."

Marsha stood up. "It was a pleasure meeting you, sir." She shook his hand and held it while making eye contact. "I hope you get closure on your case. I know what purgatory feels like." She let his hand go then. "Can you check the system on Carli," tapping her picture in his folder, "and let me know if anything pops? If she gets stopped or picked up, let patrol know this is my cell number. I'll drop everything to go to the scene."

He nodded. "Good luck"... looking at her name and cell number... "O'Shea."

"You too, Feeney."

Marsha drove to Jessalyn's sister's address on Velventos Drive in a gated community. She used the password on the keypad and her Mustang cleared the iron gates with ease. She had some time before going to Carli's address where she planned to sit on it. She rolled up on the house.

It was huge by Florida housing standards and had a fourth bedroom with its own bathroom that could double as an in-law's quarters. Jess told her this is where their mother could stay if the apartment became too much for her. Mom and daughter were happy with the "just in case" arrangement and both appreciated their distance.

Briana was home from school and was busy on her phone under the sprawling Cypress tree. It was in full bloom and shaded the teenager.

Marsha gunned the engine in Park to get her attention. Briana looked up from her phone and smiled. "Hi, Marsha."

Turning off the engine, Marsha smiled back. "Hey, Bri. Howzitgoin'?"

"Okay."

"I'm here to see both of you guys."

At that moment, the au pair came out and appeared alarmed. "Is everything alright, Briana?"

"Yes, Trudi. Marsha is our next-door neighbor."

"Your mother didn't tell me that she was expecting anybody. I will have to tell your aunt Nicole."

"Okay, Trudi," Briana replied, turning to face Marsha and rolling her eyes. Trudi marched back inside.

"Hi, Trudi, it's nice to meet you too." Marsha laughed. "Briana, after I talk to your mom, I was wondering if you could help your favorite FBI agent out on a case."

Briana's eyes widened. "Sure," she said with no hesitation.

Good thing I'm not asking her to go undercover in a prostitution sting, Marsha thought. "It's perfect for you."

Jess came out carrying a couple of glasses of sweet iced tea.

"You read my mind, girlfriend," Marsha said.

"My wonderful sister-in-law used to call me that until I got all up in her grill, especially after all that bullshit over the funeral," Jess said, handing Marsha her favorite mid-afternoon alcohol substitute.

"Listen to you, Jess, cursing and talking like a gangsta," Marsha replied.

"Lots of changes, Marsha, come sit. Bri, can you give us a little time."

"Sure, Mom. Marsha is gonna have me work on a case with her." Briana walked to the enclosed in-ground pool next to the garage where the curved driveway ended.

Marsha looked at Jess and saw assured confidence in

her demeanor. "For a tackling dummy, you actually look relaxed and happy. What happened?"

"He knocked some sense into me, Marsha. The credit counselor and Thelma had given me the roadmap and he kicked my can down the road to freedom. It's like he woke me up from a bad dream. All those years of thinking we were building something together. When he walloped me that night, I said to myself, 'I don't need this shit.' On the ride to the ER, I told Briana that we didn't have to live like second-class citizens anymore, that we would get our own apartment and start over."

"What did she say?"

"When she saw her black eye and swollen face, it took her a milli-second to agree with me. She went with me to court to get the restraining order and saw her father for the first time since he slammed her into the TV. He didn't say he was sorry and acted like he was the victim. Afterwards, she asked me if she would get her own bedroom and could she pick out some furniture. She's also gonna work with me at the restaurant Saturday nights and maybe even pick up some more hours."

"It was hard to read her, but she certainly seems to be in synch with you," Marsha opined.

"We are closer now than ever. My mom didn't put up with my father's abuse and neither am I. My daughter is not gonna be her father's punching bag either.

Her father? Marsha noticed the distancing in language, which signaled Jessalyn's determination to move forward.

"My mom put most of her furniture in storage when she sold the house and moved to her retiree community. My old bed is there and so is my sister's. There's also a couch and a dining room set. Someday when Willis is at work, I will go home and get all our clothes and kitchen stuff. God knows, he's clueless beyond the microwave."

"I'll go with you and we'll bring Shira's ride."

"I'll let you know when the coast is clear. My break is over. I've got to get back to the salt mine."

They hugged.

Marsha busied herself with her phone while she waited for Briana. She saw that a Philadelphia police chief inspector's son was shot dead at FDR park after a Phillies game. On an impulse, she dialed a familiar number.

"How's my favorite karaoke cowboy doing?"

"Hi, Marsha, give me a second," Ramit said.

Ramit Ravikant was the intelligence analyst and techie whiz with her unit at the FBI back in Philly.

"What's the good word?" he asked in their practiced patter.

"Thunderbird," she replied.

"How's the wine?" he retorted.

"Mighty fine."

This routine was passed down from Philly cops in district cars rolling upon each other in deserted parking lots to their children for generations Marsha guessed. At first, Ramit was confused by the question, but as their affinity for Karaoke night at country and western bars around Philly blossomed, it became their inside greeting.

"Marsha," Ramit began in hushed tones. "You couldn't have called at a better time. The suits from the headquarters interviewed me this morning without Jingles in the room. I told them everything again. They went for coffee and came back and have been at him all day."

Jingles was Daryl Stocker, her supervisor, who earned his moniker when he was a younger supervisor and had his charges call in regularly from payphones.

God forbid that one of his agents didn't have a pocket full of dimes jingling in their pockets.

"The wheels of justice turn slow sometimes, Ramit, but it sounds good. I'd like to be a fly in that room."

"You should have given me some notice."

"Bugging the boss's office? Heaven's forbid, Ramit, I have been a bad influence on you."

He began a line from the song about if being wrong, he didn't want to be right that she helped him finish. It was one of their after-too-many-beers favorites to sing.

"I got a call from Mike Hollins. Not sure what he's gonna do. Right now, he can't lift his left arm high enough to pick his nose, but he's pissed and he's not gonna let them railroad us if he can help it," Marsha said.

Ramit asked the obvious question.

"When are you coming back?" Ramit asked the obvious question.

"Dunno, mi amigo. I'm keeping out of trouble down here and am working under the table for my old ASIC from my Miami days. He's a PI now."

"That's good, Marsha." It went unsaid what the "trouble" was. He had his concerns about her drinking and urged her to get some warmth and sunshine while getting away from the shit storm their case had created.

Marsha saw Briana round the corner. "Listen, Ramit, I gotta go. You keep your head down and take care now."

"You, too, Marsha. Call me if you need anything. Drone strikes or satellite tracking might take me a few days, though."

She ended the call and looked at Briana. "I have to find a runaway down here and wondered if you could be my eyes and ears on social media. Her name is Carli Ertz. I don't want to make up a fictitious account and spook her."

Marsha showed her the picture from her file and said, "Her best friend back in St. Paul is still in contact with her on Snap." Marsha showed her the girlfriend's Snap profile. "Carli's brother was friends with her girlfriend Demi and that's how we got her profile."

"What about Instagram," Briana asked.

Marsha shrugged. "Do your magic."

In a few minutes of watching magic thumbs whirling on the smartphone, Marsha realized that she was being left behind in the connection age. She was too young to think of herself as a dinosaur getting trapped in the tar pits.

Briana finished. "I'm now friends with Demi and am chatting her up. We are both advanced placement in Biology. Lots of geeky stuff to talk about. I told her this weekend I was playing volleyball on the beach. That might connect me to Carli."

"Soon as that happens, let me know. Text me." Marsha gave Briana her cell phone number and seconds later they were connected. "You are a natural for this. Briana, Did you ever think about joining the FBI?"

"No, but I will now." Her eyes were like saucers.

Marsha finished her sweet tea and gave Briana a quick hug and a peck on the cheek. "I can only pay you when we connect her to her family. Is that okay?"

"Sure, Marsha, no problem."

Marsha drove away to Carli's address, given on the service order. It was in an upscale condo and timeshare community on the water.

* * *

Briana waited until Marsha was out of sight and opened her Instagram app. She confirmed that Demi was connected to Carli and also to Briana's friend Rose whom she had met at the mall the day she almost ran away. The pictures of Rose and Carli standing by Carli's car were recent.

CHAPTER 24

"I'M gonna stay at my sister's house until the end of the month. We were able to find a two-bedroom in the school district. I passed the credit check on my own pay stubs." Jessalyn was the happiest she'd been in years.

"Nice," Thelma said.

"I had to twist my mom's arm to lend me the first-month rent and security deposit, and that's when I called Briana into the living room where we were parlaying. She took one look at her granddaughter's black eye and she whipped out her checkbook and said she would give it to me as a 'divorce present.'"

Both women grinned at that. The beat-up desks outside of Thelma's office at Legal Aid were still busy during the dinner hour, as new clients and their reluctant attorneys talked about navigating the legal system, which seemed to favor the people who could pay to play.

Thelma was back to business now. "He hasn't answered the divorce filing yet. He's got time. Anything on your end?"

"Not a peep. I think he's still in denial," Jess replied.

"Filing for bankruptcy is going to get his attention.

When he realizes that you are not there to cover your portion of the mortgage or credit card, the math will become apparent."

They began the process of filing the forms out. Thelma walked and talked her through the process. If the divorce went through in the normal course of time, the bankruptcy judge would have a simple job of splitting up the debts 50-50.

"All of this could have been avoided if he had agreed to cut back on all the toys and trips," Jessalyn said as they uploaded the filings.

"Be thankful this didn't go on for another twenty or thirty years. Many older women feel trapped and then become resigned to a miserable life."

* * *

"I took a chance with the nice old lady that lived next door to Carli's last known address. It got to be eight o'clock and I hadn't seen the Sonata or Carli," Marsha explained to Charlie on a phone update. The quirks of condo ownership in tax assessor rolls had hidden the owner's name from their online search. "The lady said the condo was owned by a professor on a sabbatical to Spain. His name matched the voter registration rolls. She recognized Carli as the house cleaner who came in every other week. Carli would come by every so often to water the plants and had a key to get in."

"Sounds like she's using the address as a mail drop while the professor is away. It's a nice way to get mail without paying for a P. O. box. What else?" Charlie said.

"I was surprised the missing persons detective called me back. He checked and didn't have her in their system for any field stops or complaints as a victim or a witness. He reminded me that she is almost eighteen and is not in any danger here."

Charlie said, "Still, she is in the system now and we can only hope they pinch her for a motor violation. I can tell you the client won't go for sitting on a house where she might visit once a week to water the plants."

"Darn," Marsha replied. "I have all these books on tape I could listen to. They would pay you for me to catch up on my steamy romance novels."

Ignoring that last comment, Charlie asked, "What else?"

"I've got Briana making friends with Carli's best friend on Snapchat. Maybe we can get some leads on how to find her without tipping her off. This weekend, we are going to visit the condo and time-share communities. Saturday after ten a. m. when all the renters have to vacate is the time to look for Carli's Sonata until about 3 p. m. when the new renters come in."

"You thinking about calling bone crusher tomorrow?" Charlie said, referring to the car dealership general manager.

Marsha winced as her hand still throbbed from the handshake that morning. "Yeah, I'll tell him the X-rays were negative. That will spark the conversation and that he owes me."

"Remember this way of chatting up people when you get your credentials and gun back, Marsh," he said.

"Looks promising, Charlie. I heard that the suits were bending my supervisor over the table today. It sounds like I wasn't such a loose cannon after all."

"Just don't leave me hanging me on this one, kiddo, okay?" Charlie asked.

"You've got my word on it, Mr. Akers," Marsha replied.

"Where you headed now, Ms. O'Shea?" he returned the formality.

"The Threshers are in extra-innings. I'm hoping to catch the ending and maybe see if DiNatale is hungry. I haven't eaten since after my workout today and I am starved. Besides, it's my turn to pay."

"If he lets you, I will have to have a talk with him," Charlie said.

"I have to offer, Charlie, so he knows we're just friends."

"Yeah, right. Don't bullshit a bullshitter, Marsha."

***

"He gave me a black eye." Briana was in mid-Snapchat with Rose. She decided to work Marsha's case a little differently.

"That's terrible," Rose replied.

"Yeah, he's not even sorry. It's like it's my fault or something?"

"What's happening now?"

"My mom and I moved out. We're staying with my aunt. She's got a beautiful place, but my aunt is really uptight."

"It's not like you wanted to move in with her. It sounds like you didn't have much choice."

"My mom found us an apartment near my school. It's okay, but that's all we can afford right now."

"Better than a shelter," Rose said.

"You ever had to stay at one?" Briana asked.

"When I was younger. People have problems with boundaries there too."

"Sorry... but you are good now, right?"

"Yeah, I make good money, saving up for my own place and a better car."

Rose had told Briana the day they met that she made ridiculous money working nights as a cocktail waitress at a high-end club. Briana probably needed to be an adult to work there.

Briana said, "My mom is getting me a job where she waits on tables, but I could use some extra work. Does your roommate need any help cleaning houses?"

* * *

Grayson Stanfield had just two case files on his otherwise pristine walnut desk. As the deputy director of the FBI, he was in charge of overseeing field investigations. He could request updates on any case and his assistants would make them magically appear in his executive assistant's in-bin. He still liked paper files with the tabs and two-pronged reports along with copies of the field 302s.

The latest reports contained in the thicker file from Philadelphia looked as though he had found the solution for the thinner file from Detroit, which disturbed him more. He had time to make his decision. He never rushed his decisions and always weighed the politics against the best way to get the job done. He was a field agent at heart and recognized good talent when he saw it. He could kill three birds with one stone.

* * *

The clay pigeons disintegrated when the birdshot from the shooter's double-barrel competition-grade shotgun caught them in flight.

"Pull."

The camera caught the gunner shoot left, swing right and shoot again with a practiced nonchalance of a marksman. He opened the breech and dumped the spent shells. He placed fresh ones in the barrels before snapping the gun shut. The scene shifted to the other cameras that recorded the demise of these two round discs as well.

With eyes half-open, Willis snoozed in his lounger. Empty General Tso take-out cartons and egg roll wrappers sat next to his now-warm Mountain Dew, leaving rings on the coffee table. He forewent coasters and trays in silent protest.

CHAPTER 25

THE CALL CAME in from a local line to her VoIP for the mortgage company. Jess would typically answer the phone after the caller had entered their account number into the system. It saved precious seconds of having to re-keystroke the information and possibly getting it wrong. She had trouble with some Caribbean accents and was hoping it was an English-first speaker.

No screen came up. It happened sometimes and she would then re-direct the call. She hadn't forgotten her chat with her boss about how taking the time to give excellent customer service had gotten her in trouble.

"Zephyr Mortgage and Loans. This is Jess speaking. How may I help you?"

She recognized the voice before long and gritted her teeth. *It's starting.*

"Hi, Jess."

She recognized the voice before long and gritted her teeth. *It's starting.*

"We haven't seen you at worship recently and we were wondering how you are doing."

"I've been taking muscle relaxants for my back spasms. I'm able to sit at my chair and take calls for work, but I'm really tired by the end of the day."

"That's good, I guess."

Jess couldn't help herself now. "With a little bit of make-up now, Briana's black eye is not as noticeable."

"Oh, that's good too."

Pastor Rick isn't used to backpedaling, it seems.

"We're okay, but the police blotter entry in the newspaper doesn't tell the whole story. Is that what you're calling about?"

"Well, actually, I was calling—"

"I'm on the clock, Pastor Rick, but why don't you Google 'Willis Teesdale,' plus 'Clearwater Police,' plus 'assault.' I can wait for a minute."

When he came back on the line, she preempted him. "I can't really talk about his case as the charges are still pending, but when it is over, I would be more than happy to discuss with you starting a battered woman's ministry. How does that sound?" She reached for her divorce paperwork while he stammered to form a cogent reply.

"Well, that's certainly something we can bring to the programming committee."

"Thank you, Pastor Rick, I appreciate the opportunity to help other women feel God's compassion and love when they are so alone. In the meantime, if you could keep me in your personal prayers, I would appreciate it, and if you want to discuss this more, you can call my attorney. Here is her number." She spit it out quickly. "The divorce filing is online and you can get it there. Oops, that's my next call, I've got to get back to work."

She disconnected and ripped the headset off and stood up to catch her breath.

About that time, her sister Nicole walked into the in-law's fourth bedroom without knocking or announcing herself. This wasn't the first time, and it was a clear signal that Jess and Briana were needy family and not guests. She was still in her nursing scrubs from working an overnight shift on the Ob-Gyn floor.

"That was my pastor on the phone. It seems like Willis is trying to communicate with me through him."

"We had a stillbirth last night and I stayed with the mother and father until the grief counselors came in to take over. It's the worst part of my job."

"I'm sorry to hear that. You get to see the miracle of birth and then this. What happened?"

"It wasn't a difficult labor, but all of a sudden, the baby just stopped—"

Jess put her arms around her younger sister and let her cry on her shoulder. Of course, the callers kept calling and Jess had to let them rollover. Mr. Miele will be sure to note that at their next teleconference.

Sniffling and red-eyed, Nicole continued. "I came back to my locker and found my phone was blowing up with text and voice messages from your in-laws." Nicole reached into her shirt pocket, pulled out her cell phone and waggled it at Jess.

"I'm sorry, Nicole. You didn't need my shit on top of your own. Just one question. Did any of them ask how Briana was doing?"

She shook her head.

Jess took the phone and composed a simple message. *Please contact Attorney Thelma Madsen at 813-555-4567 if you wish to discuss the criminal or civil cases brought against Willis.*

Each call and text were responded to this way along

with a photo of Briana's swollen face and blackened eye. Jess received Nicole's permission each time.

Jessalyn's personal phone rang, and she showed the caller ID to Nicole, they both rolled their eyes. It was their mother calling.

"Hi, Mom, I am sitting with Nicole right now and have you on speakerphone."

"Hi, Nicole, how are the kids?"

"They're good, Mommy, how are you?" Nicole, the youngest, always called her that.

She coughed. "I'm okay, could be better. How's Jake?"

"He's doing great. He's in line for the regional sales manager's job. Let's keep our fingers crossed."

"That's great, Nicole. Send them all my love.

How's Briana holding up, Jess?"

"About as good as a teenager going to school with a black eye and her father's name in the police blotter, I suppose," Jess said.

"Good thing those kids at school don't read the paper," she said.

"What's up, Mom?"

"I got a call from Willis's father. I don't think I've talked to that old coot since Briana's christening."

"What did he have to say?"

"He said that it was all a big misunderstanding and that Willis wants to talk. He said that you needed to lift the restraining order so that he could do that."

"What did you say, Mom?"

"I told him that if Willis came anywhere near my daughter or granddaughter that I would give him an enema with my oxygen bottle."

Both daughters laughed for the first time that day.

"Of course, I used language that he would understand, him being a Georgia cracker 'n all."

"I'm sure you did, Mom. I'm sure you did. I don't think we are going to get any more calls. I told the rest of the family to contact my attorney."

* * *

"Ain't getting no divorce attorney, cuz I ain't getting no divorce," Willis said.

"That family is just bad news. The sooner you walk away, the sooner you can find a woman that will listen to you," his father said.

"It ain't all her fault, Dad. She's got all these women chirping in her ear. I'm sure if I talk to her alone, we can straighten this out. I can't believe it's gotten this far."

"You saw the way they acted at the funeral. Townsfolk paid better respects to your mama than they did."

"I know, Dad, they did just enough to say that they came." Willis hadn't told any of his family that he purposely didn't tell Jess that he was rushing home to see his mother before she died. He was still grieving her loss and so was his father. This wasn't the time to set the record straight.

"Well, we tried talking to her, Willis. She told everybody to talk to her female attorney and sent everybody the picture of Briana's face so we could get the point."

"Yeah, she told our pastor to leave her alone in pretty much the same way."

"She had quite the shiner, Willis," his father said.

"Like I told the cops, when I tried stopping Briana from knocking down my stuffed coyote from our last trip, Jess blind-sided me and knocked me off balance and I bumped Briana into the TV. It wasn't even my fault, Dad. She's making it like I punched my daughter in the face. I would never do that."

"Girl's gotta respect a man's property. You were protecting what was yours. You gonna be able to get it fixed?"

"Yeah, like new, and I already replaced the TV, so all I need to do is to talk to her about coming home and get things back to the way they were."

"Well, Willis, I can tell you that they are not welcome up here, but you gotta do what you gotta do, I guess." The old man gave his final admonitions.

"Yeah, Dad. It's time for me to take charge and stop all of this foolishness."

He rolled up on his next job.

CHAPTER 26

WILLIS AVOIDED eye contact with Marty, his truck salesman, while he was in the service customer lounge waiting for them to finish his oil change. Every 3,000 miles, just like clockwork, didn't matter that he was going to turn it in for another one next month, it was part of the free service.

This Saturday, he was planning to go to the gun range and dope out his new scope for his .308 Ruger deer rifle. He liked the range. He could shut everything out and concentrate on his shooting. He had his arsenal sitting with him. He had pulled his Colt 1911 from under the seat. He didn't want any car jockey getting sticky fingers. Others sitting there pretended to watch TV as they nervously glanced at his weapons.

Screw them.

His phone rang, it was Lisa.

"Hey, Willis."

It was a rare weekend call. "Hey, Lisa. What's up?"

"Sorry to bother you on your day off. Lane can't handle an emergency call out. You are next on my list as we promised."

"Sure, what's the story?" He was not going to let this overtime opportunity pass to the next technician.

"Everything went dead at a commercial alarm and camera combo out on Oakmont Drive. The cops gave the monitoring team the all-clear. The weekend staff didn't even know their security system went down. Can you go out and see what's up?"

Willis didn't recognize the address for any jobs he might have done there.

"I'm just getting my oil changed now. I'll bring up on their system specs when I get to the office to see what I might need to take out."

"Okay, thanks, Willis. I'll text you the account info."

"Glad to help, Lisa."

Right then, Willis decided that this OT check would go to paying off his personal credit card. No need to tell Jess about that.

His truck was ready just then. He paid his bill and he loaded his long guns into the extended cab and slipped his pistol under the seat. They always washed his ride after every service visit, and it was spotless.

Just like old times, he thought as drove directly to his employer's offices and pulled into the deserted parking lot. The monitoring group was outsourced to an outfit out of state and those cubbies in his location were now collecting dust. The office had a ghostly feel to it as he walked to the workstation in the parts room.

Bringing up the account, he saw that it was for a nonprofit with the name ERP Foundation. The pictures on file were of an old, turn-of-the-century mansion. It had a gated driveway with a camera on the gate and access by permission only. The schematic showed where all the exterior and interior cameras, windows and door alarms were located.

They could control the electronic door locks remotely if a problem occurred on the premises.

Interesting.

They also had a fire suppression system installed. He had seen these mandated at state and county out-patient drug/alcohol treatment and half-way houses. If you had people living in a house that got government funding or grants, you had to have the fire package.

He was okay with the water sprinkler systems, but he had trouble with the finicky dry chemical setups in kitchens. He was hoping that was not part of the problem. They had a panic button on every floor. He couldn't tell what they did there for that level of security. He had not done the install and never had any service calls there. This was not for a wealthy family. He double-checked to be sure.

When he arrived, the GPS address put him at the end of the dead-end road. It had probably been part of the driveway for the estate from which the surrounding housing development was carved out. Willis could not see the house from this location. It was definitely off the beaten path.

The driveway went on for another hundred yards and curved to a broader turnaround. In the distance, he could make out the upper floors of the mansion. The painting was peeling and the cupola was boarded over. It had seen its better days.

The turnaround was big enough for delivery trucks. Here the gate was attached to a ten-foot-high privacy fence that surrounded the inner perimeter.

Boy, they really want their privacy in there.

In the fencing was a portal cut out for an oversized mailbox big enough to accommodate large UPS or FEDEX packages, which allowed access from both sides of the fence.

Never saw that before.

He approached the gate. He saw that it had power but couldn't send or receive communication from the buzzer box containing the keypad and camera. He opened the box with its special screwdriver and inserted his USB connection from his laptop into the port.

From the coolness of his work van, he entered the codes directly and the gates opened electronically. He disconnected and drove in. The portal automatically closed behind him. As he got closer to the mansion, he saw that the interior grounds were poorly kept and the rest of the building was rundown shabby. He had trouble reconciling the state-of-the-art security system with the state of disrepair of the building.

As he was getting his test equipment together and his tool belt on, a woman's voice came from next to his van. "Hello? Can I help you?"

He closed the rear doors and stepped towards her. He groaned inwardly. The spiky short bleach blonde hair and a barbed-wire tattoo across her right bicep completed the picture.

"I am here to fix your security system," he said.

She crossed her arms defensively to deflect his eyeballs from her bra-less breasts under her plain white T and said, "I need to see your identification, please."

He looked at the signage on his work van. "You called in for emergency repairs to your security system. I was on call."

"Thank you for your response, but do you have identification?" she said.

"My work badge is with my work shirt at home. I was

getting my oil changed when I got the call. I went straight to the office and came here."

"Again, I appreciate your response, but do you have identification?"

Shaking his head, he removed his wallet and he fished out his driver's license. "Here you go."

"I'll be right back," she said.

What is this top-secret shit? Willis was getting the feeling that it was some kind of secret agent safe house. The plantings around the foundation were severely overgrown. He was left standing there in the sun and decided to get into his truck and turn on the AC. *What's taking so long?* His cell phone rang.

It was Lisa. "Willis, the woman is going to return your ID. They have asked me to bring in a different technician. Please call me when you're off the property. I will explain it then." She hung up.

At that moment, Spiky Hair returned with a sour puss and he rolled down his window. She handed back his driver's license, and without another word, retreated into the house.

He was pissed. This would have been good money and he already had loaded up for the run and now he had to go back to the office to fetch his own ride.

Outside the gate. He dialed Lisa.

"What was all that about?" he said without a greeting.

Lisa said, "I had to find out from a client that you were arrested on two counts of domestic violence and have a restraining order on you."

"All that is going away. It was a mistake. The charges will be dropped any day now," Willis lied.

"How much of the newspaper article is true, Willis? It says you assaulted both Jess and Briana?"

He was boiling now. "What about being innocent until being proven guilty, Lisa?"

"There are some places you can't go into until you are proven innocent, Willis, and that was one of them."

"What kind of place is it? It's like I needed security clearance to walk into the place."

"They have to be careful who can be on the grounds there. If I had known you had been arrested for domestic violence, I would not have sent you there."

"That doesn't tell me what kind of place it is," Willis replied harshly.

"No, it doesn't, Willis, like I said, I had to find out from a client that you have an arrest record. It doesn't make a security company look good. The company looks like we don't know what we are doing. I was caught completely by surprise. We could lose this customer over this, Willis." Lisa was just as heated now. "One more thing, Willis, maybe it's none of my business, but you tell me that it's all gonna blow over. Right?"

"Yep. It's all going away."

"Then tell me why your wife filed for divorce?"

"You're right, Lisa, it's none of your damn business." He hung up.

His temper did not cool off as he drove back to the shop and he retrieved his own truck that had been baking in the sun. All of his guns were as hot as he was. He rode to the range, still fuming.

Thirty minutes later, there may have been paper targets on the bales of hay at 200 yards, but all he saw through the scope were the faces of the spiky-haired woman, the hotel maid, the school secretary, the bitch next door, Lisa and Jessalyn.

Pulling the trigger each time, he released his anger and

frustration until he ran out of ammo for the rifle. He moved over to the pistol range and emptied out his Colt rapid-fire to end his session.

He felt surprisingly better for the first time since he fired the machine guns.

CHAPTER 27

"HOLD ON THERE. What does she want?" The gruff voice grumbled from deep inside the trailer. Marsha heard the blaring TV get turned down from a jet-taking-off decibel level to just plain loud.

She hated when the conversation at the door got interrupted by somebody from the interior of the residence. She would now have to deal with two people from her perch on the rickety wooden steps leading up to the mobile home. She glanced around and realized that it hadn't been mobile since the day that it was plopped down in what would not so lovingly be described as the ass end of town.

There were not one, but two "planters" in the yard next to the gravel driveway where Briana sat in the Mustang. The planters were two Chevy pick-ups with knee-high weeds surrounding the rusted bodies. The engines had been removed and from the hoodless engine compartment sprouted all forms of fauna and flora.

"Hello, sir. I was just asking the Missus how I could contact Rose."

Marsha was staring at a sullen, scar-faced middle-aged man with a sweat-stained shirt that hadn't seen the inside of a washing machine recently. His nicotine and whiskey-soaked body odor competed with the stench from the interior of the trailer. Marsha vowed not to go in there under any circumstance.

He had pushed "the Missus" to the side and was now leering out at Marsha, not bothering to hide his stare to between her neck and her navel.

"Wha' fer?"

"I'd love to tell you that she won the Florida Mega-Million Lottery, but sadly, that is not the case. She's not in any kind of trouble, sir, I assure you. I'm looking for a runaway from up North and I think she is roommates with Rose." She paused. "If I talk to Rose, I can find the runaway." Marsha was talking to him but looking at his wife and held Carli's photograph out for both of them to see. "Can you help me out?"

"She lit out of here a couple of years ago and ain't come back since."

The woman behind him began to sob. "Yeah, not so much as a birthday card for her mother."

The controlling claustrophobic cretin continued, "Yeah, when you find her, tell her to call her mother, will ya?" He slammed the door in Marsha's face.

That went swell. Marsha walked back to the car seeing Briana busy on her cell phone. When Marsha got closer, Briana stopped abruptly, causing Marsha to take note. "The roommate's parents hadn't heard from her in two years. I can't blame her for leaving that shit hole."

"Maybe Carli had a good reason for running away too," Briana said.

Marsha fired up the Mustang. "Neither one has spoken

to their parents since the day they ran away. I kinda understand why Rose left this place and never looked back, but I can't understand why Carli left home. As far as I know, she had a great life. Solid family, lots of friends, doing great in sports and academics. Then one day, she just up and left town."

"Umm, Marsha, I don't know if I'm supposed to ask, but how did you find her roommate?"

They wheeled from gravel road to the access road onto the interstate and Marsha talked loudly over the wind scream. "The car dealership where Carli took her car for repairs had video of Rose's beater when she dropped Carli off. We got the license plate. Once we had her name, we were able to get her driver's license photo. This was the address on both and it looks to be a dead end. I don't know many people down here, but I swear I've seen Rose before."

Marsha let that hang in the air.

Briana tucked her phone into her jacket pocket and looked away towards the construction workers twisting wrenches on the new guardrails replacing the mangled ones lying on the ground next to them.

Marsha had a list of property managers, Realtors, and timeshare management companies. She had rehearsed Briana to go in and ask for a job cleaning houses. Briana would tell them that Carli suggested she come in. If Carli worked for any of them, then Marsha would follow up with the photo and parent's plea to contact their daughter.

Interspersed between these office locations were the addresses for the timeshares, vacation resorts, and condo communities where they might spot Carli's Sonata. As a last resort, they had Carli's cell phone number and Marsha would get Eduardo to text her.

They ran down the leads. Briana walked nervously into

the offices and walked out, dejectedly telling Marsha the bad news. At each timeshare, vacation resort and condo complex, it was move -out, clean and move-in Saturday. Marsha got out of the Mustang every time she spotted a cleaner to ask them if they recognized the tall, blonde highschooler in the photo.

This was old-fashioned shoe leather. Each visit, each interview held the promise of a lead or a thread to a lead. Pulling into each complex held the hope of spotting Carli or her car.

Briana had checked with Demi, Carli's bestie in Minnesota, a few times to mention that she lived in Clearwater and was thinking of checking out the same colleges that Demi was accepted at. According to Briana, Demi was not forthcoming with any clues about Carli's whereabouts.

Marsha was dictating her report as they made the rounds. She wanted to show the parents that they were going about this runaway case logically, thoroughly and cost-effectively.

They arrived at the car dealership just as Eduardo was finishing up. They met him in the parking lot of the nearby quickie-mart, so as not to incur the wrath of his service manager or the general manager.

After introducing Briana to him, Marsha said, "Hi, Eduardo, do you think you can do me a small favor?"

"Sure. What do you need?" His excitement about being brought into the case was palpable.

"Is there a quick-fix safety recall item that you can pretend that the girl needs to come in for? You know, something that takes like fifteen minutes to swap a part out for. I would even pay for it if you needed me to do that."

Eduardo thought a moment, then said, "Yeah, I can tell

her that the fuel filters for her make and model are being recalled because they leak gas into the hot engine compartment and could cause a fire. We can replace her fuel filter for about a hundred bucks for parts and labor."

"I can give you the cash. Can you text her and try to schedule a visit for Monday morning?"

Eduardo pulled out his cell phone and texted Carli's number from the service order with the make-believe recall notice and the free repair. She replied instantly that she didn't want her car to catch fire. The appointment was set for Monday morning at 8:30 a. m.

"Thank you so much, Eduardo. If she cancels, here is my cell."

He then connected with Marsha.

"But there is one more thing." Marsha hesitated and turned to Briana. "Can you sit in the driver's seat of my car and rev the engine? I want him to listen to the motor." She handed her the keys.

"Sure." Briana perked up.

Marsha showed her the hood release and how to start the car. It turned over immediately. Eduardo and Marsha stood shielded by the hood. "Okay, rev the engine."

Briana was tentative at first but slowly pushed down on the gas pedal until Marsha gave her the hold sign.

Marsha then said to Eduardo over the din. "There's an additional fifty bucks for you if you can put a GPS tracker on the car. The parents are the sole owners and they would not have a problem with that at all. I don't think Briana would like hearing about spying on the girl."

He thought about it and nodded.

"One more time, Briana." She revved the engine again. "Okay, that's enough. Turn it off."

Eduardo closed the hood and said, "We can switch you over to synthetic oil, that will help with the knocks."

"Thanks, Eduardo. No, Briana, you can't drive home, your mom would kill me. Hop out."

CHAPTER 28

SUNDAYS WERE Carli's only day off. She worked for an upscale cleaning company during the week. She connected well with the snowbirds and retirees. Some even left her house keys to water their plants and feed their cats, birds and fish while they were away. It was a friendly cash side business. Saturdays were somewhat easier and paid better.

She worked four hours for a luxury timeshare in nearby Dunedin, cleaning and getting the units ready for the next week's occupants. Most of the people were responsible, but occasionally she would arrive to find the units fresh from a night of drinking and debauchery. She donned rubber gloves to gingerly pick up wet clothes and towels from around the beds and nightstands. Used condoms didn't always make it to the trashcan or toilet. Ditto for marijuana roaches. The booze left behind was much more expensive than what her friends drank when their parents were not home or when then got into an unlocked lake cabin. The vacationers had every right to party, but it still triggered memories from St. Paul.

Her roommate had gotten home around four in the

morning and didn't bring home any company. Carli had made a mistake one morning of walking out to the kitchen for a drink of water in a bra and panties only to make eye contact with a guy kneeling down between Rose's legs splayed out on the couch. She never asked Rose why he was humming a Queen song.

Turning eighteen in another week, she would schedule her GED, then claim her transcripts from Laurel Valley High School as an adult and immediately enroll in Hillsborough Community College. She was determined to get her high school diploma and go to college. She had always wanted to teach young kids and her life circumstance was not going to change that.

Carli had been saving and could afford the first semester's tuition. Her roommate was planning to go to a technical school to become a blood draw technician and then maybe even nursing school, but those plans seemed to be always "next semester."

There were mornings when Rose was asleep and had left her tips on the kitchen table. Carli was curious and counted between four hundred and five hundred in cash on those occasions. Rose worked four nights a week and was making two grand a week. They never talked about what Rose did with all that cash.

Sunday brunch for roommates were cheesy scrambled eggs, bacon, and toast with strawberry jam. She didn't pay as much for rent as Rose, but cooked for them and cleaned as part of the trade-off. The smell of bacon and fresh-perked coffee usually was enough to entice her roomie from her slumber.

"Good morning, sunshine," Carli said as Rose sniffled and shuffled her way to the coffee pot and poured wake-up juice into her Disneyworld *Pirates of the Caribbean* coffee mug.

"Morning," Rose replied.

"How many guys bought you shots last night?" Carli asked.

"Too many." Came her answer. "Getting too old for this shit."

Barely twenty, Rose had learned quickly that having surreptitious shots with a big-spender at the club was good for tips, but bad for her head and liver.

Carli placed the plates of steaming goodness on the table while the toaster was doing its thing.

Rose dug in and closed her eyes. "Promise you will teach my future husband how to cook, Carli Ertz."

This was a standard joke between them. The toaster popped and Carli gave one to Rose and one to herself. They took turns lathering on the jam. Carli refilled the toaster.

"Hey, I almost forgot. Do you remember that girl I met at the mall last month, who was a runaway for a day?"

"Yeah, her mom showed up with a friend and talked her into coming back home. They were the same women that you recognized from a night at the club."

"Yep, you got a good memory. Anyway, she told me that a car mechanic showed up where they live and wanted to take her out. Jesus, she's only fifteen but looks older. Her mom complained to the car dealership where he worked, saying it was not good that he knew where they lived. He said that she invited him to come over while she waited for her mom to pay for the repairs. The manager didn't believe her mom. It was her word against his."

"We know how that works." Carli put her fork down to receive Rose's phone being slid across the table. "What am I looking at?"

"Briana is her name. She was going to shame them on Facebook, but I told her not to until I talked to you."

"Why?"

"Look at the photos."

Carli recognized the Google map photo of the Hyundai dealership and the Facebook profile of her mechanic Eduardo.

"Isn't this where I picked you up and dropped you off?"

"He doesn't know where I live, but he has my cell number," Carli muttered.

"You think maybe that's why you have that free recall fix tomorrow?" Rose suggested as she negotiated a bite of toast with too much jam into her mouth, pushing the excess jam with her fingers onto her tongue.

Carli and Rose ate and played junior detectives on the internet and could not find a recall for fuel filters for Carli's Sonata or any year Sonata, for that matter.

"This is creepy," Carli said while polishing off her third piece of toast.

* * *

Charlie had left that morning to fly to Milwaukee to testify in the Wisconsin worker's comp case where he had gotten daily video of the Cheesehead twisting, bending, lifting, swimming in the amusement park wave pools, heaving heavy suitcases around like they were styrofoam and riding rollercoasters with all their G-force turns and drops. All of this physical activity with a supposedly bad back that rendered him totally and temporarily disabled from a high-paying union job.

Marsha stepped out of bed and padded to the bathroom. *Gee, a Bloody Mary would be swell right about now.*

There was no booze in the house, not even mouthwash. She couldn't even call Sully back in Bensalem to ask him how he had gotten over the gag reflex to earn the nom de plume *Listerine Man* when he was a homeless and hopeless drunk living on the streets of Philadelphia. They hadn't talked since that day by the pool with all the dead bodies around them.

Shira came over a few hours later and worked with Marsha on knife attacks. Each simulated attack was preceded by lung-busting drills. It demonstrated the need to react when her body wanted to surrender.

After showers, both women devoured their egg rolls, wonton soup, shrimp over pork-fried rice Chinese delivery. Marsha told Shira about the recurring nightmares.

"I am trying to deal with everything by keeping busy with what Charlie has me doing and you kicking my ass. I'm too exhausted to let my emotions sneak in."

"Have you talked to your parents since it happened?"

"My father is in denial."

"And your mother?"

"She's taking sides with my dad."

"Call your mother. Ask her how's she's doing. Knowing how she feels is better than guessing. Then you can start dealing with all those things. What do you call them?"

"Feelings?" Marsha asked.

"Yes, those things," Shira replied. "Be thankful you still have parents and those things."

***

"Just being good-looking with a tight top and low-cut jeans will make you more money on a good night than you'd make in a week of your house-cleaning job. We'd just have to get you the right bras to wear under your shirt that leaves just enough to their imaginations. Going braless or wearing a push-up would ruin your look," Rose said as they walked into *Roxanne's Redlight* that Sunday night.

"Just think, no student debt, a more reliable car, and a real checking account. I am telling you, you don't have to play up to the guys the way I do. You are so fucking innocent they will throw money at you. Telling them that you are working two jobs to pay for college to be a schoolteacher will have them reaching for their wallets."

Carli laughed and they entered the dark cavernous building. She was immediately introduced to the bouncers as Rose's roomie.

Rose now went into tough girl transformation for the first time in front of Carli. The Hooter's-like top and hot pants over pristine white low cut *Chucks* painted the picture of the cheerleader gone bad. The rose tattoo, in all its glory, was her bad-girl business card. Now she was in her role for the night.

That is how most of the dancers dealt with the mind-numbing cavemen come-ons and sophisticated sweet talk. Nonetheless, the tough-talking no-nonsense server would push drinks on the guys, all the while letting them ogle her rose.

"My 'I might let you take me home act' is just an act," Rose said as she prepared her set-ups for the tables and regaled Carli with how she played guys right to that point when they put her tip on their tab. By pre-determined staging.

Rose would be chatting up Happy Harry and then one of the bulging bicep black-jacket guys with the secret-service earbuds would walk up to them and ask her if she was ready to go home.

"You see, Carli, it is never my fault that I can't sneak off with them for a romp in a nearby no-tell motel or in the back of their cars. I've played some guys more than a couple of times. It's hilarious."

"I could still do cleanings in the afternoon and take care of bringing the mail in and feeding the pets, right?" Carli asked when she was seated by the server station.

"Sure, sure. We could work the same shift. I would have your back and won't let any of the customers give you any shit."

Later that night, after sneaking Carli a couple vodkas and sodas, she asked her roomie to walk out with her to the tables while she served. She introduced Carli as Chrissy and told them that she was in training. Next, Rose introduced "Chrissy" to the nicer dancers as they came off the dance floor. Rose could tell that Carli was getting more comfortable talking with the totally naked girls.

Before the evening ended, Rose had promises from most of the girls that they would celebrate "Chrissy's" eighteenth birthday. A little more vodka and soda and more funny stories about the clients made Carli agreeable to all the attention and the thought of having her new friends throw her a party.

This is how Rose recruited new talent for the club. First, as a roommate, then as a cocktail waitress, and finally as a dancer. The club owners loved Rose for having an excellent eye for talent and paid her a $500 finder's fee per girl every month that they worked at *Roxanne's*. In a couple years, Briana would be ready too.

CHAPTER 29

"HI, MOM."

"Marsha? Is that you?"

"Yeah, Mom. I was calling to see how you were doing."

"Your father would be so upset if he knew you called."

"It's Sunday afternoon, Mom. He is at the FOP lodge watching the game with his cronies. I wanted to see how you're doing," Marsha repeated.

"Your father is furious, Marsha. He's been coming home drunk a lot since, since Nicky... since the funeral. He just sits on the front porch, drinking beer and listening to the game. I try to talk to him or bring him a piece of cake and he just stares out on the street."

"I get that, Mom. I was hoping we could talk a little bit. Just you and me."

"Where are you? Are you back in Philly?"

"No, I am still in Clearwater. Matter of fact, I am at the spring training stadium watching the minor league team getting clobbered. They are bringing another pitcher in and I thought I'd give you a call. So can you talk with me?"

There was a pause then tearfully, she said. "There's not

much to talk about. Your brother is dead and your father is completely lost and I don't know how to reach him." She started to sob.

"I'm sorry I called, Mom. In case you were wondering, I am torn up about everything too. You know why I couldn't come to the funeral, right?"

"Because all the cops would have told you, Marsha, that you had no business sticking your nose in their investigation. They would have told you that Nicky is dead because of you." She said it like she was reading an indictment.

"And what do you think, Mom?"

"I think that I am going to hang up now. A month ago, we were a happy family and now...." She began crying harder and then for both of them, mercifully ended the call.

Marsha stared at the draft beers being poured out at the Tiki-Bar in the left-field food pavilion. *I love you too, Mom.*

***

"It's going to take time, Marsha, you'll see. She will come around."

Joe and Marsha sat at an outdoor table by the Gulf at The Shrimp Shack, a secret only the locals knew about. Peeling all you can eat shrimp and drinking sweet iced tea by the pitcher, they talked in subdued voices the way couples often do.

"I never realized how much of her sense of worth was based upon being a wife and a mother. Asking her to tell me how she was feeling was like pulling teeth," Marsha said as she expertly stripped the shrimp down to the good stuff.

She stole glances at the other tables. Beer bottles and mixed drinks with the miniature parasols sticking out of them cluttered the butcher paper-covered table. People were having fun, shucking mussels and clams and having few or more bottles. She looked over at Joe and realized what could have been between them.

He was everything she wanted in a man; confident, but not pushy, self-made, but not ostentatious, and it didn't hurt that he was drop-dead gorgeous.

"Sorry, I am such a party-pooper. It's a beautiful evening. It's a warm night in South Florida and I'm sitting here sulking because nobody loves me." Marsha peeked over the rim of her glass.

Joe shook his head. "When the truth comes out about your brother, you may still not get back your parent's love. You did what was right, you had no idea that he was dirty. We all make mistakes, but you didn't do anything wrong. He chose to sleep with the devil. Why do you have to rent a room in hell too?"

"That's the trouble I am having, Joe. One side of me is really angry. He was protecting his dirty business, but even then, I think he was trying to protect me from getting too close and getting hurt. I can't sort my feelings out about that while simply grieving the loss of my big brother."

"I am sure he loved you very much. Pick those memories, and when the darkness starts to close in, just focus on the good times. The other stuff will just eat you alive from inside."

She nodded distractedly. "You're right. Let's talk about how your pitchers couldn't find the plate without their *Waze* app."

Their conversation got lighter and the banter between old friends returned. Joe paid the check over Marsha's half-hearted protestations. They walked without hurry to their cars. Marsha told Joe about the dealership surveillance plans for the following morning.

It was during a gentle hug in the gravel parking lot when Joe said, "Just grieve your brother's loss. You can't be expected to figure out all the other stuff. Nobody should be forced to deal with all that other crap."

Driving to Charlie's house, she knew that she would be alone. She stopped for gas, always wanting to have her tank topped off before a surveillance day, not knowing where she was going to follow Carli and for how long.

She couldn't get her credit card to work at the pump and had to go inside. She got the pump authorization, filled her tank, and came back in to complete the transaction.

The TV mounted over the counter to keep customers occupied while the retiree haggled with the clerk over playing the lottery numbers boxed or straight. The next guy had to have his exact brand of cigarettes in the box, not in a soft pack.

Marsha's eyes drifted to the screen to see the news about the latest shooting in a Texas border town and in the Rust Belt within hours of each other. The graphic then showed more Americans were killed by gun violence in those two mass shootings than in the entire country of Japan for the whole year. She was numb to the carnage.

When it came time to settle up on her pump, she hoisted two six-packs of Corona Light onto the counter and walked out on auto-pilot. She was going to get drunk. Nobody would know about it or why and she would set two alarms for the morning to prevent over-sleeping. She justified it all very easy to herself. She was surprised by how her willpower disintegrated as she thought back on her phone conversation with her mother.

She pulled into the driveway next to the neighbor's truck. *Don't mess with me tonight buddy boy. I will seriously fuck you up.*

It would have been nice to talk to Jess, but she was still at her sister's house. Jess was not coming back except maybe to grab the rest of her clothes and some furniture.

Marsha carried her package under her arm, trying to make it invisible to anybody walking by. She would remember to erase the CCTV footage before Charlie got back in several days.

She closed the door and set her package on the coffee table and went to pee. No sooner than she was seated and releasing about a half-gallon of sweet ice tea did she hear someone knocking on the front door. The knocking got louder.

If it's that pissant, I kick his balls up to his throat.

"Hold on!" she yelled as she made her way back down the hall, pulling up her panties and smoothing out her skirt. She flung open the door to see Joe standing there. *What the hell?*

He walked past her and picked up the six-packs and turned to her and said, "I know a couple sore-armed pitchers that could use these while their coach tells them that tomorrow is another day."

He stopped at the doorway that she speechlessly held open. He closed the distance and, with his free arm, pulled her close. They stood eye to eye and he slowly closed his and their lips touched.

This was a kiss twenty-some years in the making and she didn't want to let go. Finally, Joe broke the kiss and the firm embrace. He looked at her with soft eyes and said, "You are very lovable, Marsha O'Shea, don't you ever forget that."

He returned to his idling car in the driveway and backed out leaving her speechless for the first time in a very long time.

CHAPTER 30

MARSHA HAD trouble shaking off her fatigue that morning. Between Joe catching her red-handed with the six-packs and flat-footed for "the kiss," her emotions bounced around like pinballs. It was a nightmare game where she couldn't keep track of all of them and work the flippers fastest enough to keep them all from draining.

Shame was dominant. She was only fooling herself when she justified thinking she could get half in the bag after her mother's rebuff. Hiding her drinking was definitely a warning sign. How many more curveballs was her life going to throw at her? She had to be ready for the next time. She had set herself up to drown her sorrows this time. She gave herself all the excuses to get herself shit-faced.

She still couldn't believe how Joe swooped in and nearly swept her off her feet. That led to some lustful thoughts until she finally gave in to those urges. Twice. That added to her shame knowing her friend was spoken for. Who was she kidding?

* * *

Carli was late for her appointment. Marsha had positioned Charlie's plain wrapper sedan by the entrance to the Hyundai dealership's service department. Her plan was to cozy up to Carli in the visitor's waiting area and keep her occupied while Eduardo put the GPS tracker on her parents-owned car for which Marsha had their permission. They were home in Minnesota, both delaying their morning routines to hear from her. She would tell Carli that her parents were able to monitor the car's appointments at any dealership and had asked Marsha to talk to her and possibly put them on the phone with their daughter.

Carli would become an adult on Saturday and this was the last chance to connect them while she was a juvenile. The thought of getting the police to enforce the laws on a runaway kid just days away from her eighteenth birthday was laughable.

Maybe they could talk and Charlie could broker a meeting when he got back? If that failed, they would learn her address from the tracker and fly down to talk to her in person. Marsha had warned the parents not to call her while the game was afoot.

8:30 a.m. became 8:45 a.m. and then 9:00 a.m. The country radio station news came on. They talked about how the state had passed legislation allowing persons to openly carry guns into churches and other meeting places.

Praise the Lord and pass the ammunition, she sighed.

Eduardo came out to her car at a nervous half-trot carrying a plastic bag. She got out and met him on the side shielded from the dealership.

"I don't want any part of this. Take your stuff and get out of here and don't come back." He thrust the tracker and the money into her hands.

"What wrong?" Marsha asked.

He showed her his phone. In response to his text asking her if she forgot her appointment, Carli replied: *IF you text me again, I will report you to your manager and this time, he will take action. I know what you are doing. Don't contact me again.*

"This doesn't make any sense," Marsha said as the plans for a happy reunion evaporated like the steam escaping from a boiling kettle.

"What is she talking about my manager will take action this time? Do I have a complaint against me that I don't know anything about it? How does she know what I am doing?"

Marsha immediately thought of Briana, and now the teenager's reticence to help out was clearly evident.

"I'll find out, Eduardo, and let you know," she said.

She rolled out of the dealership and called Charlie and filled him in.

"Shit," he said.

"Double shit," she said.

"The service writer was really spooked. It could have only been Briana. She knew the plan and was one-step away from Carli. She had been withdrawn that day that we went hunting for her and I couldn't put my finger on why. Maybe she knows more than she's telling me."

"On the other hand, we can use that to our advantage by telling Briana that the case is closed after Carli didn't show and keep her out of the loop. Give them a false sense that we are done looking for her."

"You're right, Charlie. We can chat with Briana later."

They bantered about some options. Charlie had one more idea. His database provider had a brand new feature that was perfect for this case and he would fire up his laptop when they disconnected. It was agreed that she would tell Briana that the case was over.

It's better than the bad news about the failed meeting comes from the license-holder Charlie if this last idea didn't pan out. They all needed a Hail Mary right about now.

* * *

"Hello?"

"Hi, Jess. This is Willis. I hope I'm not calling at a bad time?"

"Willis..." Jess automatically reached for the record call app on her phone and started recording.

"Just listen to me for a second. I have been trying to get in touch with you through everybody that I know. We have to work this out."

"Willis, you need to get a lawyer and you need your lawyer to talk to my lawyer, is that clear?" Jess said. She saw the recording was working.

"Look, Jess. I can't pay for any more lawyers. I am sure that if we sit down, we can work things out."

"You have a restraining order on you and cannot contact me. Do you understand that?" she asked.

Ignoring her, he went on. "Jess, we can start over, like it was before we started fighting over the bills. I got some overtime last week and I'm sure that I will get some more. Get your lawyer to drop the restraining order and the charges and come home. I miss you and Briana."

"I can't do that. That ship has sailed, Willis. You don't get it. You need to get off the phone now; otherwise, I will tell my lawyer that you have violated the order."

"Why, so I can have another woman yell at me? I am tired of getting put down all the time when it's not even my fault. I can't even breathe without some bitch getting in my face." He was hot.

"Willis, I have told you twice already that you can't talk to me and that you have a court order against you. I am hanging up the phone now. Goodbye."

* * *

"Jess... Jess.. **JESSALYN!**" He wanted to slam his shooting-range buddy's phone against the counter at the luncheonette, but people had stopped eating and were looking at him again. *This is how Homer Simpson always feels in public,* he thought.

"Everything alright," his buddy asked, looking relieved that his phone was still in one piece.

"Just peachy." Willis handed him the phone back, and they walked wordlessly out to their trucks.

Willis had no intention of hiring a lawyer or talking to his wife's female lawyer. He was going to see her face to face and tell her to drop the restraining order and the arrest charges. He would make her come to her senses. This was not his fault.

It was Briana who tried to destroy his personal property. It was Jess who was boxing him into a corner about what he could do and what he couldn't. His anger and frustration mounted. He was seething as he drove to his next work install.

He began to believe his family's anger towards his wife and daughter for their hit-and-run at his mother's funeral was justified and he fed off their anger as well. He felt ashamed as he thought about his father and brothers scolding him about his inability to control his women.

He had bottled up all his emotions during his campaign

of silence and they exploded out of him when Briana acted like a destructive brat. He felt his face flushing and he couldn't get the AC cranked up high enough to cool him down.

He didn't know how long he was lost in his rage when his phone rang. He saw that it was Lisa.

"Hi, Lisa," he answered evenly.

It was not Lisa but their boss, Mr. Keller, on the phone. Willis had talked with the owner at parties and at the company-wide meeting and knew him to be a businessman first and foremost.

"Willis. No, it's me, Bernie. Have you started that install yet over at the industrial center?"

"No, Mr. Keller, I am almost there now."

"Good. I will call Lane out to take it over. I need you to come back to the office now."

Willis was confused. "Why? I've got all the parts and the work order with me."

"Never mind, just come back to the office. I will explain everything to you when you get here," he said.

Willis's mind raced. *What's going on? Why does Lane have to take over the job?* He double-checked the work order and made sure that it was not the gated mansion that he was asked to leave.

He pulled into the parking lot behind the work bays where materials and parts could be easily picked and walked out to the trucks. The other installers were still out on jobs and their spots were empty. As he exited the work truck, he spotted Lane pulling his Uber car into the employee parking spot next to Willis's personal vehicle.

He waited until Lane got out and started walking towards him.

"Hey, Lane, what's going on?" he asked.

"Beats me. I got a call from Lisa telling me that they needed a rush install. Thank God I wasn't running a tourist from the airport to Busch Gardens. Is everything in your truck?"

"Yeah, I was about five minutes away from the job when Mr. Keller called me," Willis replied.

"Mr. Keller called you back to the office," Lane said.

"Creeping me out too. Can't figure it out either."

Lane stopped their progress to the door. "I don't want to know. Give me the keys and a little head start. Call me after the dust settles."

Willis flipped his mentor the keys and watched as Lane scurried to the work truck, fired it up and sped off like he was fleeing a quarantine area.

He walked into the building and was motioned by Keller into the conference room.

"Have a seat." He guided Willis to sit in a chair facing away from the door and towards the whiteboard and flip charts at the end of the table.

A few minutes went by and neither Lisa nor Mr. Keller entered the room. Willis became more uncomfortable as the wait dragged on. Then, in a flurry of activity, Keller, Lisa, and the HR manager made their way into the room and took up positions facing him and behind him the only door in and out of the drab conference room.

Mr. Keller was the first to speak. "I will make this short and to the point. I will not entertain any discussion on this matter. You are being told what is happening. As of today, you are placed on indefinite suspension until your arrest and restraining order are resolved. We cannot have you interacting with our customers, particularly our female customers, until we feel it is safe for us to allow you to do so. We would face serious liability if you were to commit any violence towards our clients, now that we are aware of the full circumstances."

Lisa was next to speak. "We had warning signs from when the hotel manager contacted us and we didn't act then, given that you were injured in the fall."

The HR manager, an older woman that he met on his first day on the job, just stared at him with contempt.

"You gotta be kidding me. This is all a big mistake. I can explain everything." Willis was interrupted when he saw Keller nod his head to someone standing behind him.

He turned around and saw two uniformed Clearwater police officers entering. The larger of the two stated in a no-nonsense tone, "Mr. Teesdale, you are under arrest for the first-degree misdemeanor of violating the court injunction of no contact with Mrs. Teesdale. Please place your hands behind your back."

Willis looked at them and then at his employers, who now stood as far from him as they could on the other side of the room. He closed his eyes and tried to calm his breathing. He thought he was about to blackout.

He teetered to his feet and submitted. They walked him out of his employer's office, in front of the most influential people in his world at the moment, and knew instantly why Lane didn't want to come in.

As the big cop led him to the back seat of their cruiser, he muttered under his breath, *"Just you wait, Jessalyn, you will get yours."*

CHAPTER 31

"WILLIS, you need a divorce lawyer if you want to talk to your wife. I can't do both," his lawyer said after they cleared the police station.

"Why not? You're a lawyer, aren't you," Willis complained.

"Your wife and daughter are victims of an alleged crime. I represent you for that and now for the violation of the restraining order. I can only talk to them in that context, and since she is represented by an attorney, I can only talk to Attorney Madsen about the charges. The divorce is best handled by a different attorney. That attorney can only talk about the divorce case. If they were to talk about the criminal cases, they could get in trouble. I don't want to give the prosecutor any reason to get hard-ass on you. You don't want to poke the bear, Willis."

"But I have a right to see my kid, don't I? She doesn't have a lawyer." His indignation was increasing.

"You have a separate restraining order on you for her too. It would be cleaner if you got the other attorney to talk with your wife's attorney about that."

"I've got the mortgage note and my truck payment is due this month. My wife has to send me money for those. I need to talk to her about holding up her share."

"Mail a copy of the bills to her attorney. That's all you can do until you decide on another attorney. You have to play by the rules. You can't take any more chances with trying to get messages to her or contacting her directly."

Willis was not listening and waited until his expensive do-nothing lawyer stopped talking. "I got suspended from my job because of this garbage. Can I sue them to get back to work? I need to get paid."

"I am sorry to hear that, Willis. I don't handle employment law. That is a separate practice specialty."

Willis groaned. "They made up some stuff about me not being good around women, and if I were to have a problem with another *female* customer, they could be held liable, knowing about my arrest and the other stuff."

"Sounds reasonable to me. The best you can hope for is to get your charges nolled and dropped, so you can return to work. Would you really want to sue your employer? How do you think that would go over? I just need to remind you that if we can't dispose of your charges before trial, I will need another $10,000 upfront."

"$10,000! I don't have that kind of money. You are telling me to get another lawyer, that costs money. I've got bills that I have to pay and I don't have a job." Willis was yelling now.

"You hired me to keep you out of jail. Do you know what they do to child abusers in prison, Willis?" the attorney quickly retorted.

He got Willis's attention with that zinger.

Willis was silent while he mulled the thoughts of

getting his ass kicked while many of his friends from the range, who were corrections officers, turned a blind eye.

"I know you are upset, Willis, but I have given you good advice. You need to keep your nose clean while I work on the prosecutor. I can argue that you were blind-sided when you were served the divorce papers, but there cannot be another violation of the restraining orders.

"Get an attorney to work on your divorce case. That attorney can talk to her attorney to try to get the restraining orders dropped or modified.

I will remind you, once again, that you can't talk to your wife about dropping the charges. That is witness tampering and no prosecutor or judge will look kindly on that."

Willis remained silent.

"I've got a client waiting for me at court, Willis. I've got to go."

Without even saying goodbye, the attorney left Willis in a swirling rage at his impotence in the situation.

He took a taxi to his employer, where his truck sat with a dusty film from all the pollen of two days. He made no eye contact with anyone in the building and drove home with his tail between his legs.

He walked into the empty house. In the good old days, he would come home between jobs and his bride and he would occasionally sneak in a quickie while their daughter was in school.

Not today Willis.

He wanted to ball up his paperwork and chuck it into the trash overflowing from the kitchen garbage can, but he knew that would only add to his woeful predicament. He looked around the living room.

Pizza boxes and other fast food take-out containers were stacked on the coffee table. The countertops were stacked with half-eaten frozen dinners for the microwave. The kitchen table was the depository of unpaid bills. His work clothes were dropped in a heap by the bathroom door. Sitting on the couch in gym shorts and a Remington shotgun patent T-shirt, he had trouble even concentrating on his breathing.

Action movies aside, visions of hardened lifers tuning him up left him genuinely frightened. Going to jail had not even occurred to him up this point. He was protecting his treasured trophy from his crazy daughter. He had believed that this whole mess would blow over. He had been convinced that if he talked to them, Jess would come back to him and Briana would have learned her lesson to respect other people's property. They would have gone back to the way things were before he lost his overtime.

That wasn't his fault. He was a good worker and had worked as much OT as he wanted. Getting him arrested made his boss nervous about him working for their female clients. He would still be working if it wasn't for Jess being a tattle-tale. All he had wanted to do was talk with her. He was civil on the phone and didn't say anything that would cause her to do that. He had no money to pay for a trial. He didn't want to go to his family for a loan. The shame would be unbearable.

Maybe he could represent himself in the divorce hearings. He had seen the TV and billboard ads for low-cost lawyers to get divorced, but he didn't want a divorce. He wanted the life he had before all those women started putting ideas in his wife's head.

Moving to the kitchen, he found the divorce papers under the Taco Bell wrappers. *Damn it.* He had gotten some extra hot sauce on the summons. He called the lawyer's number, and the receptionist took a handwritten message. Next, he called his truck salesman.

"Hey, Marty, how you doing? This is Willis."

"Great, how are you doing, Willis? Are you ready to trade up? That fully-loaded Ram has been waiting for you to come in for a test ride."

"No can do, Marty, I am going to bring my truck in a little early and talk to you about getting a beater."

The banter ended quickly. "You still have a month left on the lease. I am not sure we can do that."

"Don't bullshit me, Marty, you were tripping all over yourself to put me in a new lease on the Ram. I can put the last month on my credit card and get me into somebody's trade-in before you send it to the auction. How many years have I been leasing from you without a problem?"

"Why? What's the problem, Willis? A beater? You must be kidding. Talk to me."

"I'm not going into all the gory details, but let's just say that I have had a financial setback. That sounds about right. Yes, I have had a financial setback. You can either help a loyal customer out or I can drop the truck off with the keys under the floor mat tonight and make the last payment by phone. What do you want to do, Marty?"

"I just took a twelve-year-old black Silverado on a trade-in. I've known the owner for years and we serviced it religiously. We can do the deal. Come in and I'll make it happen for you." Marty said.

"How much?"

"We can do the numbers when you come in," Marty replied.

"You said yourself that you just took it in yourself. How much?" Willis was more forceful.

"I gotta run the numbers, Willis," Marty said.

"Last chance, Marty."

"$5,000 Willis and I don't make anything on it."

"How much have you made on me over the years, Marty?"

Just then, his phone rang with another caller. He looked at the caller ID *Jess Lawyer* came up.

"I'll be in later today, Marty. Wash it and do an oil change and you've got a deal." He hung up happy with himself for the first time in a long time. He took the other call.

"Hello?" He took the other call.

"This is attorney Thelma Madsen. I am returning your call, Mr. Teesdale."

"Yes, ma'am, I've decided to represent myself in this divorce. I am sure that if you could set it up for me to talk with her, we can give our marriage another try."

"Thank you, Mr. Teesdale. I must advise you to get an attorney and have that attorney answer the complaint. The due date is next Monday."

"I can't afford another attorney and there is something else I have to mention too," he said.

"You then have to go to the court and file what is called *Pro Se*. Once the court has accepted your petition to represent yourself, I can then talk to you. However, I must remind you that you still have the restraining order and not to contact Mrs. Teesdale or your daughter directly or indirectly through family or friends until it is lifted or modified."

"How do we do that?" he asked.

"As I said, either hire an attorney or go into court and answer the complaint *Pro Se*. Then a discussion can be had about the restraining order."

"So everything has to be done real legal-like. Is that it?"

"That's it, Mr. Teesdale. You have been sued in court. Your wife is suing for divorce. You have a restraining order by the court. Everything has to be done by court permission."

Willis stewed on this news, thinking that he could make everything go away with a quick meeting with Jess.

"What was the other thing, Mr. Teesdale?"

"The truck payment and mortgage is due and I need her to pay her part," he said.

"Please send me the information and I will share it with your wife. Is the truck listed in both of your names?"

"No, just mine."

"As her attorney, I can tell you that she is not legally obligated to help you with the truck payment. The contract is between you and the seller."

"Our paycheck always went into the same checking account. That's how we paid our bills."

"That may be true, but that is not how it goes now. Mrs. Teesdale gains no benefit from the truck as she now resides away from the marital home."

Rather than argue about a truck he was turning in, Willis asked, "What about the mortgage?"

"As I said, send a copy of the payment coupon to me. Please do answer the complaint; otherwise, you will be in default. I have a client waiting for me now and must go."

"Tell Jess and Briana that I love them." He was talking to dead air. She had already disconnected. *These lawyers and their waiting clients.*

He began going through the mail stacked up on the table, looking for the mortgage bill. He came across an unopened letter addressed to Jess from a property management company that his alarm company did business with. He had installed cameras and alarms at their clubhouse and the pool area of their sprawling apartment complex. It was across the street from the high school.

What's this?

At first, he thought about forwarding all her junk mail, but then his curiosity got the best of him. He opened her mail and had to re-read it to be sure of its content. The property management group told her that her security deposit was received. She needed to arrange a time to pick up her door keys, mailbox key and key fob for the main gate before the following weekend, which was the first of the month. They had even assigned her a parking space number and listed her car color, make, and license plate.

What the hell?

He saw that the envelope was marked as undeliverable to her sister's address and was returned to sender. They must have sent it here instead.

No. No. No! This is not happening.

He stuffed the envelope into his gym shorts and grabbed his wallet and keys. He punched his sister-in-law's address into his GPS as he got on the highway. At the first red light, he felt for his Colt under the seat and recognized its leather holster before touching the rosewood checkerboard grip.

Shit. I don't have a belt to clip it onto.

The contemporary Christian station he was listening to carried the syndicated newsfeed story of the Senate's continued stance of not letting the bi-partisan House bills on universal background checks be introduced into the Senate. It was followed by the local station's announcer giving the weather report. She then followed it with a piece about the mass shootings in West Texas, where a rifle-toting shooter was cornered in a cinema parking lot and killed by responding police.

Willis turned to the hard rock station and cranked up

the bass. He was determined to talk sense to his wife. He'd tell her that he was trading the truck in for basic transportation. He'd start looking for a job right away.

Hell, I'd even do Uber!

Maybe she could also get her security deposit back. As the thoughts of going safari hunting evaporated like mist off a lake, he even thought, *She can put me on an allowance for all I care.* Willis believed that if she got her own car and an apartment that she didn't need him around anymore. *How did it get so far out of hand?*

He punched the numbers in the keypad at the gate and rolled in. Briana would still be at school, and hopefully, Nicole, Jessalyn's sister, would be at the hospital delivering a baby. As he got out of his truck, he spotted Jess's car parked in the furthest part of the driveway, where it would not interfere with Jake and Nicole's cars backing out of the garage.

Real cozy set up.

The Colt was too heavy on his gym shorts, pulling them down over his right hip. He debated putting it back in the truck but instead held it in place with his hand.

He stood sideways on the step as he rang the bell. Soft footsteps on the plush carpet preceded the whoosh of the door opening.

The au-pair stared through the screen door at him.

"I'm sorry I forget your name. I'm Willis, Jess's husband, and I am here to talk to her."

"One minute, I will get her."

The door closed as he asked, "Aren't you going to invite me in?"

Willis stood on the steps and admired his brother-in-law's house. It was well-maintained. The yard didn't have a single weed in it. The driveway was resealed regularly. The curb line was edged and the flower beds all had fresh mulch. The smell of cocoa in the mulch always reminded him of the hot-chocolate that his mother used to make. He began to think of how he missed her and how she could have talked Jess into giving Willis another chance.

Where was Jess? He heard the soft footfalls again over the birdsong from the canopy of mature trees, then the click of the deadbolt.

She locked the frigging door.

"Jess. It's me, Willis. I just want to talk to you. Open up."

No reply, the house was quiet and the birds stopped their merry sounds as if anticipating what was to happen next. He pulled out his cell phone and clumsily brought her number up on speed dial with his left hand. The phone rang four times before going to voicemail. He tried it again. This time it went immediately to voice mail. He punched the door ringer repeatedly.

"C'mon, Jess, All I want to do is talk. Jess, please."

No answer. He began pounding on the reinforced door with his hand, then he raised the Colt up and started pounding on the door with the butt of the gun.

"Jess! Jessalyn Teesdale, you have to talk to me at some point. I need to talk to you!" He kept pounding on the door.

Two police vehicles pulled up in front of the house. Willis turned with the automatic pistol raised above his head.

The one male officer shielded by his car door in the road barked, "Freeze!"

The other, standing in combat stance on the driveway, kept yelling. "Put down the gun! Put the gun down! Put the fucking gun down!" He presented a small target with the gun being the focus of Willis's attention.

Willis kept his gun pointing up with his gun hand raised above his head and looked at both turning his head slightly from one to the other and saw their frenetic energy. If he pointed it towards them, his troubles would be over, but he didn't cause this mess. He wasn't going down for just wanting to talk to his wife. This was absurd. He realized that these guys would pump him full of lead if he even twitched. He began to observe the situation like a drone camera from above as it circled the stand-off. Each cop was jabbering at him non-stop.

His face grinned, his shoulders shrugged and his voice said, "Can you boys just make up your mind and decide what you want me to do?"

CHAPTER 32

HE JUST PUT a twenty-dollar tip on a thirty dollar bar tab. Carli/Chrissy thought as she broke the fifty with her own growing wad of cash and returned the rest to the cashier. "Is it always this easy?" she asked as the cashier who just smiled knowingly.

She didn't have to wiggle her boobs in the guy's face or shake her ass on the pole. She was taking drink orders, chatting briefly (letting the men know she was working two jobs to go to college to become a schoolteacher) and moved the drinks and empties quickly. She was the good girl and dressed just the part.

She learned from Rose how to time her entrances between songs and her chat time between sets. She had time at the drink station to huddle with Rose when she needed to ask what the ingredients of some of the more exotic drinks were. "What is the fixation with single malt Scotch," she asked Rose.

"The younger guys think that they are sophisticated when they order. Say something like "good choice" and give them a nod when they do. Those are top-shelf drinks and the bigger the bar bill, the bigger the tip. Slow down visiting them when they start ordering beer. That's your signal that they are running out of money—your money."

Rose side-stepped Carli with a full tray of micro-pub beers for a table celebrating the last hours of bachelorhood for a loopy drunk who the bouncers had to warn twice about getting too touchy-feely with the dancers.

Carli's evening was flying by and she stopped at midnight when there was a lull to count her tips. She had received $275 at that point and that didn't even count what was accrued on charge cards. They would cash her out at closing. She was buzzing from the free drinks and the energy of making more money in a single night than a week of cleaning rich people's houses.

Hand them a drink and give them a wink. Rose had told her. *Sure beats cleaning toilets.* She agreed with Rose on that one.

A few times, she had to politely shake a hand away from one overly friendly customer who grabbed her arm. This guy made it clear that he was in love with her. Whether it was the alcohol, the naked dancers or "Chrissy's" cheery attitude, Mr. Polo shirt and Italian jeans stayed after his friend went home and he seemed less interested in the stage activities and rebuffed the dancers who made the rounds when they bounced off stage wearing the skimpiest of silk robes. He wanted to chat with *Chrissy* longer and longer when she brought him his drinks.

He intercepted her on his way back from the bathrooms and started hugging her. He tried kissing her and her drink tray went crashing to the floor when she tried pushing him off. He was surprisingly strong. Bad flashbacks started firing in her brain.

Rose signaled a bouncer and two of them grabbed him

roughly walked him back to the door where he settled his tab with Rose. They remained with him until the bar tab was paid. He didn't argue the 20% extra added for Carli's tip. They walked him out of the double doors into the parking lot.

Carli waited for Rose in one of the VIP rooms. She was shaking.

"Nobody has touched me like that since....." Carli began crying on the plush red sofa.

Rose and Brandi, a dancer of thirty-two who acted like an older sister to the dancers, both hugged Carli and made soothing sounds.

Carli was not placated. "Call me an Uber. I am done with this. I can't do it."

"It is not your fault, Chrissy, but you have to keep an eye on that kind of guy when you're working. It's your first night. You just have to be alert for the drunk lover boys. It won't happen again." Brandi lied.

"That's why I ran away and you know that Rose." Carli cried into her roommate's shoulder.

She stiffened her resolve. "Call me an Uber and get my charge card tips, Rose. I am not doing this again."

"No, Carli, take my car. I'll get one of our guys to give me a ride home later." Rose handed Carli her keys. "I'm sorry tonight didn't work out. It's my fault for not telling you how to keep your head on a swivel while you're working.

* * *

Carli made her way to where they had parked the car earlier that night. Away from *Roxanne's Redlight* glitter, the building was a drab converted warehouse. She turned the corner to employee parking on the darkened side. All the times that she had driven Rose's car, she fumbled for the right key that opened the car door. As she tried the ignition key into the door lock, a shadow overcame her.

He came out of nowhere and slammed her against the car, pinning her arms.

"Don't play goody-goody with me, I know you want it." He began to lift her shirt up with one hand and held his other over her mouth while dragging her towards his BMW nearby. "Wha..?"

The jab into his armpit released his grip from Carli's mouth. Then two hands raked his eyes from behind, pulling his head and torso back as a knee slammed into his midback. He released Carli as he fell hard to the ground. A foot found his genitals and nearly lifted him off the ground with the speed and force of the kick.

Then another to his ribs and then another and another.

Marsha jumped around the crumpled and moaning rapist-no-longer and grabbed the motionless Carli who had just witnessed the savage beatdown. "Let's get out of here."

She led Carli to Charlie's car and settled her in the front passenger seat, buckling her in. She fired up the sedan and sped out of the parking lot before anyone was the wiser. "Are you okay?" she asked.

"Who are you?" Carli asked.

"I'm Marsha. I was keeping tabs on my no-good boyfriend when I saw that guy sneak up on you," she lied. "What's your name?"

"Carli. Carli Ertz. How'd you do that?"

"I take self-defense classes a couple of times a week. Looks like I got my money's worth," Marsha said with satisfaction. Somebody got what they deserved and it felt good to do it. "Where am I driving you?"

"It's not far, I'll show you."

Marsha parked next to Carli's Sonata. She was invited in and followed her to the apartment. *Finally, I have an address,* Marsha thought.

Carli disappeared down the hall while Marsha took in the living room. Simple and clean. Neither girl had any photos of family, boyfriends or pets about.

The brand-new vehicle registration sighting feature on Charlie's Private Investigator database listed the dates and times Rose's car had been spotted at *Roxanne's* street address. Looking for scofflaws and vehicles to be repossessed was becoming big business, and license plate readers fed the database that was now being repackaged for private investigators and insurance companies.

When Marsha entered the address in her phone GPS, the Google Maps picture showed a drab, windowless warehouse from the street view. She didn't realize she had been there before until she arrived at its side entrance. That's when it all clicked.

This is where she had seen Carli's roommate before. Marsha couldn't ring up Eduardo to see if Carli's "slutty" roommate had a rose tattoo on her breast, but she was pretty sure it was the same girl. She now connected Rose with being the girl that Briana was sitting with at the mall the day she tried to run away. Marsha had a better idea now of how Carli was warned off from the dealership.

Marsha had put that all together while she staked out Rose's car that evening and was surprised to see Carli, not Rose, approach Rose's car. In those few seconds of startling recognition of the girl in the photograph coming to life, she didn't have time to process it all before she saw the guy get out of his car and sneak up behind the high schooler from St. Paul.

She was out of Charlie's car and silently fast-walked her

sneakers for her surprise attack. She had no time to think, only to react. It happened so very quickly. Shira would be so proud of her.

Wearing a Minnesota Golden Gophers jersey and yoga pants, Carli walked barefoot to the kitchen and had the coffee brewing in no time.

"Did you go to school there?" Marsha asked.

"No. It was the local college where I grew up. I was hoping to go there someday."

"Where was that?"

"Minneapolis." Carli had her back turned and apparently was going to leave it at that.

Marsha would try another tack and waited until Carli had brought out two steaming mugs of coffee, the creamers, and sugar packets on a tray. "I played against the Gophers when I was at Penn State for the Division One volleyball championship a long time ago."

Marsha had played volleyball on a full-ride scholarship, but they never got to the finals. Sometimes you had to give a little to get a little.

"Who won?"

"They did, but it was a close game that could have gone either way," Marsha fibbed again.

"I played volleyball in high school," Carli replied.

They talked about how the game had changed over the years. Carli began to relax in their conversation.

"So what brings you to the Sunshine State, Carli?"

Carli hesitated before saying, "I am going to the local community college to get all my general credits. I am going to be a schoolteacher."

Marsha acted perplexed. "Why were you there? Are you a stripper?" She used that word on purpose.

Carli's face flushed red. "No, my roommate works there

as a cocktail waitress. That was my first night on the job and my last. She made it seem so easy and exciting. I made more in one night than last week cleaning houses, but I guess there is a price to pay for that. That guy was a customer that I served. I helped him get drunk so I could get a bigger tip. Maybe I smiled and showed too much interest in him."

"Is that what you do, clean houses?" Marsha quickly moved on.

"Yeah, houses, timeshares whatever. I worked my way down here, cleaning motel rooms in exchange for rooms and meal money."

"Does your family know that is how you're living?"

Carli shook her head no. "I left under a dark cloud."

Marsha nodded. "Me too. I will tell you my story if you tell me yours, is that a deal?"

She reached out her coffee mug for Carli to toast. Carli reciprocated and they made a pact.

CHAPTER 33

"THIS PLACE SUCKS, MOM."

Jessalyn tried to soothe her daughter. "It's only until we know he can't do anything to harm us."

The visage of the police drawing down on her soon to be ex-husband was not far from her memory. Trudi and Jess had peeked out the shades as more cops swarmed the quiet street. They saw Willis drop the gun into her sister's azaleas and began laughing as they rushed him.

She didn't want him dead. She just wanted him to leave her alone and let her and Briana get on with their lives.

"After what you told me about him banging on Aunt Nickie's front door with his gun, I can't believe the cops let him out of jail."

"They wanted him to stay locked up, but the judge released him to Uncle Bryce on a stiff bail. They were able to confiscate all his guns on an emergency protective order. If he so much as sneezes at us, the judge said he would throw him in jail and throw away the key."

"Still, Mommy, he is not right in the head."

. . .

In due course, Thelma told her that Willis had an up-to-date license to carry his sidearm. No action had been taken to revoke it previously. His new lawyer, a public defender, argued that he was just using it as a hammer to get someone's attention in the house.

The charges were piling up. This was the second violation of the restraining order and they added breach of peace and threatening to the original domestic assault.

"We will let Thelma handle everything from now on."

"We don't know where he is. Marsha said he hasn't been back to the house since the cops were there." Briana alluded to a private conversation with her neighbor.

"I talked to Marsha too. Her friend Shira was able to get us into this place, remember?" Jess replied.

Nicole and Jake didn't want to take the chance of their children being caught in the crossfire. Her mother said the retirement community had strict rules about family members staying with the retirees who all had been carefully screened.

"It's only until we can get the all-clear. The apartment is waiting for us. Everything will be okay then, I promise."

"Still, Mom, it's like I'm in prison. I have to have a tutor here. We can't leave. I just want to see my friends at school. I miss the Youth Group. This was the weekend that we had the three-day mission trip."

"We pretty much stopped going there, honey, when Pastor Rick told me to make a nice dinner for your father and let him take charge again. I think you are reaching a little bit there, Bri."

"No, I'm not. Those kids were my only friends at school too. They can't come here and I can't leave. I'm a prisoner and Daddy's running around free. That's not fair."

The argument was escalating. "You're right, baby, it's not fair, but we are safe for now. He can't get to us in here."

"We can't work at the restaurant either. How can we make enough money to live on?" Briana was not letting it go.

"Your Aunt Nicole said that she and Uncle Jake can lend us a little money until we get back on our feet. They told me that they were secretly happy when I told them that I was divorcing your father. I guess our eyes are open now to what they saw all along. You don't deserve this, but it will be over soon, you'll see, I promise."

Jess hugged her daughter and Briana returned her mother's hug and said, "I've got a test to study for, Mom."

Back in the room, they shared with two other mothers and their children, she sat on her cot and typed a message.

Hey, Carli, this is Rose's friend Briana wazup?

* * *

"Hey, Charlie, you'll never guess who I bumped into last night," Marsha was filling him in over breakfast.

Charlie had returned home the previous night from Wisconsin. When the worker's comp judge saw the videotape Charlie introduced into evidence at the Cheesehead's hearing, he immediately halted the proceedings. He advised the worker's attorney that his client needed a criminal attorney. He then read the Miranda Rights to the slumped over man and said that he was duty-bound to forward this video to the Economic Crime Unit of the District Attorney's office.

The man's attorney acted as affronted and surprised as he could when he quickly realized that he had failed to ask for discovery of any videotape on his client before allowing his client to make incriminating statements during the hearing in front of the now-incensed judge.

"Rose?"

"Close. Carli Ertz, in the flesh, coming out of the location where Rose's car was spotted."

"You've got my attention now, O'Shea. Fill me in."

"Do you remember the strip club that was pirating the pay-per-view feed where Jess and I got the video?"

"Yeah?"

"It's one and the same. The map view just shows a dingy warehouse, but on the side of the building. This is what you see." She slid her phone across the table to the familiar photo of *Roxanne's Redlight* they had used for the piracy case.

"No kidding."

"Even better, the cocktail waitress that served Jess and I had a red rose tattooed on one of her ta-tas."

"Rose is the girl with the red rose tattoo? This is getting better." Charlie liked a good story and his storyteller was happy to oblige him.

"Do you remember when Briana ran away from school that day and Jess and I found her at the mall? Guess who she was with?"

"The girl with the red rose tattoo. That's incredible."

"Not if that is where you recruit your talent. That is where Rose met Carli and just so happened to have a spare bedroom at the time. I was in that apartment last night."

"No shit?"

"I shit you not, *kemosabe*.

Anyway, I had no sooner set up on Rose's car in the back parking lot of the club, when who walked out and tried the key in the door lock. I was thinking to myself, *Holy cannoli. That's Carli*, when this creep gets out his car sneaks up to her and starts to drag her back to his car."

"I take it things didn't go well for the ne'er do well."

"Let's just say he will be singing in the alto section for awhile if his ribs aren't broken too badly."

"Ouch." Charlie winced.

"Yeah. I got Carli to your car and we beat feet outta Dodge back to her place."

"Case solved. Way to go, Marsha!"

"Whoa, Trigger. There's more to the story."

* * *

Fired by text message. They're making a direct deposit of my last check. I'm supposed to meet Lane and give him my keys that they forgot to take from me when they suspended me. My good buddy Lane who took away my overtime. I wouldn't have these problems if I had my overtime. Fat chance of them getting those keys back anytime soon. They might come in handy later.

Willis chuckled to himself. Unlawfully entering a burglar alarm and security company had a nice feel to it.

At least, my vacation pay will be in there, along with all my unused sick time.

He had checked his online account a few times, and when the money cleared, he would visit a different branch and clean it out. He was able to get his truck out of the impound lot where the cops had towed it.

I'll get some travel money and Marty can pick up my truck at the end of May.

CHAPTER 34

"CHARLIE, she is turning eighteen on Saturday," Marsha said.

"What are we supposed to say to the client? 'I am sorry, Mr. and Mrs. Ertz, we couldn't find your daughter until she became an adult. We will return to you $8,437.28.' You know that won't fly and that is beside the point." Charlie had the file and looked at running expense sheet for their $10,000.00 retainer.

"And the point is?" she asked.

"The point is we were hired by the client to find their daughter who ran away with their car five months ago. We found her while she was still juvie. We tell them where they can collect her."

"And then what?" Marsha insisted.

"They take her back home. Case closed."

"It's more complicated than that, Charlie, and we both know it. She can refuse to return, and by the time they have a hearing, she would be an adult and can tell them to kiss her ass. They would lose her again."

"That's not our problem. We worked this case and found her before she turned eighteen. We get paid."

"I'll give you the fucking money if that is what you are worried about."

"Marsha, you know it doesn't have a damn thing to do with the money, it's about doing the job we are getting paid for."

Both were getting heated for their own reasons.

"Look, I know a little about running away from ones problems. I think I can talk her into going back to St. Paul on her own terms and she can start living her life without having to clean houses or work at a strip joint. She wouldn't be anywhere near a place like that if she was back home. She almost got raped for Christ's sake. She'd be cruising towards graduation right now, maybe getting ready for her senior prom, picking out a prom dress instead of cleaning up after strangers. She has enough credits to graduate and start her freshman year at the University of Minnesota, not a community college."

"I don't know, Marsha. Do you think you can pull that off? Let's look at the downside. She can say no to your ideas and then run again."

"Charlie, explain to the parents that there are compelling reasons why she ran away and that we might be able to talk her into going back. Unless her chicken-shit brother has told them why she left, they are still clueless. If they came down here, not knowing the whole story, they would go home without her. She doesn't know I am working for you. Woman to woman, I think I can talk her into returning. More about her being able to get on with her life rather than running away from it. Maybe for her, life doesn't have to be a shit-sandwich."

"What if we clue them in and they make a surprise visit

here, knowing what needs to be done back home?" he suggested.

Marsha the woman, whom Carli confided in, was in conflict with Marsha the operative for Charlie Akers. She knew along that it would come to this. She was outside of *Roxanne's Redlight* for a reason and it was not to be the savior of sex workers. Charlie was paid to do a job, this was very clear.

"The goal is to have Carli safe at home in Minnesota. If I can't talk her into going back, then I would say give Plan B a shot, but that presupposes that they want her to come back to town once they know. Remember, my folks, think I was responsible for my brother's death. I don't see me going back home to reconcile with them anytime soon."

By trading stories with Carli, she was able to see her own situation with more clarity. She knew that there would be a day of reckoning in Philly, but some other pieces had to fall into place first.

Charlie considered the idea carefully, then made the call. Marsha could only hear his side of the conversation. The parents were happy to learn that she had been located and that she was safe and not in harm's way. They were delighted to learn that their daughter's refusal to answer their calls or text messages was not due to anything they had done or didn't do. It was a much harder sell to explain to them why his female operative could talk her back home, rather than them.

He explained that if Marsha couldn't get their daughter on a direct-flight home, they would be welcome to come down. He would supply them with her address then. If they asked why she left town in the first place, Charlie didn't say anything about her reasons.

As the conversation went back and forth. Marsha was

glad that they weren't told. If word got back to Carli that her reasons for leaving were exposed before she was ready to deal with them, that might force her into deeper hiding. So far, only Rose, Briana, and that angel FBI agent on administrative leave knew the sordid details.

It wouldn't take Carli long to figure out that Marsha had told them. Regular folks need time to process new information intellectually, as well as emotionally. So Charlie had to go over the news a couple of different ways for them. In the end, he got the reprieve for Marsha to work her magic.

When he disconnected, he said, "Well, I guess I still have paying clients. This better work O'Shea."

"I'll do my best, Charlie." Glancing at her watch. "I've got to get ready for my appointment with Shira at the shelter. I am her practice dummy. I will connect with Carli tonight after Rose leaves for work."

"Say hi to Jess and Briana for me," Charlie said. Marsha had filled him in on the latest with their neighbors and how Shira had found them a spot at the women's shelter.

***

The hour-long class was geared to escaping holds both standing up and on the ground. It was not as physically punishing as a workout, but playing the attacker had no upside. Time and time again, Shira moved Marsha around like a tackling dummy with swift sureness and pulled her strikes within a whisper of causing severe and permanent harm. Neither of Charlie's neighbors attended the session, but the women who did appreciated the chance to practice on Shira and Marsha.

The moves were clumsy at first, but later, paired off with each other, the movements became smoother and more assured. This training was not about earning a black belt, it was about learning how to avoid a beating or worse. They were practicing how to buy time, by surprising their assailant and then escaping or calling for help before their attacker could recover. Today, Shira concentrated on teaching them how to quickly move out of attacks from all sides.

The one thing she couldn't simulate with these women was getting punched in the face. Former heavyweight boxing champion Mike Tyson said it best: "Everyone has a plan until they get punched in the face."

Not surprisingly, several of those gathered already knew what that felt like, including Marsha. So, Shira's plan was for them to feel the pain, feel the shock and surprise, then set their feet and lunge back quickly with a strike to the throat or to the groin. The padded headgear she provided allowed either Shira or Marsha to slap the left cheek pads with a hard-right cross.

Since Marsha was as tall as the average man, she threw most of the haymakers. The women took the shot, reeled back, set their feet and came back with the counter-strikes. Shira wanted to end this training with the women defending themselves. If any of them were to encounter an attack at home or on the street, having these several moves in muscle memory could be the difference between life or death.

* * *

Marsha checked in with Jess and Briana. The tutor from the high school had left minutes earlier. In this short-term arrangement, she really had not much to do but bring Briana her assignments, collect her homework, or babysit her while Briana took tests or quizzes. School would be over in less than six weeks and she would only have to make up lab assignments.

Jess had appropriated a walk-in closet in their shared living area. Using her phone as a hotspot, she was able to connect her laptop and its VoIP headset to the internet and worked off a card table. It wasn't the first time a home office was set up in a walk-in closet, Marsha thought.

"We had to shut down the case." Marsha handed Briana $200 in twenties fresh from the ATM she had stopped at on the way. "When the girl from up North didn't show up at the car dealership, we ran out of leads. The family doesn't have a way to track her unless she brings the car in again for an overnight repair."

Marsha had to play her neighbor's daughter if she wanted to keep her from interfering further. Marsha's anger gave way to compassion when she understood why Briana was protective of Rose's friend, as she had heard the whole story of Briana's warning from Carli.

Marsha talked about how Briana could keep studying biology and chemistry in college and try to get into the FBI laboratory as a first step to becoming an agent. Marsha saw that the sullen teenager was mollified by the money and that she had successfully kept Briana from causing worse damage.

"Marsha, can I stay with you and Charlie while they fix the problem between Mommy and my father? I hate this place. I feel trapped here. I'm going stir-crazy."

Jess had finished her call and gave Marsha the head shake. *No.*

"The last time he came to visit you and your mother, he brought a handgun and was banging on your aunt's door with it. He was acting really strange when they arrested him. This is just temporary, you'll see. Everything will work out just fine. You will be able to live in your new apartment without him bothering you anymore."

"When?"

"I don't know, Briana, your mother's attorney will know better than anyone. I'm sure your mom doesn't like it any better here than you do."

Shira came back and the women all said their goodbyes.

Marsha and Shira lugged the canvass bags of props and headgear out to Shira's car. It would be May soon in South Florida and a car didn't have to sit long outside even with the windows down to be boiling hot.

Marsha's cell phone under the floor mat was turned off. When it came back on, she had a voice message from a number in DC she didn't recognize.

"What was that about?" Shira asked her passenger who was sitting motionless with the phone still to her ear as she stared out the windshield after playing it three times.

"It was the number-two guy in the FBI wanting to see me in his offices in DC at 10 a. m. Monday morning."

"What did you do this time, Marsha O'Shea?"

CHAPTER 35

CROSSING the Saint Marys River north of Jacksonville was a violation of his bail agreements, as if that even mattered. Back home in Georgia now, Willis was five miles from where he grew up in Folkston. His excitement was building. Anything that he cared about from his house was laying in the truck bed under a tarp.

The cops didn't take his fishing equipment or his hunting clothes. Eventually, he'd get his guns back, but that might cause his do-nothing lawyer to do some work. The lawyer had kept the entire retainer Willis gave him arguing that he earned it.

With no job and the stiff arm from his wife and daughter, he now realized that leaving his roots to chase Jessalyn was a mistake. He would go back for court hearings and pick up his prized coyote. He'd get his probation and let her have her divorce. All they had to split up was bills.

He'd start over and never step foot in Florida again, except to go saltwater fishing with his brothers. Her uppity lawyer would be more than happy to agree to him not returning to South Florida. Let them try to sue him for child support.

He'd stay at his familial home until he could get his own place and work for his brother's electrical company under the table until the divorce was finished.

His church back home didn't know anything about the charges and he'd start attending worship as soon as he could. The youth pastor was now the lead pastor and had done the funeral service for his mother. He'd make that connection right away. Being a sober church-going man had its plusses in this neck of the woods and he'd have no trouble finding a girlfriend.

His father didn't seem really excited to see him. The old man was on disability and getting VA benefits for exposure to Agent Orange in Vietnam. The family home was well-worn, but well-kept, thanks to his brothers and brothers-in-law. The inside was tidy as his sisters and sisters-in-law took turns coming over.

Hard to believe that five kids were raised in this house. No one had their own room, except for Bryce, who had moved into the basement when Willis was old enough to climb out of his crib.

"So how long are you planning to stay?" his father asked.

"Probably until I can get my own place," Willis replied.

"I was thinking of selling the house. It's too big for me now. I can get a spot over at Riverview where they will be able to take care of me."

"Sure, Dad, I understand. That will take a little while and by then, I should be settled."

"I don't know. Brenda and her husband were thinking of buying it to use as a rental. They know what needs fixing and what they can let slide."

"Well, it will take some time for Mom's estate to probate. They can buy it then, right?"

"Your mom's name was not on the deed. She never worked a day out of the house the whole time we lived here."

"I guess I could put a camper top on the truck and live out of there for a bit if I don't get a place before you move out."

Willis was annoyed. The thought of buying the house or even renting it from his brother-in-law was out of the question. He couldn't afford either option. Willis started to move his belongings into his old room while his father watched him.

The room was full of boxes and junk. His bed and box spring had been turned on its side to make room for the hoarding. His sleeping bag would have to do until he could get to Walmart.

He brought his stuff in and started to carry out boxes so that he could lower his bed. His father blocked the door.

"I haven't gone through that stuff, Willis." His father blocked the door.

Standing there with two boxes and a broken lamp in his arms. "Geez, Dad, I am just making room for me to have a place to lay down. Is that okay?"

"Where are you taking it?"

"To the girls' room, I guess."

The old man grudgingly moved aside while Willis brought them to what had been his sisters' room only to find it as cluttered. This was going to be a lot of work.

"First thing tomorrow, I will start going through it all for you, Dad."

"I'm not ready for that, Willis. I am having trouble letting your Mom go. You come here with little warning and expect to live here and change things. I don't know about that. I am kinda partial to my routines."

"Where would you like me to go, Dad? Uncle Willis could stay at Brenda's house when we visited, but this has to be a little longer than a holiday weekend or such."

"I don't know, Willis, where you can stay. That's not my problem."

"Is it my fault that my wife and daughter don't know how to respect a man's property? They didn't have the decency to come up with me when Mom was sick. I am coming back home to start over. I should have stayed in Folkston and not gotten married to Jess."

"We told you that before you married her and you wouldn't listen. You done closed the barn door after the horse has bolted."

Both men stared at each other.

Finally, the old man spoke as he walked back to the blaring TV in the living room. "I'm not saying that you are not welcome, but you need to make other arrangements sooner than later."

Out of earshot, Willis replied, "Gee, thanks, Dad."

* * *

The following morning, he carefully stepped around the clutter as his father watched his every move. He showered quickly using a threadbare towel he had to find on his own in the linen closet. Driving to the diner to meet his brothers, he was hoping for better news than the news on the radio.

The West Texas mass shooter had failed a background check at a retailer but was able to buy his rifle from a personal seller, a deadly loophole in the laws governing gun sales. This fact just flowed over Willis like water over a dam. His thoughts were about meeting his brothers for their first serious sit-down since the funeral.

Bryce was first to lay into him. "Well, well, the Prodigal Son has returned."

"Not really, Bryce. I didn't take a damn thing away from y'all. It seems to me you got the business and the nice house. I am returning home for a fresh start. That's all."

"Yeah, I heard. Dad didn't seem real happy about that. Since Mom died, he's been really off."

"Yeah, no kidding. My old room became the junk room. I had to negotiate for everything I moved out of there just so I could sleep last night."

"Couldn't control your women, huh, Willis? Gotta come home with your tail between your legs," Bryce continued baiting his little brother.

"What can I say, Bryce? The cops down there would arrest me for picking my nose." This is how the put-downs went with the Teesdale boys. *Never miss an opportunity to stick it to little ole Willis. Do I really want to work for this jag-off?*

"You are planning to pay me back, right, li'l bro?"

"I was hoping to work it off, big bro," Willis replied.

"What? Work for me? You gotta be kidding, right? It would never work out."

"Wait a minute, Bryce, this is a family business. Dad turned it over to you when he got sick. I trained in electrical and it wouldn't take me long to catch up. I've been working with the latest alarm and security systems and we can add that piece to the business."

Teesdale Electric was the company to turn to for commercial and residential electrical wiring and repairs in southern Georgia and the greater Jacksonville area. Both were still growing areas with persons and companies moving out of the Northeast and the Rust Belt for more sunshine, less government interference and lower taxes.

"You're always bragging about how you are growing and making stupid money. I've got the skills to slide right in."

"Slide right into what? This is not a charity ward. I am running a tight ship. I can afford to go hunting and fishing when I want because I have people that can run the business in my absence. It's more than knowing where the wires go. I've actually learned how to run the company as a real business. Dad ran it like Spanky's Clubhouse."

Willis put his fork down, stopped chewing and looked at his older brothers. He couldn't believe what he was hearing. The company had his last name on it and his oldest brother couldn't throw him a bone.

"I'm willing to start at the bottom and work for one of *your* trusted lieutenants. The only time we have to see each other is at company and family picnics."

"If I start hiring family, everybody will expect me to hire their family. I can't do that." Bryce dug in.

"It ain't like you are some big corporation, Bryce. My last name is on that truck sitting out there." He waved toward the tricked out GMC Envoy.

"And you done worked for none of it, Willis." Bryce pushed back.

Realizing that the parachute was not opening and he was in free fall, Willis asked, "What about your suppliers? Can you put a good word in with them?"

"What? Call them up and tell them that my screwed-up little brother who will be on probation for domestic violence and who had his guns taken away from him would be an excellent candidate for their next job opening?"

Willis looked around to see if anyone else in the diner heard the insult. "Screwed-up little brother, huh? Their records check would only be on Georgia if they bothered to look. You know that if I can pass a piss test, I can get a job anywhere."

"So don't look for me to bail you out again. Go get your job on your own then." Bryce stood up, peeled off a twenty from a wad in his shirt pocket and threw it on the table. "Gotta go. Got a business to run."

Willis stared at his brother and realized that he was just a joke in his big brother's eyes. All the insults, jabs and jibes from the time he was a little kid surfaced in the awareness of the present moment.

His stare turned to Jazz.

"Don't look at me," Jasper said. "You know you need a CDL license to drive a long-haul truck."

"What about at the freight depot? They need guys to transfer pallets, don't they?"

"You need to know how to run a forklift. Besides, we've got laborers with more seniority waiting for their turn," Jazz said. "Get your CDL, then talk to me. I'll see what I can do then."

Willis was not hungry anymore and pushed his farmer's country breakfast onto Bryce's plate.

* * *

He waited in line at the Department of Driver Services in Kingsland to get his Georgia driver's license and to get the paperwork for his commercial driver's license. He would have to go to a school to learn how to drive the big rigs, but it was worth it in this economy. They could not get enough long-haul truckers who could regularly pass a drug test.

He handed the bored clerk his birth certificate, social

security card and his Florida license. Minutes later, he had a new driver's license in the state where he grew up.

* * *

"Willis, you can't just go barging into his office demanding to see him." Brenda, his oldest sister, was angry with him.

"He was sitting in his office alone, looking at his computer screen. I could see that from the sidewalk. When I told the receptionist that I was in town and I wanted to say hello to my brother-in-law, she went into his office and they both peeked out the door. A few minutes later, she came back and said that he was in a meeting."

"He told me you yelled at her. What is wrong with you? She had to go home for the day."

"All I said that she was a—oh, never mind. What's the point. All I wanted to do is see how I could get a highway job. He is the superintendent of highways last time I checked."

"You apply online like everybody else, Willis, but seeing how you acted today, I wouldn't hold my breath. That's the attitude that got you in trouble down in Florida, isn't it?"

"You're right, Brenda, it's my terrible temper and my poor attitude. Your husband is alone in his office watching porn or cat videos on his computer and he has no time to visit with his brother-in-law from out of state. He could have come out, shook my hand and told me exactly what you just did.

"I'd ask him about his last fishing trip and he'd ask me how long I was in town for and that would be that. Instead, he treated me like a leper. Am I a leper? Do I have leprosy? What is it that y'all are afraid you are gonna catch from me?" He upped his volume with each question.

"You don't dare yell at me, Willis. You don't go barging into people's offices and insult their employees."

He lowered his voice to a restrained, "I asked to see my brother-in-law, politely. I didn't know that I needed an appointment. SOR-REE."

He hung up the phone.

He walked into his old high school. Classes were over for the day and he found his way to the principal's office. Lots of bad memories there, and after exchanging pleasantries with his oldest sister, he was bracing for yet another smackdown from his other sister Millie's husband.

"Willis Teesdale, Class of 2002 hoping to say hello to the principal on my first visit in a long time."

"One second, Mr. Teesdale."

She is a lot nicer than that witch at Briana's school.

He spotted the trophies for the year that Bryce captained the varsity football and baseball teams to a regional championship. He remembered idolizing his big brother while in grade school. Being shy and not athletic in grade school only compounded his nervousness of being Bryce's youngest brother.

"Hi, Willis. What brings you back to your old school?" the principal grinned.

Finally, somebody that understands how to treat me with respect.

Playing into the role of returning alumnus, Willis said. "Well, sir, I loved it so much when I went to school here, that I thought it would be neat to return and help out with electrical, mechanical and janitorial."

He said the last word softly. *Yes, even janitorial. Willis Teesdale, the high school janitor. How low will I go?*

"Hold on a second." He grabbed a piece of scrap paper from the recycle bin next to the photocopier. As he was writing, he said, "See Dolores Trombauer at human resources in the Board of Education building. She can take your application. Right now, the budget is at an impasse and we won't know until the summer if there will be any openings or vacancies. Some kindergarten teachers aides may not be called back if we can't get the funding."

"Thanks, Scott." Willis pumped his hand a little too vigorously and held it for longer than necessary until he said, "I will do that and I will tell her you sent me."

He smiled broadly to the school principal, who looked relieved that his brother-in-law let go of his hand.

No leprosy was transmitted in the handshake.

Willis walked easily down the halls where he had felt so much misery as a gawky adolescent standing in the shadow of his revered older brother. He knew that he would not be walking down those halls ever again as he loitered in the parking lot.

He was glad that he didn't get the hand-out while he was getting the hand-job from Millie's husband.

* * *

"Pastor Jason, it is good to see you again."

"Hello, Willis. What brings you back to Folkston?"

"My wife and I were having money troubles after my job cut my overtime and they didn't give her a raise because of poor work performance. She refused to follow the counseling from our pastor at Clearwater Church of the Rock. She and my daughter took their anger out on my possessions and made it impossible for me to talk to them. I couldn't live like that anymore. I am getting a divorce and decided to return to worship here and help out where I can. I just need to start over."

"Where you staying?"

"With my dad, I am keeping him company. He feels really alone since Mom died."

The pastor nodded. "Have any job prospects?"

"Got my feelers out with the county and the Board of Ed," Willis lied. "I was hoping that you might put a good word in with the folks that attend worship," he said truthfully.

"I'll keep my ear to the ground, Willis. You were a good kid when you were here. It shouldn't be hard to find something for you when the time comes."

"Small towns have a way of taking care of their own. That's for sure," Willis said, missing the cue.

"Yes, but they also talk." Pastor Jason was more direct. "When you get all those arrest charges dropped and restraining orders lifted, Willis, we will be glad to have you join us again." The smile had become a grim, stone-cold set jaw.

"Whaddya mean?" he implored. "I can't come to church?" He implored.

"Times have changed, Willis. Domestic violence involving guns is not something I can turn a blind eye to. To ignore those issues puts my congregation at risk. The church board and I could be held personally liable for anything that happens in the sanctuary or at church-sponsored events."

"You gotta be kidding me? In all the years that you've known me, you know that I wouldn't hurt a fly."

Pastor Jason shook his head and reached for his cell phone. It didn't take him but a few seconds until he pushed it across the table and asked, "How do you explain your daughter's black eye, then?"

* * *

His father didn't bother to get up from his recliner. The expert on *Fox News* was explaining how the uptick in mass shootings was due to the teaching of evolution in the schools. A different expert added that video-gaming was linked to the violent behaviors of loners that spend all day in their basements gaming. Willis caught his eye. The old man reached for the remote, turned the volume higher as if his youngest child was not standing there.

Willis trudged back to his room and walked in to find his bed upended on its side against the wall and the boxes and broken lamp were put back where they had been the previous day. His belongings were stuffed into two large black plastic bags.

CHAPTER 36

"HOW DO I know you are telling me the truth? Briana told me all about you."

Marsha's heart slumped. Her plan to talk Carli back to Minnesota on a direct flight the next evening was evaporating like the steam from the coffee that Carli made for her.

"You're right, Carli, about some things and wrong about others." It was time to come clean. "Yes, I set you up at the dealership. At the time, it was the only way we knew how to connect with you. I was there, but I didn't know then why you had run away."

"And what about at the club?"

"We had gotten Rose's license plates from the security camera feed when she picked you up. Her car had been spotted at the club several times and I set up surveillance at the club expecting to follow her home. And it was a good thing that I did, wasn't it?"

Carli looked away to a book bag on the table. "I printed these off at the library today. Everything you told me about happened to you was true. You weren't making that up."

She pulled them out. For Marsha, it was like separating gauze bandages from the scabs over her heart.

Looking at the print outs of *Philadelphia Sun* headlines and screenshots of the local TV reporters talking about the bloodbath in Lower Merion six weeks earlier brought back all the memories.

"Yep, I had a good reason to run away too. I am not saying I will never go back, but some things have to happen first, like knowing whether or not I'm washed up as an FBI agent."

They both took sips of their coffee.

"Reading how your brother died...really made me sad for you," Carli said.

"That's what I have to start dealing with. I can't change what my parents think of me. I didn't know that he was going to invite himself to the party that night. I have to stop wishing that I can change the past." Carli had done a great job of changing the subject and Marsha had to bring her back. "You can't change the past either, Carli, but you don't have to be a victim of it either. I told the private detective who I am staying with that you should be trying on prom dresses and getting excited about graduating at this time of your life, not working three jobs."

"Briana said his name is Charlie. Does that make you one of Charlie's Angels?" Carli smiled for the first time.

"No, I've been a real pain in the ass for him. You see, I convinced him not to tell your parents where you live. Otherwise, it would have been them and not me knocking on your door tonight."

"How do I know that? Did he tell them what I told you?"

"No, I made sure that he didn't. I was there when he called them and told them that I wanted to talk to you first."

Marsha was slowly gaining the teenager's trust by talking about her own shit and then flipping the conversation around. "So you see, it doesn't matter if I was working for him or just happened to be sitting in strip club parking lot when you needed me to be there, I would still tell you the same thing. You've got to go home and face the people that caused you to run in the first place. They need to be held accountable for what they did. I am prepared to go with you. I will stand by your side until you are finished telling your story to your parents, the school, and the authorities." Marsha slipped the plane tickets on the table. "You can have the window seat."

"I'm not ready for this, Marsha." Carli recoiled.

Marsha stood up and gently reached for the girl's arm and sat her back down. They sat side by side on the couch. "You've been fortunate so far, Carli, being on your own and staying out of trouble. Maybe I was an angel sent here to protect you and get you home safe. Did you ever stop to think there might be a reason you and I were meant to meet?"

"You did play for Penn State, but the Golden Gophers never went to the Final Four."

"Okay, Carli, that was a fib. Some detective habits just don't go away." Marsha was still hoping for a home-run.

"I don't know, Marsha, I have to think about it."

"We can do this together, girlfriend. I've got your back, Carli Ertz."

***

The ten-year-old cowered in the corner. Her mother glared at Briana.

"I want my stuff back." Briana moved closer.

The mother got between them. "Keep your hands off my daughter."

"She's a thief and I want what she stole back. I caught her going through my backpack."

The girl kept her body slightly turned from them.

Jess entered the room wrapped in her shower towel, hair, and legs dripping water on the hardwood floor. "Briana Jane! Leave the little girl alone."

Briana's anger exploded. "I hate this place and these fucking people. That little shit was going through my things. I want it back," she yelled.

The mother went to her daughter and began prying something out of her hands. As soon as it was free, the girl bolted from the room. The mother was left holding a stuffed pink piggy.

Jess recognized it as Briana's favorite stuffed animal when she was a toddler, she had carried it everywhere. How many times had she made Briana's bed as a child and placed the piggy on the throw pillows?

The mother tossed it to Briana, fearful of getting closer to the raging teenager.

"I hate this fucking place. I want to leave. I hate this fucking place. I HATE THIS PLACE."

Briana tore out of the room, hugging her piggy.

Jess couldn't even console her daughter. Letting go of the towel would cause problems. Their apartment would be ready tomorrow, but they did not have a clue where Willis was, and until his court appearance on Monday, they would have to sit tight.

The puddle of water beneath her was growing.

CHAPTER 37

WILLIS MET his brothers at the Valdosta Gun Show hosted by Western Gun Shows and held every year at the Jonas Darkcloud Conference Center. Five thousand people descended on this pretty "Old South" town twice a year to walk aisles of dealers stalls. Serious dealers and regular folks who wanted to clean out their gun cabinets took tables at this show. Bargains could be had.

Willis was a little sore from sleeping in his truck overnight, but had a good breakfast with lots of coffee. It was going to be a long day. He was in a good mood with his new purpose, letting the tension between siblings from the day before slide off his shoulders like water off a duck's tail feathers. They talked about old times and some of his fondest memories. They talked about future Teesdale boys adventures. They were surrounded by guns. Antiques, estate collections, handguns of every make and model and tons of rifles from old muskets to the later military-style assault rifles.

He told his brothers how he handled the M-60 on full ammo night at the gun range. He handled the World War II

German Lugers and shouldered the American M1 Garand rifles. The smell of gun oil permeated the air. It was an elixir for all those attending. They paused at a table that was surprisingly bare, but staged well.

"Whoa, that's some serious firepower," Jazz said.

"Kept me safe all those years. Nobody was coming into my house without a serious fight," the old man said.

"Why you letting it go then?" Bryce asked.

"The big C is kicking my skinny ass. Sixty years of smoking. Throat cancer. No excuses. I did it to myself. I've got no kids. My only sister had all girls." Looking around the large hall, he said, "This is my family. I know my guns would be in good hands."

Willis handed the Bushmaster QRC AR-15 Semi Auto with a thirty-round magazine and collapsible stock to his middle brother.

Bringing it to his shoulder, Jazz tucked it in and said with his eye on the open sights, "This would definitely stop a lot of bad guys."

The Remington over-under twelve gauge sat in its gun case next to a Smith & Wesson Police Chief Special, a reliable bed stand-point-and-shoot. That was the old man's whole display of guns.

Jazz handed it over to Bryce. "It's a beauty." He balanced it in one hand. "It's lighter than I imagined. How much you asking?"

"$1,000 for the whole table. $750 for that baby and these."

He pulled two additional thirty-round magazines from under the table.

Bryce, blew air out of his checks and moaned, "That's a lot of money."

Willis had heard the line so many times from his brother that he learned to keep a straight face.

With an even response, the seller looked Bryce straight in the eye. "I worked in a retail business for forty years. I wish I had a nickel for every time I heard somebody say that to me. You know that I am not here to make a lot of money and probably won't be here next year. It's a fair price and y'all know it."

Bryce said, "We were just asking that's all. We want to look around some more." He set the Bushmaster down and started to walk away.

Willis stayed there and looked at the man.

"Are you coming, Willis?" Jazz asked.

"I'll catch up with you guys. You go ahead."

The background check took less than fifteen minutes. It helped that Willis had a Georgia license and a birth certificate showing the same address. His record was clean in this state, except for an underage drinking citation which was wiped off long ago. There was no universal background check to surface his ERPO or pending charges in Florida. No three-day waiting period. Nothing was done to bring up his divorce and the two affidavits supporting his restraining orders. This was an all-American gun show—land of the flag-waving free, home of the brave.

Willis handed the man the money the man for the AR-15 and ammo. "Where did you get the holster?" The worn tanned leather had a faded emblem on it.

"I was a special deputy. The county was so poor we had to buy our own guns and holsters."

"What kind of stuff did you do as a special deputy?"

"We'd get called out for traffic details on bad wrecks,

homecomings and the county fair—stuff like that. Best times were when a chain gang prisoner escaped from a work detail. Now that was some good hunting. We'd get the dogs out and have ourselves a good ole time."

"I bet. It must be hard letting go of the memories," Willis said.

Both men started at the revolver on the table.

"Here you go, son, take it." The old man slid the gun and holster across the table.

"No I couldn't."

"Sure you can, and tell your smarty-pants brother that I gave it to you."

"That I can do." Wills grinned.

The Teesdale boys enjoyed walking around the show. The old man must have sold the shotgun because his spot was empty when they made a second pass. Willis would have liked to nod and wink at the only person to treat him decent in the short time he was back home.

Willis surprised his brothers at the end when he picked up guns at the holding area. He was in rare form. "Let's go to our favorite spot down by the river and shoot this bad boy, then I will treat you to lunch."

"Alright," Jazz said.

Bryce looked at his young brother quizzically and said, "You musta really knocked that guy down."

Willis just nodded as they headed to the parking lot and their separate trucks.

The Saint Marys was moving fast this time of year. Too much rain. It had been a very wet Spring. Today, though, was a perfect May day. Light breeze, warm and getting warmer, but in the shade of this secluded part of the river, it brought back memories of fishing and blinking at tin cans with their .22s.

Far away from any farmer or off-the-grid survivalist, they could enjoy their make shift targets. Tin cans on pallets served as the targets. They all took turns with the thirty rounds from the first magazine. Willis ejected it and reached into the bag for the second mag. He also took his belt partially off and fastened the holster with the Smith & Wesson onto his hip.

He slipped the magazine in, sighted a can at forty yards, and sent it spinning off the pallet with one shot. He then turned the gun onto Bryce and shot him in the left knee. Before Jasper could utter even a gasp from his open mouth, Willis shot him in the stomach twice.

Both of the Teesdale brothers lay on the ground writhing and moaning in pain.

"Shhh. It will be over soon. Just one shot to the heart. I can hold my hand steady. You'll see Jazz."

Jazz was holding the stomach with both hands, but couldn't stem the bleeding. He tried to stand up, but Willis pushed him down hard and pointed the revolver at his face. Jazz's hands flew instinctively to ward off the shot, but Wills lowered the gun and pressed the trigger when the tip of the barrel touched his middle brother's mid-line.

"Faked you out." It was Jasper's favorite line when he punched Willis in the groin all those times when they were teenagers.

Bryce had gotten up and was hobbling towards his truck. He would have made it except for Willis taking a kneeling position over his dead brother and firing again and hitting Bryce mid-back. Unlike the movies, Bryce dropped like a sack of potatoes and was barely breathing when Willis kicked him over.

"Who's screwed up now, Bryce? At least I won't have to drag you far to your truck. You made it easier for me."

The lifetime of torment was over with a single shot to the head.

Willis lifted his dead brothers into their trucks and then got the pick-ups rolling fast enough to go swimming in the river. Both trucks floated for a bit before finally disappearing below the surface.

This will buy me some time to finish what I'm gonna start.

He opened the revolver and counted three bullets.

Enough for Jess and Briana and me.

He got in his truck and nosed it down the dirt path leading to the country road that took him to the highway which got him to the interstate heading south to Clearwater. He sang along with the radio.

CHAPTER 38

MARSHA INTRODUCED Charlie and Joe to Shira, who already knew about the call from the FBI. This could be Marsha's last day in Clearwater. She was either flying to Minneapolis tonight with Carli and then on to DC, or driving to DC on Sunday.

Charlie was first to chime in when she told them. "For a bureaucracy, the bureau moved pretty quick on this one. It's even stranger because the state police investigation into an officer-involved death is not finished and won't be until every ounce of overtime can be squeezed out of it."

"Do you think that they are going to fire you?" Joe asked.

"Hard to tell. What do you think, Charlie?"

"I don't think so. They would have had your boss in Philly be the hatchet man. They don't dirty their hands in Washington with firing a street agent."

"Some kind of proposition, then?" Shira asked.

"I'm afraid they will bury me behind some desk in the Swamp shuffling papers and dying a slow death from a thousand paper cuts."

"What'll you do if that is the case?" Joe asked.

"Take it and wait until everything that's gonna come out comes out. Then I will push for a transfer to somewhere I can still use my brains again until it's time to pull the pin. I want to finish my career on the street. Believe it or not, Charlie, I really liked working for you out in the field again."

"Being on 'the case' is a good cure for the blues," he said, knowing what else it was a cure for.

They all nodded.

"Have you heard from Jess at all?" Charlie asked.

"She's hanging in there, but Briana is flipping out. It's so unfair. She's a prisoner there while her father runs around God knows where," Marsha said.

"But necessary," Charlie added. "Her husband is still MIA since the cops cleared the house of all his guns. We check the security tapes every night, and he hasn't been back. I always thought the guy was a few bricks short of a load." Charlie said between sips of his Diet Coke.

The plate of nachos, with everything imaginable on top, arrived at the table along with a double order of wings.

"He has to show up Monday. Jess's attorney will have a few questions for him," Marsha said as Shira filled a plate heaped high enough for two people.

Marsha had become accustomed to her friend eating like a foraging bear and just as easily understood how Shira kept the weight off with punishing Krav Maga workouts.

As her friends all dug in, Marsha realized how fortunate she was. Staying with Charlie, keeping her mind off her problems with the work, and Shira's workouts was precisely what was needed to remain on the straight and narrow.

Just for kicks, she waited until Joe almost had a heaping mound of the Nacho Bomb into his mouth and gave his thigh a playful squeeze. He started to eject from his seat but sat quickly and pretended the concoction was too hot for his mouth.

"Hot, hot, hot." He set it back on his plate and reached for his non-alcoholic beer and his flushed face receded back to normal.

It was better to leave things unsaid between them for now. Both of their lives were in major-league flux. She promised herself to stay close to her college friend, sort of wishing him happy with the nurse from Queens, but deep down inside, hoping that they could circle the bases together someday.

The banter was lively and friendly. She would miss her angels. That's what they were. Angels sent down to protect her and give her strength to carry on when all she wanted to do was crawl into a bottle and hide.

Joe and Charlie argued over the check and Joe won Rock, Paper, Scissors two out of three times.

In the parking lot, Joe gave her a gentle hug and Marsha played nice and gave him a peck on the cheek.

Charlie was next. "If I don't see you tonight, I know you are on an airplane and I will let you handle the family when you touch down."

"You saved me, Charlie, how can I ever repay you?"

He pointed to his bumper sticker: *One day at a time.*

"Call me the next time you feel like drinking. Promise me that."

"That's a deal, boss."

The hug between them was exquisite. Mentor and apprentice. They'd fought the Miami Cartel Wars together when they both were younger and carried that swagger. Sponsor and drunk. Surrogate father to a girl desperately in need of fatherly love, but too tough on the outside to show it.

Shira busied herself on her cell phone until Marsha got in the car and fastened her seatbelt.

Shira had offered to give Marsha and Carli a ride to the airport so that Marsha didn't have to pay long-term parking rates for who knew how long.

Marsha had a travel bag and her laptop. The rest of her belongings were crammed in the back of her Mustang at Shira's condo guest parking.

They rode in comfortable silence to Carli's apartment. The Sonata was not in its spot. *Not a good sign.*

"You were right, Shira, I think she went rabbit on us."

Rose's car was still there. Her shift at the club hadn't started yet.

Rose opened the door to Marsha and Shira and looked at both of them and said to Marsha, "New girlfriend?"

"Cute, Rose, I am here to take Carli to the airport. Do you know when she will be back?"

"Yeah, never. You can go fuck yourself, Ms. FBI agent." She started to close the door on them.

Shira kicked it in and planted Rose between the now wide-open door and herself. "That's no way to talk. Let's try this again. Where is your roommate?"

"She packed all her shit and left about an hour ago. Go look for yourself."

Marsha was clear to say for the benefit of the recording on her cell phone. "That is very nice of you to invite us in, Rose."

Rose, better with words than fists, said, "You spooked her bad. You know what happened back in St. Paul and you wanted her to go back. You get paid for a job well done and she would have to relive her nightmare over again and again and again."

Shira came back and nodded. "How do you Americans say it? She has flown the coop."

Marsha turned to look squarely at Rose. "I get where you are coming from. I've been to your home. I've met your father and mother. I would never in a million years talk to you about going back to that shit show, but Carli has parents that treated her decent and who still don't know why their daughter ran away. Your world now has to be ten times better than what you had, but Carli still has a chance to make things right."

Rose considered and rejected the argument. "She's gone. She left. She gave me back her keys and gave back all the keys to the people she was watering plants for. That's what took her most of the day. She moved out and is moving on and she wouldn't even tell me where knowing that you would keep looking for her. She gave me zero notice. I still have to pay rent for this place." Rose waved her hands around.

"How strong is her connection to Briana?"

"Who?"

"Who? Who? The girl at the mall, you know who I mean. The girl who warned you off about taking Carli's car back for the safety recall. The girl that you talk to on Snapchat all the time."

"She's a hormonal teenager. Nice kid but wouldn't last a minute on the streets. I keep telling her to hang in there. It's a better place than I was ever put in."

"And she's too young to become your next roommate. Ain't that right, Rose? You can't recruit her. She's too young. Got it?"

Regaining her courage now that what was said and

what done was done. Rose said, "If you ladies are done acting tough with me, I've gotta go to work. Do you mind leaving now? You got what you wanted."

As Marsha followed Shira from the apartment, she noticed that Rose's rose was a little redder than she remembered it from the day at the mall.

That girl is lying.

Back in the car, Shira asked, "Where next, Marsha?"

Getting her laptop out, she replied, "I'll tell you in a minute."

CHAPTER 39

WILLIS THOUGHT about some more unfinished business with the man sitting in a recliner, hooked up to an oxygen bottle back in Folkston. Maybe making him clean Willis's room at gunpoint until he collapsed, gasping for breath. Then poke him to keep working some more with the muzzle of his new toy until he died from respiratory arrest. It was only the urgings of his dead mother to leave the bastard alone that kept Willis's truck pointing south on I-75.

The shock, and then fear, in his brothers' eyes as he prepared to kill them balanced out the years of belittling and bullying that he had suffered. Two older brothers ganging upon him in the bedroom while his parents were downstairs and pretended not to hear his pleas. The belly punches hard slaps across his face and knees to the groin all faded when their trucks disappeared into the swollen Saint Marys. He no longer had to suffer as the klutzy adolescent trying to keep us with his older brothers when they went hunting.

Even as adults, the jabs were no longer physical, but the

spoken words hurt just the same. He evened the score with them. Thoughts of firebombing his old high school flashed in his head. It would be easy enough to break in and wouldn't take more than a couple of five-gallon cans of gas to get things cooking, but that would take him away from his higher calling.

Ditto for Pastor Jason and Pastor Rick. Where was God when he needed The Almighty most? Those two were more concerned about the image of successful houses of worship than Willis.

Thoughts of shooting both in the throat so they could never preach or sing with the praise band again would be perfect, but those thoughts veered him away from his higher purpose. He reminded himself of the real cause for his problems. Well, sort of.

How could it all go to hell in such a short period, he wondered. His women made his life miserable, all because of a broken washing machine. They blamed him for all their problems, and they got one smart-ass woman after another to keep sticking it to him. The credit counselor, the lawyer, the female cops, Lisa, the hotel room cleaner and the school secretary had all pushed his buttons on purpose.

Everything would have been just fine if he had been in control of the situation.

He always wanted to go on safari. Now he was gonna hunt the female of his species.

Oh yes, people will know my name. Willis James Teesdale.

He never used his middle name or middle initial. Still, all the great killers had their middle names elevated into history. He had a good guess where they were and needed to use that key from the office that he never returned.

Now that would be a good use of the jerry cans of gasoline. Kill two birds with one stone. He liked that thought.

* * *

"Briana, I said I would talk to you, but you really need to give this a lot of thought." Carli had parked her car next to the fence of the woman's shelter and they talked through the fencing. It was the first meeting between the girls.

"I need to breathe for a while. I promise I won't be in the way, and I can even help you. It won't be forever. I promise."

"What about school?" Carli insisted.

"What about it? I have straight A's and all my homework is in. A week or two won't matter. I just need to get out of that place. They are stealing my things."

"Can you stay with your grandmother?"

"No, she is in some kinda special housing for the elderly. If they find me there, they will kick both of us out."

"You can't stay at my old apartment either. That is the first place they would look," Carli added.

"C'mon, Carli. It would only be for a couple of weeks. I have money, too." She showed her the cash Marsha had given her.

"How are you going to get out?" she asked.

"We have to try an experiment." Briana moved over to the steel box protruding through both sides of the fence and opened her side door and placed her backpack in there. "Now, open your side." Carli opened it and pulled the backpack out.

"I think I can fit in there and close the door behind me."

"Hand me your laundry bag first," Carli said.

Briana complied, and she was about ready to squeeze into the box when she looked past Carli and said, "Oh shit."

* * *

"We know this address, Shira. We were there this week."

Both women were staring at the Google Maps photo of the address where Carli's car and the GPS tracker that Marsha had placed on it was parked.

* * *

It was kind of them not to change the locks, Willis thought when he went into his former employer's place of business late Saturday afternoon. In the office he was able to bring up the camera feeds of the building the spiked-hair girl wouldn't let him step foot into. He saw that there were twenty women and about as many kids in the converted mansion.

He grabbed a laptop that would allow him to open the gate, disable the alarms, and, most importantly, lock the doors remotely, except for the one he would enter. Jess had been with another woman in the kitchen, making dinner. Briana was stuffing her laundry bag at the time.

It's about time she learned how to do laundry, he thought.

About seven minutes after he had departed the building, give or take, he spotted police cars and fire trucks screaming with red lights and sirens towards where he had just come from.

It was *incredibly simple* how the lit cigarette, acting as a simple timer, when burnt down into the pack of matches under a tent of recycled photocopy paper leaning against the open five-gallon gasoline container could kill two birds with one stone.

He glanced one more time at his Bushmaster in the bag next to him as he rounded the corner to see a black Sonata by the service entrance of the shelter.

We have company, my little friend.

CHAPTER 40

"IT'S MY DAD. How did he find us here?" Briana gasped.

"Call the cops," Carli said.

"No. You don't understand. He had a gun and was banging on my aunt's door with it to let him in. You gotta get away."

Carli looked at the locked gates and delivery chute. "That's not going to work."

Briana was backing away and started breaking into a run back to the house. "Get out of here."

Carli looked at the approaching truck and could make out the driver in the slanting sun. She jumped on her bumper, scrambled up the hood to the roof of her car and climbed to the top of the fence. She grabbed the top of the wall with both hands, continued to lift her body upwards and swung her legs over the top, and fell on her feet on the opposite side. In the gymnastics of life or death, she stuck a perfect landing and sprinted to catch up with Briana.

They entered the service entrance and ran to the main desk. It was the same woman who had rebuffed Willis a couple weeks earlier.

"My father found us. He's at the back gate."

"He can't get in," she said. "I'll call the police."

The weekend manager zoomed the camera on Willis's truck just as the picture went blank and the power flickered in the building. She picked up the landline. It was dead. She pressed the panic button under the desk that would summon the police. She looked at her panel showing green or red lights for the status of the door locks. It was dark. There was no way she would get the callback, confirming that the police got her panic call. She had no way of knowing if the signal was sent. She looked at her panel showing green or red lights for the status of the door locks. It was dark.

Both girls looked at each other. Briana's phone was in her backpack, Carli's was in her car.

"Get everybody to the safe room," the spike-haired woman said.

Briana had practiced that stupid drill when they first arrived and again a couple days earlier. She grabbed Carli and said, "It's my mom's turn to cook, I'll tell her."

Rushing into the kitchen with Carli in tow, Briana wailed, "Mommy, Mommy, Daddy is here. I was talking to my friend here at the back gate when I saw his truck. I know it's him."

"What? Your friend? He couldn't have found us. Are you sure?"

"Yes, I am sure. The lady at the desk said to go to the safe room."

Turning to the frightened woman cutting vegetables, Jess said, "Mi esposo es aqui. Tiene a..a... gun." Jess made the hand gesture for a pistol.

The woman held onto the knife and wasted time running to her children.

Jess looked at Briana and said, "My phone is charging on my nightstand. Get it and call 9-1-1. Meet us in the safe room. Hurry."

* * *

Willis had opened the gate after shutting off their alarms and cameras remotely from the laptop and drove to the same doors that Briana and Carli had run through. They were locked. The first-floor windows had security bars across them.

He holstered his revolver, adjusted his boot, and pulled out the Bushmaster from the bag. He fished out the extra magazine and slipped it into his cargo pants lower left pocket. When it came time to eject the spent magazine, he could reach down and load up another thirty rounds in no time.

He walked around to the basement door. It was set and framed with heavy timber surrounded by the stone that made up the foundation. He turned the handle easily and slipped in. He had programmed this door to remain unlocked. Every other exterior remained electronically locked.

His eyes had to adjust to the darkness, but he made his way across the damp partial-dirt floor to the electric panel.

* * *

Briana connected with the 9-1-1 operator from their bedroom. Carli went to the window and opened it. It was thirty feet to the ground. She went back to watch the hallway.

"Nine-one-one. What is your emergency?"

"My father found us and coming after us. Come quick."

"What is your name?"

"My name is Briana Teesdale."

"Where are you?"

"In the bedroom."

"The address, I mean. What is the address?"

Briana didn't know it without her phone and looked at Carli. "What's the address here?"

Carli reached for her phantom phone and said, "It's on my GPS in my car."

"I don't know. It's a big white house where women and their children are hidden from their husbands who beat them up."

"Is it the Women's Shelter?"

"Yes. Yes. It's the Women's Shelter. Hurry up. He was not supposed to know the address but he found us."

"Do you know what town?"

Briana didn't know and began to panic. "Carli, do you know what town this is?"

"Clearwater," she replied.

"Clearwater," Briana yelled into the phone.

"Did he have a gun? Can you describe him?"

"I didn't see a gun. They were supposed to take away his guns. He's my father."

"What's his name?"

"Willis Teesdale."

"Stay on the line. Don't hang up."

Briana looked at Carli. Both girls knew precious seconds were passing by.

"We don't have anything on a William Teasdale," the 9-1-1 operator said.

"That's crazy! He was arrested for beating me and my

mom up, and he got arrested again last week for banging on my aunt's door with a gun. He has restraining orders on him."

"Did you see a gun?"

"No, I told you that already," Briana snapped. "I saw his truck coming and I ran into the house where we are staying."

"What's your mother's name?"

"Jessalyn Teesdale."

"Hold the line. Don't hang up."

* * *

Jess gathered with the other woman and children in the safe room.

The weekend manager came in and closed the door.

"I've seen that truck before. Does he work for a security and alarm company?"

Jess nodded.

"Stocky guy, short brown hair?"

Jess nodded again.

"Lousy attitude?"

Jess agreed, "yep."

"That explains why the cameras went down. I am not sure if the panic call went through."

At that moment, the power went out and the room was plunged into semi-darkness, thanks to the LED lighting in case that happened. The safe room was surrounded by reinforced steel sheets. The wall phone was dead. Cell phones were useless in there. The panic room would be a shooting gallery.

* * *

The hallway and bedroom lights went out. The setting sun plunged them into soft gray.

"Oh shit, the lights just went out," Briana said to the 9-1-1 operator.

"Still nothing. What's your aunt's name?"

"Nicky, Nicole Frazier. Her husband is Jake. I think they live in Clearwater too." Briana was slowly melting down.

"Hold, please. Stay on the line and don't hang up. Okay, Briana?"

Briana sniffled. "Okay."

The 9-1-1 operator came back on the line. "We have it here. Is your father's name Willis?

"Yes! Yes!"

"I thought you said William, and your last name is spelled T-E-E-S-D-A-L-E, not Teasdale."

"That's right." Briana exhaled.

"We have the report here." There was silence on the line. "Okay, we will dispatch a car now."

* * *

Willis had made his way out of the basement and onto the main floor. He wanted to clear those rooms first, just in case some of the hens had decided to fly the coop. He knew exactly where the safe room was located, thanks to the schematics on file. The house was locked tight, and the room that was supposed to be safe—wasn't.

* * *

Shira and Marsha pulled up to the open gate lazily swinging in the cooling evening breeze. They observed

Carli's empty Sonata and Briana's backpack, recognizable by school ID on the flap.

"This is not good." Shira sped down the driveway.

"No, it's not. That's Jessalyn's husband's truck."

Marsha dialed 9-1-1 and gave the operator her name, the GPS address and the situation. The operator held her on the line and said that a unit was responding.

"This doesn't look good, you better send more than one car," She said.

"Sorry, Agent O'Shea, our other cars are tied up at a structure fire," came the reply.

"Roger that," Marsha lapsed into cop-speak.

Shira hopped out of her car and climbed into Willis's unlocked truck while Marsha called Jess.

* * *

Briana picked up. "Marsha! Thank God, it's you."

That got Carli's attention.

"Have you seen your father?" Marsha asked. "Does he have a gun?"

Carli saw a shadow coming up the stairs and shushed Briana and pushed her into the walk-in closet.

"Somebody's coming, Marsha," Briana whispered.

Willis made his way up the stairs and walked to the rooms at the head of the stairs down the hall from them.

Carli took the folding card table that served as Jess's work station and wedged it under the doorknob. Both girls then retreated into the racks of clothing.

* * *

Shira came back to the car, waving a slip of paper. It was the receipt for the AR-15. "We can't wait. We have to go in."

Marsha disconnected with Briana and they walked to the service entrance door and pressed against the building. They were not armed. Shira was supposed to take Marsha and Carli to the airport. All Shira had was a short billy club that she kept in her car for road-ragers. The safe thing would have been to wait for the cops and let them handle it.

Marsha got 9-1-1 again on the line. It was a different dispatcher.

"Nine-one-one. What's your emergency?"

"This is Agent Marsha O'Shea of the FBI, I am at the woman's shelter on Oakmont Drive. I called a minute ago. One of the women's husband's truck is inside the compound. He is not allowed to be here. It's empty. He's inside the house. I've got proof that he bought an AR-15 at a gun show this morning. You better send more back up and the SWAT team."

"Hold the line."

Shira tried the front door, but it was locked. Marsha motioned her to follow to the rear of the house. They came upon the basement door. Shira pointed to the wet footprints in front of it. She gently turned the knob and pushed the door open. The interior was dark and musty.

The operator came back on the line. "Yes, we got your earlier call and have had a call from the man's daughter and a car is en route."

"We can't wait. We are going in. Get everybody or bring body bags."

Marsha hung up. She knew that a small town SWAT mobilization would take time. More uniforms were needed right away unless they could buy some time.

Both women had worked urban situations before; Shira, with the Israeli Defense Force, and Marsha with tactical teams in Miami. They made their way cautiously in the darkened basement. If they turned the power back on, they would alert Willis. Stealth was in their favor. He was not expecting them.

The main floor was now in twilight, a cloudless spring day had given them a minute or two more of light.

Two shots rang out upstairs. Both women ducked then quietly climbed the stairs.

* * *

Jess heard the shots as dull thuds through the nearly sound-proof walls of the safe room and reached for the door.

"No, you can't go out there," the woman in charge said. "You are jeopardizing the lives of others in here."

Jess hesitated.

"My daughter is out there," she said and pushed her way past the weekend manager.

* * *

Willis had encountered the locked door of his wife and daughter's bedroom walk-in closet. He splintered the cheap lock and was kicking the door, but it still didn't budge. He fired several times again chest-high should the door be held back by humans, splintering it.

* * *

Marsha was first up the stairs and turned in the direction of the gunfire. Shira was right behind her.

"My daughter is out there," Jess said and pushed her way past the weekend manager.

Marsha crossed the threshold and nodded to Shira that they were in the right room. Shira didn't hesitate and closed the distance to Willis in near darkness, only to stumble on a black suitcase on the floor.

Startled, Willis wheeled around, firing as he turned.

Shira threw the billy club into his face as she rose from the floor into the barrel of the still firing gun.

Marsha swooped in from the right side, hopping onto a bed and then launched at him, reaching her thumbs for his eyes.

Shira held the gun into her stomach, taking another round and pushed it down until it was pointing it at the floor. She wasn't allowing him to lift the weapon to square off on Marsha.

Willis let go of the gun as Marsha's thumbs gouged his eyes. He reached up to her arms.

Marsha then grabbed the back of his sweaty head with both hands and pulled herself towards his face, head-butting him in the nose with a sickening crunch. In close quarters and with Shira below her, she had to hit high and hit hard.

He threw her to the side.

Shira now lay on the rifle, pushing it back with her remaining strength away from the raging bear.

Willis, nearly blind and bleeding from his broken nose, reached for his revolver to shoot Marsha as she charged him again.

* * *

Carli had heard the women attack the armed man and, looking through the cracks in the door, she saw him reach for the holstered gun. She exploded out of the closet and clamped both her hands over the leather flap.

Willis could not lift the gun out of his holster, try as he might. It was stuck.

He tried to fend off Marsha, who was standing and throwing hard jabs at his throat, kidneys, and solar plexus. He twisted away from Marsha and Carli, freeing himself as the gun slipped from the holster and out of his bloody hands.

Carli was behind him now and Marsha to his front, Shira on the floor to his right, still blanketing the AR-15.

"You're not gonna win this time, bitch," he roared.

Willis reached his left hand into his left boot and unsheathed the double-edged dagger, aptly called a boot knife, that he had bought at the gun show. He lunged at Marsha, who dove to her right.

Willis staggered forward and raised it up to plunge the razor-sharp blade into Marsha who was trapped between the wall and the bed.

There was a click of a hammer falling on an empty cylinder followed by the reports of three bullets that struck Willis in the stomach, chest, and head. He pitched backward to the floor, dropping the knife, as the silence was punctuated by more clicks from the empty revolver.

Jess was standing between the beds, still pulling the trigger of the empty revolver pointed at her dead husband.

CHAPTER 41

"DROP THE GUN, LADY. POLICE," the tall male cop yelled. "Drop it!" he yelled again.

Jess stopped clicking the Smith & Wesson. He was about to shoot, but his partner, the shorter female cop, stepped up and reached out, taking the gun gently from Jess.

"It's okay now. It's okay. Nobody is gonna hurt you." She sat Jess on the bed. They were the team that had responded to Jessalyn's house on the night of the Walmart parking lot incident.

Marsha rolled onto the floor next to Shira. "We've got wounded here," she yelled over her shoulder. Shira's eyes were closed, but she was breathing. "Let go of the gun. It's okay. He's dead. He's not gonna hurt us. Shira—SHIRA, let go of the gun. It's okay. We're safe."

She finally let go and Marsha turned her over. At least two bleeding wounds oozed in her lower abdomen. Marsha reached for the rifle and extracted the magazine and lifted it into the air for the police to take.

The weekend manager rushed in with the First Aid kit and knelt next to Shira.

It was then that Briana staggered out of the closet with blood streaming from her neck. "He shot me, Mommy."

* * *

"Marsha, I want to introduce you to my mother and father."

Seated in the ER waiting room of Tampa General Hospital, the only Level I trauma center that trains for mass-shooting incidents in the Tampa Bay region, Marsha looked up to see Stan and Greta Ertz.

"This is the woman who found me and saved my life. I wanted you to meet her."

The first thing that Carli had done when she retrieved her phone from her car was to call them.

Charlie stood up next and reached out his hand. "Charlie Akers, nice to meet you in person."

He had been on the phone with them most of the night before and during their two connector flights from Minneapolis, assuring them over and over again that Carli was indeed safe. He and Marsha agreed that it was up to Carli whether or not she wanted to tell them why she ran away.

The adrenaline dump and quickie-mart coffee had left Marsha physically exhausted, but mentally wired. "Did your daughter tell you how brave she was back there? She actually saved my life," Marsha said.

Greta Ertz spoke first. "No, she didn't, but we will have time to talk about everything, I hope. We are so thankful for you, Ms. O'Shea."

"Call me, Marsha."

"That's right, we've got a long drive home with plenty of time to talk." Stan Ertz shook her hand.

Forgotten were any recriminations. It was Charlie who had initially talked them out of coming down to Florida after he had discovered her address. If they had come down then, Carli might have shunned them, but this brush with death prompted her to call them after nearly six months of silence.

"You're safe and that's all that matters," he added.

"If it's okay with you guys, I would rather leave my car here for my friend Briana. She saved my life too. She will need a car next year when she turns sixteen. She's recovering from surgery. I want to tell her when she wakes up."

Carli walked across the room, looked at Jessalyn, and handed her the car fob. Jess was huddling with her sister and mother while they waited for Briana to wake up.

"Are you sure?" Jess asked the teenager, but also stole a look to her father.

"I'll mail you the title as soon as we get back," he said.

In reality, Jess had saved all their lives by killing her husband in their defense. That Briana was grazed by a bullet was not lost on them as they tried to process it all.

The police detectives had come and gone taking rounds of statements.

They tested everyone for gun powder residue.

A doctor in scrubs came out of the hallway leading to the operating room suites and asked, "Marsha O'Shea?"

Marsha nodded.

"Before we put her under, she said you are her sister," the puzzled trauma surgeon said.

Marsha nodded again and without missing a beat lied. "Half-sisters. Same mother, different fathers."

"Shira lost a lot of blood. It's good that we got her on the table right away. She will be in lots of pain when she wakes up. Gut shots take a long time to heal, but she will eventually recover. We had to reconstruct her intestines. There may be a possibility of infection, and we have to watch for that. The bad news is that the bullets tore her uterus to shreds. I am afraid that she won't be able to have children."

Marsha shook her head and began to cry.

Those assembled stood in silence. The woman doctor placed her hand on Marsha's shoulder as she sobbed. Charlie moved in and so did Joe DiNatale from the other side.

Marsha took in comfort. She didn't retreat or resist them. The sudden relief that Shira would live unleashed a flood of suppressed feelings. At that moment, she began to deal with all the self-inflicted second-guessing, guilt, and recriminations that she had been holding inside since the shoot-out in Philly, which sent her running here in the first place.

She no longer blamed herself for what happened there and for what happened hours ago. She stopped beating herself up. It was clear to her now that it was not her fault that people died or got hurt in either situation. Standing there, being cared for by Charlie, Joe, and the surgeon, she didn't feel the need to dive into a bottle to drown her pain.

Marsha wiped her eyes with her shirt and asked, "What else did you want to tell me, Doc?"

"She said something else, but I didn't understand it. Something about your footwork being sloppy and unbalanced?"

"My little sister is trying to teach me how to tango." Marsha shook her head with a wet grin.

CHAPTER 42

IN THE NEWS cycle the next day, the story broke how a female former Israeli soldier and Krav Maga teacher, along with an off-duty female FBI agent, thwarted a mass shooting at a women's shelter.

A deranged husband, who had purchased a military-style rifle that morning at an out of state gun show, found out where his wife and daughter were.

For once in a very long time, there were no other mass shootings reported that weekend and the story stayed in the cycle longer than usual. The police response was praised as forward-thinking and proactive.

Two days later, news broke in the Twin Cities of a group of high school football players arrested for raping an unconscious female at a post-game party.

Several college-bound players had their scholarships suspended pending the investigation. An investigation into how much the coaching staff and school administrators knew before the victim came forward, was continuing.

That same day, Jessalyn and Briana moved into their new apartment with help from Charlie and his gang of retirees. Charlie gave Jess all of the money from the pay-per-view signal piracy job as a housewarming present.

Three days after his death, Willis was cremated and his ashes were taken back to Folkston. There was no memorial service. His brothers were still missing and the small Georgia town was reeling from the shock of the press blitz. Meanwhile, the high waters of the Saint Marys River were beginning to recede.

DiNatale and Marsha hugged before she pointed her Mustang north to DC. A kiss was contemplated, but both of them knew that Joe was spoken for—again.

They promised to stay in touch.

Charlie Akers would be a daily visitor with his soon-to-be new operative at the hospital until she healed and was released.

* * *

Friday morning, Marsha was admitted to the Behavioral Analysis Unit at the FBI Quantico Training facility in the quiet Virginia suburbs on a pass approved at the highest level.

Strangely, Grayson Stanfield was alone in the dull cream-colored interview room. No phalanx of suited men and women stood between her and the number two person in the bureau. Her badge, gun, and credentials sat on the round table between them. He had a thin unmarked manila file on the table next to his cafeteria coffee cup. Her badge, gun, and credentials sat on the round table between them.

"How was your trip, Agent O'Shea?"

"Uneventful. Stayed at an Airbnb last night. Thank you for allowing me to get squared away this week in Clearwater. I needed the extra time."

"And your friend. How is she?"

"On the mend, but she has a long road to recovery. Charlie Akers is going to watch over her." She couldn't figure out his play. *Why here? Why's he alone?*

Stanfield smiled. "Charlie Akers. Good man. Old school. She's in good hands."

Marsha sat. She would wait him out. She was like this with suspects who wanted to confess but just needed the silence to help them want to fill the void. Her hands remained in her lap. *Talk to me.*

He pushed the symbols of her self-identity and life-long ambitions towards her.

Marsha's hands remained in her lap. *Talk to me.*

"We've doubled the squad in Philly to work the leads your investigation uncovered. Make no mistake, you and Hollins were right all along." He continued, "You showed remarkable resilience in the face of deception and bureaucracy, given the false flags from your brother and the interference from a supervisor, who, by the way, chose to retire rather than accept a choice assignment in Guam. You didn't quit. You got the job done."

She breathed in the sorely needed validation and vindication.

"Did you really charge into a room bare-handed against a guy with an AR-15?"

"I wasn't alone. I had help," she deadpanned.

Stanfield smiled. "Even more the reason why I need you for a specific job. You will report directly to me. Both the good and the bad, everything. You get an analyst of your choice. You two work alone; no squad to lean on or to spread leaks. You seem to work best that way anyhow, Marsha."

"Why did we meet here and not your office, sir?" she asked, not having the cojones to call him Grayson, now that they were on friendlier terms.

"The summary is for your eyes only. When you finish reading it. It goes there." He pointed to the shredder. "Too many eyes at headquarters. We need to keep this quiet."

Badge and gun were put where badges and guns usually go, and she reached for the file. "Where am I going?" she asked.

"Detroit." He stood up and glided to the door lingering there for a moment.

"Detroit?" she said as she opened up the file.

"Detroit," he said as he closed the door on his way out.

The End

Reviews are the life's blood of independent authors, please take a moment to go back to your retailer and leave an honest review. It's the best way for readers to discover their next favorite author.

Dedication
To the Written Word Writers Group of the Milford (CT) Arts Council for their encouragement and support.

ALSO BY JOHN A. HODA

Also by John A. Hoda:

Mugshots: My Favorite Detective Stories
Come ride along with veteran investigator John A. Hoda on his most memorable cases. He serves up them up like free refills at the 24-hour diner. His cases have headlined in the Philadelphia Inquirer and the New Haven Register
My Book

Odessa on the Delaware: Introducing FBI Agent Marsha O'Shea
Book one of the Marsha O'Shea series
Can Marsha stop a Russian Gang Enforcer on a murderous spree to take over the Philly mob scene. A mistake she made cost the life of a crime beat reporter and an innocent man is being framed for it. Uncovering the truth may get her killed in the final show down.

https://www.amazon.com/John-A.-Hoda/e/B00BGPXBMM

Book three in the Marsha O'Shea Series: **Detroit Wheels**

The clock is ticking as FBI Agent Marsha O'Shea tries to stop a mass murderer before he kills again on the same exact date every year, 9/11. His target: Muslim women. She and her trusted sidekick Ramit grind outside of normal channels to put together the clues. Will they stop him in time?

https://www.amazon.com/John-A.-Hoda/e/B00BGPXBMM

Book four in the Marsha O'Shea Series: **West Reading Traffick**

Sixteen year-old Irina came to America to be a model or so she thought. Can an injured and burned out FBI Agent, Marsha O'Shea and a young patrolman find her alive or before she disappears in an international sex trafficking ring?

https://www.amazon.com/John-A.-Hoda/e/B00BGPXBMM

About the Author

John A. Hoda is a real-life PI whose cases have headlined in the Philadelphia Inquirer and New Haven Register. He coaches at www. ThePICOACH.com and has written several How To books on the business of private investigations. He podcasts **My Favorite Detective Stories** can be found at your favorite pod catcher or at www.johnhoda.com where he can be reached.

John's first novel where he caught the writing bug:

Phantasy Baseball: Its About a Second Chance

A little-league coach, throwing batting practice, discovers he has a magical pitch. Joe DiNatale receives a one-in-a-million chance to try out for his beloved Philadelphia Phillies. How does this 'average joe' maintain his hometown values on his rollercoaster ride in the major leagues?

https://www.amazon.com/John-A.-Hoda/e/B00BGPXBMM

Coming Soon:

Liberty City Nights: Marsha O'Shea Prequel Novella

Mr O'Shea wants his wife to settle down and start a family. FBI agent Marsha O'Shea is working on the Bank and Fugitive squad in Miami and is making a name for herself as gunslinger when the FBI was the federal alpha dog in the fight against crime pre 9/11. There is no compromising as the sparks fly.